FREE ENTERPRISE, JUNGLE STYLE

Meeker had done a few odd jobs for Scanlon. The first time Scanlon had given him a thousand, the second time fifteen hundred, and always more of the smokes.

This time he was in for twenty-five hundred flat or a ten percent cut, whichever was more. "Ten percent of what?" Meeker had asked, back in Bangkok. Scanlon had shaken his head and laughed and given him a carton; and now it was not long before the dawn in the wide channel of the Mekong, with the rain slanting across the jungle's face.

"You want to hold on to your rifle," Scanlon said, "once we make the pickup."

"Who am I going to shoot?" Meeker asked.

Scanlon looked at him for the first time. "Whoever I say."

DENNISON'S WAR
TRIANGLE

TRIANGLE

Adam Lassiter

BANTAM BOOKS
TORONTO · NEW YORK · LONDON · SYDNEY · AUCKLAND

DENNISON'S WAR: TRIANGLE
A Bantam Book / December 1985

ISBN 0-553-25284-4

Published simultaneously in the United States and Canada

Bantam Books are published by Bantam Books, Inc. Its trademark,
consisting of the words "Bantam Books" and the portrayal of a
rooster, is Registered in U.S. Patent and Trademark Office and in
other countries. Marca Registrada. Bantam Books, Inc., 666 Fifth
Avenue, New York, New York 10103.

PRINTED IN THE UNITED STATES OF AMERICA

H   0 9 8 7 6 5 4 3 2 1

For Earl and Bernice Krauzer

In the debris of defeat 30,000 Hmong lay dead; the survivors had been driven from their homes. To translate the disaster into American terms, imagine a holocaust that wiped out 18 million of us and forced the remainder of the population to flee to Mexico.

—W. E. GARRETT in *National Geographic*, 1974.

While they have no historical archives and few written records, the Meo attach enormous importance to their collective past, and have an uncanny ability to recall precise dates and details of events that took place fifty to a hundred years ago. They view history as a causally related chain of events, thus perceiving their current problems not only in terms of the immediate past, but in terms of decisions made two or three generations ago. However, their profound sense of history is crippled by parochial vision; foreign actors have only a dimly perceived role in their pageant, even though all of the monumental decisions that have affected the Meo—from their systematic slaughter in the seventeenth through the nineteenth centuries at the hands of the Chinese to the massive bombing by the U.S. Air Force today—have been made unilaterally in the foreign capitals of great empires and superpowers. And even on this artificially restricted historical stage there are only a few leading actors; in the minds of the Meo, events are determined, not by social conditions or mass aspirations, but, as in a Greek tragedy, by the personal strength or weakness of great leaders.

—ALFRED W. MCCOY, *The Politics of Heroin in Southeast Asia*, 1971.

Armament is an important factor in war, but not the decisive factor. . . . Man, not material, forms the decisive factor.

—MAO TSE-TUNG, 1938.

Northern Laos
June 1975

The doper propped himself on an elbow and scratched at the stubble growth on his bony chin. He wore khaki fatigue pants, a white T-shirt, and newish black combat boots. He lay prone on the flat forward deck, peering through the fine steady rain that slanted across the monitor boat's bow. Thick, deep-green jungle clotted either bank. Looking upstream, the right bank was Laos, the left Thailand.

Despite the early-morning chill, there was sweat on the doper's forehead and under his arms. An M16 automatic rifle lay on the deck beside him, propped under a scrap of canvas in one of the ports where twin flamethrowers had once bee·. mounted. The doper's name was Meeker.

He did a push-up and got his legs under him. The muscles in his thighs were twitching a little. The other two watched him from the monitor's little bridge. Steel fence poles had been bolted to the sides of the circular armored enclosure, and a tarp fastened over them formed a crude wheelhouse shelter against the rain. Meeker ducked under its overhang. It was good to get out of the constant drizzle, but in the suddenly still air the sweat on Meeker's forehead turned cold. To the rear of the bridge a .50-caliber heavy machine gun was tripod mounted on the stern deck. It was the only original armament left on the monitor.

"You got any belts for that thing?" Meeker asked.

Scanlon peered upstream into the dawn dimness. He was somewhere in his thirties, with dark, close-cropped hair and a

1

bushy mustache, and had six inches and forty pounds on Meeker. "There," he said. He dragged the word out to two syllables that pivoted around a hard *R*.

He was pointing to the right, toward Laos. "Say what?" Meeker said; and then he saw them, three men in peaked caps and khaki uniforms, toting AK-47s with their distinctive banana clips. Meeker dropped to one knee behind the armor plate.

"Pathet," Scanlon said into the mist. Two months into the rainy season, the Mekong's channel ran deep and straight. Scanlon kept the bow pointed dead upstream.

The third man grunted. He was big for a Vietnamese, with a shiny moon face like Mao's on the posters, a hard barrel-shaped trunk on short thick legs, big ropy forearms, and don't-fuck-with-me eyes. He stood about five-ten and wore a Makarov 9mm pistol on a web belt. The grips of the Russian automatic sported a relief of a five-pointed star within a circle, surrounded by embossed checkering. Meeker watched the three Communist soldiers watch the monitor as it slipped past, the diesel engines muttering in a subdued deep voice.

The Vietnamese grunted again. "He speak English?" Meeker asked.

"That's a good question, son," Scanlon said, as if it had never occurred to him. "You speak English?" he asked the Vietnamese.

"No," Nguyen said. He laughed, though his hard moon-like face did not change expression. He gave Meeker the willies.

"Vietnamese, probably, is what you speak," Meeker said. "North Vietnamese, maybe." Meeker wiped the icy sweat from his forehead. "Hey, congratulations on your boys taking the pennant this year."

Scanlon said, "Under here," and tapped a bulkhead cabinet with the toe of his boot. Meeker frowned, then bent and saw the heavy ammo belt. "You can handle an M60 if you have to, right?" Scanlon asked.

"I said I could." Meeker slung the belt over his shoulder

and got a leg over the edge of the enclosure. "Where'd you get this crate?"

"I stole it, son," Scanlon said.

"I could use a smoke," Meeker said.

"It used to belong to a guy I know, name of Sam. First name Uncle. Sam gave it to the ARVN when he went home, but I had a hunch them old boys wouldn't need it much longer. You read the papers lately—looks like I was right."

"A smoke, is what I said."

Scanlon turned the wheel slightly. The inboard motors chugged smoothly enough; the boat looked like a junker, but its guts had been overhauled not too long ago, at the old U.S. base near Nakhon Phanom. They had started out from there, around midnight. Scanlon took a pack of Marlboros from the pocket of his jacket and offered it.

"You know what I need," Meeker said.

"I want you a little edgy," Scanlon said. "A little edgy is good."

Meeker took two cigarettes, put one behind his ear and the other between his lips. Nguyen watched him through his bad-ass eyes, small dark pupils floating in gelid off-yellow. The skin on his round cheeks seemed stretched too tightly. Scanlon lit Meeker's cigarette with a gold Zippo.

They'd not met previously, but when Scanlon had come into the bar in Bangkok—La Chien Andalou, the place was called—Meeker had had an odd feeling that Scanlon was looking for him, or anyway someone like him. That was a couple of months back. The Khmer Rouge were marching into Phnom Penh; the coalition in Vientiane was folding like a pup tent; and the NVA were bombing Tan Son Nhut in captured American planes, while ground troups took Saigon and the last of the American diplomats, advisers, and spies climbed to the roof of the American embassy to board the helicopters. Bangkok was a good place to be just then.

Scanlon came to his table, pulled out a chair, turned it around, and sat straddle-legged. He had long horseman's legs. Scanlon said, "Been waiting awhile, son?"

Meeker was startled. "I did my time," he said. "Sixty-nine and seventy."

"Must have been fun, you decided to hang around." Scanlon's voice was neutral.

Meeker spread his fingers over the tabletop and watched them twitch. "I knew a guy." They weren't too bad this early in the evening, his fingers. "I was going to re-up, but this guy got me a lift back without that."

A dark woman in silk pajamas put two bottles of Budweiser on the table.

"I was out ten months, a year, scrambling every day. First off, the only shit on the street was stepped on hard. I had a taste for Double U-O Globe Number Four—eighty percent pure at the worse."

"Too bad," Scanlon said neutrally.

"Then," Meeker said, "what I needed, you had to deal with niggers. Very mean niggers, kind that carry knives, razors, nickel-plated revolvers with tiny-dick barrels. Most of them learned about being mean in these very parts—Uncle taught them how to blow guys away and not have bad dreams later on. But I had to deal with them. You know?"

"I've heard, son."

"I got cut once, and I got the crap kicked out of me, and maybe around the half-dozenth time I got ripped off I said the hell with it, and I came back here where the living is easy." Meeker wiped his nose on the back of his hand. "Fish are jumping, and the cotton is high."

Meeker ran a finger down the length of the brown Budweiser bottle and studied the line it left in the condensation. "Why am I telling you this?"

Scanlon reached inside his jacket and threw a Marlboro pack on the table. There was no cellophane around it, but the foil was neatly folded down. Meeker poked at it with his forefinger. The smokes inside were machine-rolled but the paper was discolored. There was a scratchy, ticklish feeling in the back of his throat.

"Help yourself," Scanlon said.

It was wonderful stuff, clean and sharp; after that, Meeker

kept in touch. He did a few odd jobs for Scanlon. Once he flew to Rangoon to deliver a thick padded envelope—Meeker guessed it held money—to some Burmese Lahu guy. Another time Scanlon sent him upcountry to the U.S. base at Udorn to pick up a packet from an American civilian. Meeker tabbed him for a spook. The only Americans left were spooks, or guys like him, or guys like Scanlon. The first time Scanlon gave him a thousand, the second time fifteen hundred, and always more of the smokes.

This time he was in for twenty-five hundred flat or a ten-percent cut, whichever was more. Ten percent of what? Meeker had asked, back in Bangkok. Scanlon had shaken his head and laughed and given him a carton; and now it was not long before dawn in the wide channel of the Mekong, with the rain slanting across the jungle's face.

"You want to hold on to your rifle," Scanlon said, "once we make the pickup."

"Who am I going to shoot?" Meeker asked.

Scanlon looked at him for the first time. "Whoever I say."

Nguyen spotted them first. Meeker was asking Scanlon for a smoke, and Scanlon was saying no. There were eight men, twelve women, and four kids: three girls and a boy, none over ten years old. The women wore cotton blouses and loose black trousers or wraparound skirts. The rain had changed to mist and the low gray sky was a shade lighter. There was an outside chance that the fog might burn off, making for a clear run back downriver. Meeker took the Marlboro from behind his ear, straightened it, and took a light from Scanlon. The damp tobacco sputtered and caught. The men on the bank were dressed alike, in cammie flight suits. The noise of the monitor boat's engines deepened, and Scanlon swung the bow toward the shore. On the left shoulder of each man's flight suit was an American flag, on the right a Laotian flag.

Meeker drew on the cigarette. "You said refugees, I pictured old men with Fu Manchu beards, women in black pajamas, screaming babies."

"These folks are Meo," Scanlon said, watching the people on shore.

"What are Meo?"

"Meo," Scanlon drawled, "are double-tough hombres." He brought the boat around, stern to. "You want to keep that in mind at all times, son."

They were fifty feet off the little point where the two dozen people waited in the rising mist. A narrow trail cut through the tangle of vines and banana trees behind them, and an armored personnel carrier—an old American M113—was parked in it, ass-end to the river.

One man stood near it, up from the muddy shore and apart from the others. He was slight, compactly built, and he stared at the boat through dark hard eyes. One of the officers went back up the bank to him and said something. The other man nodded, keeping his eyes on the boat all the while.

"Well, I'll be goddamned," Scanlon murmured. Meeker looked at him, alarmed. Scanlon sounded surprised rather than concerned, but Meeker was in no mood for surprises.

"What's the matter?"

Scanlon peered through the mist at the compact man. "These folks are getting the VIP send-off." Scanlon pointed with his chin. "You know who that boy is?"

"What's wrong, goddammit?" Meeker's voice sounded whiny, even to himself.

Scanlon glanced at him. "Not a thing, you chickenshit. I think what we got here are some of your top-rank spook-trained SGU officers."

"I don't know what you're talking about."

"Those boys are from upcountry," Scanlon said. "Their buddies and them were running the Special Guerrilla Units for the Agency."

"What the hell is that bastard staring at?" Meeker poked his chin in the direction of the compact man by the APC.

"That there is your top Meo dog." Scanlon smiled at something. "A genuine major general, commander-in-chief of the Meo soldiers since the spooks started recruiting, back in

Camelot days. That boy ran the whole show for the last fifteen years."

"What show?"

"The *Armee Clandestine*, they used to call it. The mercs. The ones who fought our war for us hereabouts."

"They did a piss-poor job," Meeker said.

"You'd be surprised, son."

Scanlon reversed the engines. The man by the APC watched them put in toward shore. "Bastard gives me the creeps," Meeker said.

"Some folks say they were the best fighters in the whole goddamned game. Born to war, like the Gurkhas." Scanlon barked a laugh. On the riverbank, the Meo were pressing toward the water. "The major general there, he's been fighting the Commies most of his life." He glanced at Nguyen. "They hate Commies. *Ce sont des bataillons guerriers*. You know about them, right?" He spoke French with the same soft vague drawl.

"*Je m'en fous*."

"You might, though. Could be we're into some real money here." Scanlon grinned. "Anyway, you'll have the chance to get back at them 'puppet troops' your boys were always pissing and moaning about."

Nguyen shrugged. "*La guerre est finie*."

Scanlon said in English, "It will be for these folks, son. Pretty damned soon now."

Meeker stared at the man by the APC. One of the refugee officers was helping a woman into the shallow water near the bank as the monitor boat came in.

"These guys are district commanders," Scanlon said. "Those got to be their wives and kids. They hate the Pathet Lao, and the Pathet hate them. Only thing is, the Pathet are running the show now, and they know these people, who they are and what they've been doing."

"They fought on the wrong side, and they fought too well," Nguyen said. "Then their side lost—and of course the Americans walked out on them. *C'est la guerre*."

"*Ce sont les Americains*," Scanlon said.

"What'd he say?"

Scanlon idled the motors and let the boat nudge up into the muddy bottom. "He said their nuts are in the wringer, long as they're stuck in Laos, which is why they're paying us to get them out."

Meeker started working numbers in his head.

"What you want to bear in mind, son," Scanlon said, "is that these are not your ordinary gooks. You keep your rifle handy, and you do as you're told." Scanlon watched the first woman climb up on the stern. "You know the drill, Nguyen."

The big Vietnamese went astern to the tripoded M60. He did not help the woman as she scrambled aboard, or any of the others who climbed up from the knee-deep muddy water. Meeker went forward to the flat raised deck. The men and woman were young, around his age, somewhere in their twenties, and looked pretty damned healthy for refugees. They'd been eating well.

One of them said something in French to Nguyen, and Nguyen's moon face went rigid. From the bridge, Scanlon said, "What's the problem?" The Meo climbed up on the deck and stood on the other side of the armored barrier. He was about five-six and wore a thin, dark mustache. "Major Neng Houa, ranking officer," he said in English. "You wish your payment."

"I wish to haul ass out of here," Scanlon said. "We'll see to business once we're rolling."

"That man is from the North." Neng cocked his head toward the stern of the boat, where a man was handing up the small children to another man. The children looked flushed and excited, as if this were a grand adventure.

"Yeah," Scanlon said, "but he don't hold any grudges. Your one worry is the Pathet Lao."

Neng smiled very slightly. "How pleasant it would be to have one worry only."

The compact man waiting at the rear of the APC watched the last officer climb aboard, and gave Meeker a tough mean look every chance he got, the ballsy bastard . . . "Hey," Meeker hollered. "Who you staring at, bud?"

Above him on the bridge, Scanlon said, "Shut up, Meeker." But Scanlon, nibbling absently at the ends of his mustache, was watching the guy too. The compact man did not react. Maybe he only spoke gook, Meeker thought.

The compact man turned and went behind the big squarish armor-plated vehicle. He had a particularly graceful and economical walk. The APC grumbled to life and disappeared into the jungle's wet thickness. Scanlon's grin returned, and he muttered, "So long, son."

He turned and looked over the tight-packed load of passengers. "All aboard," he called, then swung the nose of the monitor boat downstream. The passengers were squeezed into the passageway along the rail and pressed close to the forward and rear gun platforms, but the boat was riding high enough in the water. They had seen plenty of deep channel coming up; there would be no problem now, Meeker figured.

Scanlon called his name. Meeker slung the M16 over his shoulder by its web strap and went back to the bridge. The rain had eased to a mist now, and sun lit one cloudless strip of sky to the west, over Thailand.

Neng was on the bridge. "Here's what happens now." Scanlon stared downriver, so for a moment Meeker did not know if he was talking to him or to the Meo officer. "There's a gunnysack in that hatch there that Meeker is going to dig out to make the collection."

The temperature had risen ten degrees in the ten minutes since the sun had begun to cut through the misty rain. Meeker leaned the M16 against the armored wall and stripped off his T-shirt. A death's-head was tattooed on his chest, with AIRBORNE above it and WE KILL FOR PEACE below it. He'd gotten the tattoo in Bangkok; in real life he'd been infantry.

"What did I tell you about holding on to that rifle?" There was something new in Scanlon's drawl, something harder and colder. Or maybe Meeker was getting a little shaky from lack of smoke. Either way, he got the idea that this was no time to screw around. He picked up the rifle, found the gunnysack, and left the wadded-up T-shirt in the hatch.

"One thousand dollars each," Neng said. "In silver, gold, or dollars. Correct?"

"Well," Scanlon said, "no."

Scanlon looked at Neng, and Neng's body stiffened. Meeker could smell violence as thick as the diesel exhaust. Right then he knew that people were going to die, and decided: *not him*. With the realization, the smoke-jones abated—deserted him—and he saw with jarring clarity the rest of what went down.

"You tell your people that we're taking everything they've got," Scanlon said to Neng. "That's just the way it is."

On the rear gun platform, Nguyen held one of the firing handles of the M60, not menacing but ready. Neng looked at him and then back at Scanlon. "Tell them," Scanlon ordered. "Soon as he's done it," Scanlon said to Meeker, "you start circulating."

Meeker slung the M16 over his shoulder and followed Neng out. Neng stared at Nguyen for a moment and said something in Vietnamese. Nguyen's eyes narrowed and he took hold of the other handle, swung the barrel of the machine gun around a little, not aiming at anyone, but checking the limits of his field of fire.

Meeker expected protest or anger or outrage, anything beyond the bland, almost bovine expressions with which the Meo listened to Neng. He was not speaking Vietnamese now, and Meeker did not think it was Laotian, either. Nguyen was frowning at Neng.

Neng turned and said to Meeker, "The people are ready. Begin your robbery." His English was good, and thick with sarcasm. Meeker stepped down and edged through the thicket of close-pressed people. A pretty woman, a little darker than the others, removed gold earrings and put them in the sack. The little boy showed him a sunshiny smile. One of the officers unzipped the leg pockets of his flight suit, took two delicate finger-sized gold bars from each, and dropped them in the bag.

Meeker watched the valuables and did not meet the eyes of the people from whom they were taken. His mind was inventorying, multiplying by ten percent. . . .

The machine gun went off with a sharp, hard, ear-straining crack. A woman screamed and someone splashed into the river.

"Goddammit," Scanlon said, not very angrily.

Meeker pressed back against the side of the raised middeck, holding the sack against his chest. At the stern, four officers, including Neng, stood in semicircle around Nguyen, poised forward on the balls of their feet, but in the moment that Meeker looked, none moved. Then Nguyen swung the barrel so that it caught one of the men in the temple very hard. The officer stumbled on shaky legs, hit the railing, and flopped overboard.

Another officer bobbed to the surface near him and floated limply, face down. Rust color swirled on the dirty water.

Above Meeker there was the duller report of a heavy-caliber handgun, and one of the three remaining officers threw out both hands and was lifted off the deck in a high flailing arch. Scanlon stood at the stern end of the armored bridge, a .45 automatic extended in both hands in firing-range position. The man Nguyen had knocked into the water took a stroke toward the boat. Scanlon shot him; the man's head snapped back, and his body rolled over like a log.

"That's it," Scanlon said in a curiously calm voice. He swung the .45 on Neng, standing within reach of Nguyen on the rear platform. "Tell them it's over or I'll kill you."

"You will kill me anyway," Neng said. "I think you plan to kill us all."

Scanlon smiled. "But you first. Right now." Scanlon waggled the gun barrel. "Tell them."

Nobody moved except Meeker, who dropped the bag and swung down his M16, wondering whom he meant to shoot. He felt awkwardly vulnerable even with the weapon cocked and aimed; they were outnumbered four or five to one, and if the Meo men and women and children became a mob, they'd be overrun in a moment.

Unless they used the automatic weapons. Unless they killed them all.

On the rear deck, Neng straightened and said something in a monotone. Scanlon snapped, "Meeker!"

"Yo." Meeker's voice cracked.

"Finish up."

Meeker kept the M16 ready in his left hand, awkwardly handling the sack with his right. He did not meet the openly hostile faces, but watched instead the hands dropping money, jewelry, or a few gold or silver bars into the sack. No one else was moving; he was the object of every eye. When he stood on the rear deck in front of Neng, the Meo officer dropped a gold Rolex into the bag and said in a low voice, "He does mean to kill us, you know. He has to, now."

Meeker had to look at him.

"What will you do when the killing starts?"

"Shut up," Meeker said, too loudly. There was murmuring behind him. Meeker turned away. It was too cold without his T-shirt. Too many clouds blocked too little sun. A breeze chilled the sweat glistening across the AIRBORNE tattoo, making him shiver. One of the little girls was sobbing, and her mother handed her a bracelet to drop into the sack, as if it were a game. The little girl grabbed at it with pudgy fingers and dumped it in. Meeker felt nauseated.

Scanlon kept eyes forward when Meeker came onto the bridge, squinting against the glare that now shimmered on the wide river's brown surface. "Put it where you found it." The easy swaggering banter was gone from his tone; his voice was mechanical, monotonal. "Look there."

Meeker looked in the direction in which they were going.

"The elbow of that bend to the left," Scanlon droned. "About a hundred meters up."

The bank jutted out, a vine-tangled mass of shubbery hiding the river beyond the bend.

Scanlon looked quickly astern. Nguyen was watching him. Scanlon nodded.

"Be ready," Scanlon said to Meeker.

"For what?"

"Soon as we round that corner, they've got to jump."

"Huh?" It made no sense, and Meeker thought he'd misunderstood.

"Put your rifle on single-shot."

"I want to know what the hell—"

"*Put your goddamned rifle on single-shot!*" Scanlon's voice was low and sibilant, deadly as venom.

Meeker put his rifle on single-shot. The monitor boat edged around the bend. From the wheel they caught the first glimpse of the soldiers, a dozen of them in their pale khaki uniforms. On the left bank—the Laos side. They carried AK-47s.

Pathet Lao. Meeker got it: Scanlon had robbed them, and now he was turning them over to the enemy. It was as good as a death sentence. "Take the wheel." Meeker snapped his head around; Scanlon was speaking to him. "Keep in the channel, about half-speed. Don't stop or change course, no matter what happens. Do it, or I'll kill you, too." Meeker took the wheel.

The Pathet Lao stood on the bank away from the cover of the brush, their rifles up, watching the monitor boat motor downriver. The Meo had seen them by now, and some of them were scrambling around to the right side of the boat. Behind Meeker, Scanlon shouted, "Tell them to jump, Neng."

Meeker could not see Neng. An officer looked up from the rail, and Scanlon shot him in the chest. The man tumbled backward into the water and disappeared. "Jump!" Scanlon screamed "*Sautez!*" One of the other officers did. A woman hesitated, then followed. Meeker looked to his left. There were eight or ten people in the water, most swimming, a few dead.

A woman grabbed up the boy as Nguyen fired three shots from the M60. The massive, slow slugs punched through the boy's small body and into his mother's. Both went into the water. There were splashes on either side now. On the left bank, the Pathet Lao soldiers stood poised and watching but did not move.

"All right," Scanlon said, so close behind him that Meeker started. Scanlon took the wheel, pushing Meeker out of the way when he did not move. Without looking back, Scanlon shouted, "Nguyen!"

The monitor boat was opposite the Pathet Lao on the shore, the Meo scattered in its wake. One of the Pathet Lao waved. The big Vietnamese swung the M60 around, gripping both handles.

Flame and smoke spouted from its muzzle, and the belt chattered through the receiver, brass casings flying through the air and flashing in the morning sun. Splashes plumed in a quick line as slugs stitched the river's sluggish surface. The line passed through the oldest of the girls, who was flailing in panic as she gulped water; when the line passed on, she was no longer panicked or flailing. The gunfire reached one of the officers, who was swimming for his life, head down, arms and legs pumping hard and rhythmically. The man's body bowed and went stiff as if shocked by high voltage, and the water around him became laced with delicate tendrils of red.

The firing stopped. Bodies floated in the monitor boat's wake. Meeker saw two of them moving: a woman whose long hair had come undone and streamed down her back, and an officer who had nearly reached the right-hand bank. He saw Nguyen switch the selector and put a single shot in the back of the woman's head. Nguyen swung the gun to the right and fired again. The officer threw out both arms, and his palms made wet slapping sounds. His body drifted toward the reeds by the bank.

Nguyen left the gun and went along the narrow walkway. Meeker saw the last little girl draped over the low rail, the back of her blouse soaked with blood. Nguyen dumped the body into the water. They were fifty meters downstream from the Pathet Lao squad now. The boat's wake lapped at the brush-covered cutbank. The two dozen bodies floated in place like leaves in a puddle.

Meeker gagged and felt bile rise up and burn his throat, but he did not vomit, because he had not eaten since the preceding evening. Scanlon heard the noise and whipped his head around. His face was ugly, contorted with rage and something else, something darker. "You're a useless sack of shit, son," he snarled.

Meeker unslung the M16, held it by the cold barrel, and flung it out over the water. It did not make much of a splash.

"Smart," Scanlon muttered. "Real goddamned smart." He suddenly sounded tired.

Scanlon shook himself like a wet dog. He reached inside his jacket and came out with a Marlboro pack, not the one he had offered earlier, but one without cellophane, the foil folded down. "Have a smoke, son," Scanlon said, and Meeker reached for it. He rarely did more than a half at a time, but he smoked one and a puff of a second, and after that he slumped on the rear deck and stared at the water and tried, with some success, not to think at all.

BOOK ONE
California

Chapter One

Berger stared with disbelief at his right foot. It was encased in a wing-tip brogan with pinhole vents, which in turn was embedded up to its gunwales in gumbo mud. Berger tried again to pull his foot out of the mud. It might as well have been stuck in concrete.

My luck, Berger thought: *if there's a dark cloud anywhere in the neighborhood, it's gonna home in, skid to a stop, and piss all over me.* It wasn't supposed to rain in Southern California in April, not like the way it was raining now, steamy drops as big as golf balls plopping into the muck of the sodden dirt roadbed. Somewhere beyond the foothills sloping away at Berger's back was Santa Barbara and the Pacific, but for now the city was hidden behind the storm's gray curtain.

Berger grabbed his right knee with both hands and pulled hard. His stockinged foot popped out of the brogan. Berger stumbled back, teetered, and nearly sat down in the gunk. The mud gurgled and the brogan disappeared. A thick bubble blossomed on the mud's surface, trembled, and burst like a drowning man's last death-throe gasp.

Berger gaped at the spot where his shoe had been. Everything he wore was sopping, from his gray fedora and gray suit and white shirt and narrow dark tie, to his cotton socks, sleeveless undershirt, and white Jockey shorts; he could not have been wetter had he fallen into a creek. For one long moment, Berger gave serious consideration to sitting down in the mire, burying his face in his hands, and sobbing hysterically.

In Central America, CIA agents were overthrowing

democratic governments. In the Middle East, CIA agents were assassinating Arabs. In Moscow, CIA agents were doubling inside the KGB. And in Santa Barbara, Berger was standing in the rain wearing one shoe. Fourteen years of loyal service didn't mean shit. One mistake and you were dogmeat. Berger's had to do with a Bulgarian tobacco broker who'd ripped him off for fifty grand while pretending to be with State Security.

"Fucking Bulgarians," Berger said aloud. It made him feel better. He lowered his head and limped forward through the rain, careful where he stepped.

The gate was around the next bend. It opened on a dozen acres of hillside surrounding a low four-bedroom ranch house, the home of a man named Vang. The way Berger understood it, Vang had been a big wheel in the Agency's Secret Army in Laos during the war—which did not halfway explain why, after the war, the Agency set him up on a spread like this. *Goddamned gook lives better than I do,* Berger thought.

Berger trudged around the bend, looked up through the thick rain, and felt nauseated. The gate was wide open, and there was no sign of his partner, Fishman.

Berger felt a burning sensation at the base of his throat, a few inches above his heart. Vang was supposed to be under a sort of house arrest, and their assignment—his and Fishman's—was to monitor Vang's activities and make sure he stayed put. Berger reached into his coat pocket, thumbed two Tums from the end of a roll, and popped them into his mouth. As far as Berger could figure, the Agency was afraid that the little bastard would cause some kind of trouble. Probably had some dirt on them—Berger did not know or care. What mattered was that this gate was supposed to be closed and locked, with Vang inside, snug in his damned ranchette while Berger shivered in the rain.

Berger clawed under his coat and dug out a little short-range transceiver. He extended the whip antenna and keyed the transmit button. "Rabinowitz, you there?" Static sizzled back at him. "Answer me, dammit."

Rabinowitz lived like a mole in a windowless underground bunker behind the house, monitoring the electronic surveillance devices installed in every room. The idea was to record Vang's activities and the contacts he made, but Vang had found every damned bug within a week of moving into the place. Within a week after that, he'd wired in an override panel that enabled him to turn the microphones on and off at will. Rabinowitz never bothered to tell the Agency that his job was pointless; for some reason, the guy actually liked it here. Living in the dark did something to the mind . . .

"Rabinowitz," Berger bleated into the transceiver.

"Yeah?" The voice was thick and dopey.

"The fucking gate is open," Berger sputtered. "The bastard's split on us again. Where the hell is Fishman?"

"Ri' here," Rabinowitz drawled. "Say 'lo, Fishman."

The radio crackled. "Hello Fishman," Fishman's voice said.

"What the hell . . . ?"

"Come on up to the house."

"But—"

"Commercial's over," Fishman cut in. "I'm gone." The static cut off abruptly.

Berger punched the button of his radio, on and off and on again. It gave off a crackling sound, a bright flash of blue spark, and the sharp smell of ozone, and then smoke began to dribble out of the plastic case where rainwater had shorted out the circuits. Berger flung the radio into the sagebrush and trudged toward the house.

He was a professionally trained intelligence agent, goddammit, and he could smell trouble like an Inquisitor could smell heresy. When the house came into sight behind the last little hill, he turned left off the driveway and circled around to the side, where a deck extended out from the side door. A gnarled juniper ten yards out gave him cover. Berger froze in place and listened hard. The only sound was rainwater dripping from the brim of his fedora.

Berger drew a rapid breath, tensed, and dashed lopsidedly for the steps to the deck. His still-shod left foot hit the bottom step and skidded on the rain-slick wood. Berger backpeddled frantically, and for a moment he was in mid-air, his arms and legs pumping madly, like Wile E. Coyote before he plummets to the foot of a two-thousand-foot cliff.

Berger flipped ass-over-teakettle into a puddle and instinctively froze once more, ears flared. He realized he was waiting for someone to laugh. When no one did, he picked himself up and climbed the stairs and jerked open the side door. *The hell with them,* he thought savagely. They could coldcock him and truss him like a Thanksgiving turkey, shoot him full of dope and ship him to Moscow and hold a Bic lighter under his nuts until he told them everything, and he would not be more miserable than he was at this moment.

But when he got inside the entryway, Berger heard indistinct but unfamiliar voices coming from somewhere deep in the house, and became the professional agent once more. *Commercial's over,* Fishman had said on the radio. It had to be some kind of code. Fishman and Rabinowitz *were* in trouble. It was up to him.

Berger pulled a short-barreled Colt .38 Police Positive from under his left arm and carefully thumbed back the hammer. He held the gun at the ready as he eased through the door into the kitchen.

On the counter by the refrigerator, a tray of melting ice cubes sat beside two half-empty bottles of 7-Up and one of Jim Beam. A fly was exploring the crusty remnants of a can of Frito-Lay bean dip, and there were a few crumbs of crushed potato chips flecked with odd-looking green flakes in the bottom of a Pyrex bowl. Berger tasted one of the chips and grinned wisely: sour-cream-and-green-onion, as he'd suspected.

Berger wiped off the potato-chip grease on his wet pants and went down the hall toward the voices, holding the revolver next to his ear with the barrel pointed at the ceiling. The volume of the voices rose, though the words remained indistinct. There was a half-flight of stairs at the end of the hall to the right, with swinging batwing doors at the bottom. The voices came from behind them.

Berger catfooted down the stairs. In the room behind the door, one of the voices said, "Hand over the six-shooter, boy."

Berger smiled grimly, without humor, his eyes squinting in a steely hard gaze. He steadied his right wrist with his left hand, drew a deep breath, let half of it out, held the rest.

Berger hit the swinging door with his left shoulder and brought the gun down as he went through, dropping into a crouch in the same motion, sweeping the room with the revolver. "Freeze, scumbags," he barked.

"Scumbags?" Fishman looked at Rabinowitz. "What kind of talk is that?"

Rabinowitz said something that sounded like "Whuzza?"

On the TV screen, Sheriff Andy held out his hand as he pinned Opie with a glare. Opie had him covered.

"Mexican standoff," Fishman said thickly.

"Sshh," Rabinowitz hissed.

On the screen, Opie shot his dad in the bridge of the nose with the water pistol. Andy fished a checkered handkerchief the size of a tablecloth out of his back pocket and mopped comically at his phiz.

Fishman shook his head in awed appreciation. "Them folks in Mayberry really know how to live."

Berger gaped at the two men. This finished basement space was something like what his parents had called their rumpus room. Fishman was sprawled in a leather-upholstered Barcalounger. On the table next to him were an empty highball glass and a full ashtray. His eyes had the glassy sheen of a dead carp.

Rabinowitz lay supine on a leather sofa, one leg draped over the edge. The TV's remote control was on his chest. He looked at Berger, who remained in a firing-range crouch with the Colt extended. Rabinowitz said something that sounded like "Whaffa?" He was as drunk as a human being could get and still survive for the hangover.

Berger had been speaking to Rabinowitz on the radio since the trouble with the Bulgarian had begun—six months ago—but he had never actually seen the guy. According to

Fishman, Rabinowitz only came out once a year, on the second of February, to look for his shadow. Berger believed him.

Living underground seemed to have wrought subtle evolutionary changes in Rabinowitz. His skin was the color of a mushroom cap. His eyes were small, yellow tinged, and set close together, but his nose was large and sharply pointed. His head was covered with a skullcap of tight, curly dark hair, as were the backs of his hands and the V of chest at the neckline of his shirt.

On the TV screen, Aunt Bea said, "My land, but don't you boys carry on. . . ."

"Holy Christ," Berger hissed. "What the hell is going on?"

"Opie stole a nickel from Floyd the barber," Fishman answered, "but Andy made him give it back." His voice was slurring a little now. On the screen, the closing credits rolled as Andy and Opie headed for the ol' fishing hole. Fishman looked Berger over. "You look like reheated dog piss."

"Where's . . . ?"

"Who you gonna shoot?" Fishman nodded at the Colt in Berger's hand. Rabinowitz pushed a button at random on the remote control. On the screen, Ward, immaculately dressed for breakfast in coat and tie, was moving his mouth at Wally and the Beav. For some reason, the sound was off now.

Berger forgot that the Colt was cocked. Its hammer caught the rim of his shoulder holster as he put it back, slipped off cock, and discharged the loaded chamber. Rabinowitz came off the sofa and rose three feet into the air. He landed in his original position. The bullet cored into the cushion of a vacant chair. Kapok puffed from the hole.

"You need a drink." Fishman sucked the melted ice from his glass and lurched to his feet. "We all need a drink. Don't step on no pink snakes while I'm gone." Fishman staggered through the door.

"Rabinowitz," Berger said. "Please . . ."

Rabinowitz said something that sounded like "Wubba-bubba."

Fishman returned presently, balancing a bottle of beer and two highballs. He held the beer out to Rabinowitz, who stared through his rodent eyes, then made three grabs for it before connecting. Fishman offered one of the highballs to Berger, who shook his head.

"Come on, let your hair down," Fishman said. "Be one of the girls."

Berger took the glass and drank. "Jesus," he said. His eyes were watering. "What is this?"

"My special four-to-one highball," Fishman said. "Four parts bourbon to one part 7-Up, dash of bitters." Fishman drank from his own glass and sighed with satisfaction. "Lemme guess," Fishman said. "The Jeep broke down."

"Flat tire."

"Fucking G.I. shit," Fishman said sympathetically. "Let's have a drink."

"We got a drink," Berger said, gesturing with his glass. "Where's Vang?"

Fishman waved a hand airily. "He hadda go somewhere."

On the sofa, Rabinowitz passed out. The beer bottle fell from his lifeless fingers, thumped to the floor, and began to pulse out beer onto the indoor-outdoor carpeting.

"Where?" Berger asked.

"Where what?"

"Where did Vang go?"

"Didn't say."

"Oh God," Berger moaned. He sank into the chair with the bullet hole in the back. "We're supposed to keep the son of a bitch here. Jesus, if he causes any trouble, the Agency'll crucify us."

"The Old Man'll pound in the nails personally," Fishman agreed pleasantly. "But not to worry. Vang promised he'd be good."

"Why the hell didn't you keep him here?"

Fishman furrowed his brow shrewdly. "Hey, Rabinowitz, didn't we tell him he had to stick around?"

Rabinowitz lay limp as a washrag. Berger wondered if he was dead.

"Well, we did," Fishman insisted. He was beginning to go into a sulk.

"They'll kill us," Berger whined. "They'll send us to Mars." He took a big slug of his drink and made a choking noise.

"Naw," Fishman said. "No one'll know. Vang promised. He said, c'mon in, make ourselves to home. Heck of a guy, that Vang."

"You should have stopped him," Berger said, and drank some more bourbon. "That's our job. That's why the Agency set him up in this place. The son of a bitch is supposed to stay put."

"Aw, you know how it is," Fishman said. "How you gonna keep 'em down on the ranch, after they've seen Paree?" He squinted, trying to focus more clearly on Berger. "Hey, you're only wearing one shoe. What are you, half-Jap?"

As Berger was embarking on a long swim through Vang's liquor supply, his host was no more than ten miles away, in the back office of a Hmong community center that was located on the second floor of a building that had begun life as an Odd Fellows Hall, in the days when Santa Barbara was younger and less self-conscious. Despite Vang's demurral, his host had insisted he take the chair behind the desk, the seat of honor. The gesture was acknowledgment of his leadership position among the Hmong people in the United States, as he has been their leader in Laos.

The man sitting across the desk in the straight-backed wooden chair was named Chue Pao. He was somewhere in his fifties, more than ten years Vang's senior. A clan headman in his highlands district, he continued in that role for the transplanted Hmong. Vang listened patiently, without interrupting, as Chue told him the good news—new babies, young people in college, families who had lately managed down payments on homes of their own. When Chue finished, Vang smiled and nodded and waited for Chue to explain why he had asked Vang to come here this day.

"I wish to speak of our people." Chue had a low, musical voice. "We have a message from Bangkok, bringing word from Xianghoang."

"Good news, I hope," Vang said, as he always did at this point in the conversation. Chue pursed his lips and shrugged, as he always did.

The exchange was ritual, ceremonial. It was not news, really, but an iteration, an assurance. Vang listened to Chue tell him once more about the small guerrilla bands of their people who still roamed the mist-shrouded mountain ridges above the Plain of Jars, digging in during the long months of the rainy season soon to begin, reemerging each autumn to harass Pathet Lao patrols. When Vang had led the Hmong warriors, they were armed by the United States; now, in the most whimsically Orwellian irony, their patron was China, because the Chinese were presently at cold war with the Vietnamese, who were closely allied with the ruling Laotian People's Revolutionary party. The Hmong, in turn, were less interested in ideology than in the liberation of their tribal homeland in northern Laos and the eventual repatriation of all Hmong, in the United States and around the world.

"Of course we look forward to returning home," Vang said neutrally. "But for now . . ."

"Yes," Chue said. "We must live in the present."

"We are fortunate." Vang had a hunch where this was leading. "But there are others. . . ." He paused to let Chue get to his point.

"Every month, a few more of our people manage to cross the Mekong into Thailand," Chue said. "They have been settled in camps outside Bangkok, but they cannot be comfortable or safe there for very long. We have too many enemies in Southeast Asia today, even in Bangkok."

"How many?"

"There are women, children, old people." Chue looked at the wall above Vang's head. "Can you obtain permission for them to enter this country?"

"Possibly."

"Perhaps five hundred," Chue said softly.

Vang stared neutrally at Chue. The problem wasn't Immigration and Naturalization Service red tape; the Hmong had become expert in navigating that bureaucratic maze, and

Vang had developed some expedient shortcuts. The problem was money. Everything had its price, and the price of liberating one refugee from the steaming lowland camps in the swampy delta of southern Thailand began at two thousand dollars. That covered airfare and processing; shelter, clothing, and subsistence in this country were extra.

Vang multiplied familiar figures in his head. "I will see what I can arrange." He placed his hands on the desktop and stood. *Two million dollars, minimum,* he thought. *Dennison . . . but Dennison is no sorcerer. Even he'd have trouble producing that amount of money out of the ether. But Dennison might be the place to start.*

"Thank you." Chue shook Vang's offered hand. "Come." Chue held open the door of the barren office and gestured. Vang went out, turning over alternatives in his head. He absently noted the man at the foot of the stairs, but the implacable problem of the high cost of relief preoccupied him. He glanced at the man and nodded pleasantly.

The young man said, "Sir!" and clicked his heels together and saluted smartly.

Vang drew up. The man was Hmong, about thirty years old, dressed in jeans and a plain black T-shirt. Vang peered at him.

"Neng?"

"Yes, sir."

"I thought . . ." Vang shook his head. "I was told that everyone . . ."

"I must speak with you, General." The young man still held the salute.

Vang returned it, and felt his eyes mist.

"Yes," Vang said. "We have a great deal to discuss."

The Laotians called them "Meo," a bastardization of the Chinese word for *barbarian.* They called themselves Hmong, "free men." They had never been barbarians, and in the present century they had rarely been free men.

The earliest *bataillons guerriers* were organized in the last months of the 1950s by U.S. Special Forces training squads who called themselves "White Star civic action teams." Were anyone to ask, they would have described their missions as "relief work."

No one ever did. The arms shipments, ferried to the highlands by "private" contract airlines financed and controlled by the Central Intelligence Agency, had little to do with "relief." The mandate of the Hmong Secret Army was to fight Communists—in Laos, across the frontier in North Vietnam, and along the Ho Chi Minh trail into Cambodia. In return, the Hmong had the CIA's solemn promise of aid in the establishment of an autonomous state, a homeland.

As early as 1961, when U.S. newspaper mention of the Second Indochina War was still relegated to a couple of paragraphs below the fold on an inside page, nine thousand Hmong had been armed, equipped, and trained. In the next fifteen years, nearly four times as many Hmong men—and women, and boys as young as thirteen—would die fighting communism for the United States.

In the end there was neither homeland nor victory. The dominoes fell to the Communists, and the United States pulled out, abandoning a number of one-time allies including the Hmong. Vang's forces managed to hang on until the spring of 1975, when the Pathet Lao advanced on the seat of the coalition government. Along the way, in their first stage of "liberation," the Communists began to fire on the "indigenous enemies of the people's state"—the tens of thousands of Hmong civilians fleeing from the northern highlands south toward Vientiane.

From the beginning, Vang viewed CIA sponsorship with open eyes. He understood—perhaps better than did the Agency—the nature of their relationship. For the time being, they shared a common enemy. But, correctly predicting that the political winds would shift and the U.S. war effort become undermined, Vang arranged a fallback. Amassing enough documented evidence of the CIA involvement in the opium traffic to deeply embarrass the Agency, Vang pressured his contact officer, Vientiane chief of station Peter Chamberlain. Vang was able to save nearly fifteen hundred of his people, mostly women, children, and the elderly, in the first weeks of that bloody spring.

With the fall of the coalition a few months later, Chamberlain was recalled to the U.S. air base at Udorn in Thailand. It was not Chamberlain's fault; he was as much a pawn as were the Hmong.

Among those who remained in the few Hmong strongholds, Vang and his officers were the most vulnerable; they were walking dead men. The Pathet Lao called them traitors, quislings, collaborationists, and worse; their association with the United States and the CIA made them the perfect object of Communist propaganda—and Communist genocide.

Toward the end of that last dry season in '75, Vang's officers and their families began coming in from the field to Long Tieng, 150 klics north of Vientiane. During the war, Long Tieng was nominally the staging center for missions to rescue pilots downed over North Vietnam. It was also the secret base of the CIA-sponsored Hmong operations throughout northern Laos.

It was near Long Tieng, ten years earlier, that Vang had last seen Neng.

At one side of the open meeting room in the Santa Barbara Hmong community center, a grandmotherly woman was demonstrating the *lamvong* to three little girls. The woman was thin and astonishingly graceful, her feet moving slowly through the intricate steps, her arms and fingers twisting sinuously. The oldest girl was six, and all three had been born in California. They laughed gaily and clapped when the woman was finished, and let her hold their arms as she guided them through the movements of the dance.

Neng said, "Do you know what happened that morning on the Mekong?" He sat straddling a metal folding chair.

"No." Vang watched the little girls for a moment. "I heard a story: the boat was ambushed by Pathet Lao, and twenty-four of our people died."

Neng smiled faintly. "Twenty-three." His smile faded. "But the others were not killed by the Pathet."

Vang stared through unfocused eyes at the laughing, awkward children, and listened to Neng's story of that early rainy-season morning ten years before. His expression was neutral, but his mind was a turmoil of outrage and self-reproach.

He had almost made the Thailand bank of the Mekong, Neng told Vang in a soft monotone, when he was shot in the fleshy part of his thigh. There was a lot of blood, and he lay in the water on his back and played dead until the monitor boat disappeared downstream and the Pathet patrol lost interest and withdrew. On shore, he fashioned a bandage from a sleeve of his flight suit and waited. He was lucky: only a day passed before he was discovered by two teenaged Thai soldiers nervously patrolling the border. Since then he had been "resettled" in several different refugee camps, from Kauk Soung and Bangkok in Thailand, then to Pulau Bidong island off Malaysia. A year ago, Neng told Vang, he had managed to contact a relative, whose sponsorship had enabled him to immigrate to the United States.

"My friend," Vang said when Neng finished. "Why didn't you come to me when you arrived?"

Neng shook his head. "I learned as soon as I arrived: no man works harder for our people. I did not wish to burden you with . . . other concerns."

Vang stiffened. Neng was trying to spare his feelings.

"All right," Vang said in a harder voice than he intended. "Why did you seek me out now?"

The grandmotherly woman lifted the hands of one of the girls over her head, gently playing the girl's fingers into the patterns of the dance. "There were three men on that monitor boat," Neng said. "One was Vietnamese."

"A refugee?"

"*North* Vietnamese," Neng said.

Vang's eyebrows rose. "The other two?"

"Both were American." Neng looked up at Vang. "Two days ago, I think I saw one of them."

Chapter Two

The tenement was in the Boyle Heights district of Los Angeles, off First Street not far from the cemetery. It was three stories tall and two apartments wide, of dirty stucco trimmed with vaguely Spanish-style pink scalloping. Three black kids were beating time with hands and feet around a large sheet of cardboard carton; on it, a fourth was spinning perfectly on the nape of his neck. A huge stereo cassette deck was blasting out an upbeat Pointer Sisters' number.

Vang parked the rented Mercury across the street. A pint-sized kid with an inflated Afro scampered up as Vang and Neng got out. "Watch your car, mister?"

"Do you think it needs watching?" Vang said solemnly.

"Sure do, man. And right here you got the best car watcher in East L.A." The kid could not have been older than six or seven.

"What does it cost to have a car watched these days?" Vang asked.

The kid looked him over shrewdly, as if gauging how much Vang was good for. "Four bits," the kid said judiciously.

Vang dug two quarters from a pocket and flipped them to the kid. The kid snatched the coins out of the air, neat as a frog pinning a fly. He gave Vang a big grin, then leaned against the car's fender, arms crossed and feet apart, on duty.

Vang waited for a twenty-year-old Caddy convertible, as big as a boat, to rumble past before he and Neng crossed toward the break dancers. He felt curiously detached, now that he'd heard the rest of Neng's story, now that he knew what had to be done. If Neng was right about the American, it was the key to taking care of business that had been pending for too

32

many years. If not, Vang would find other ways to pay this old debt. . . .

Neng had been given the Agency's field-medicine course training, he had reminded Vang as they drove south along the coast from Santa Barbara. A few months after he'd arrived in California, Neng had landed a job as an orderly at the Veterans Administration Hospital near the San Diego Freeway in West Los Angeles. Until he built some seniority, he was working the graveyard shift in the E.R.

Two nights earlier, around eleven, the cops had brought in a man with a bleeding head wound. The man was glassy-eyed and stunk of booze, and the cops assumed he'd been mugged, until Neng found a wallet on him. There was still a little money in it, which meant he'd probably fallen off a curb or staggered into a door. The E.R. doctor stitched the cut and ordered the man admitted for twenty-four hours of observation.

But a half-hour later, while the man was still in recovery awaiting a room assignment, he'd come to and rung the buzzer. Neng found him sitting up, looking almost sober and demanding his clothing. Neng paged the doctor and stayed there to keep an eye on the guy. That was standard procedure in that kind of situation.

But there was another reason: seeing the man conscious for the first time, Neng had an uncanny feeling that they'd met before.

The E.R. doctor recited the pro forma admonition against leaving, had the patient sign a release, and told Neng to bring the man's clothing. When Neng returned, the man was sitting on the gurney in his shorts.

"That was when I saw the tattoo," Neng told Vang as he decelerated for the Wilshire off-ramp. A death's-head with AIRBORNE above it and WE KILL FOR PEACE below it; faded somewhat, the skin slackened with age, but still recognizable: the same design Neng had seen on the skinny chest of the American with the heroin-red eyes. . . .

"They called him Meeker," Neng said in the car. "When

he was admitted, he gave his name as William Mears, the same name as on the cards and driver's license in the wallet I found."

On his admissions form, Mears had given the address of this sad stucco building behind the gyrating break dancers.

"I'm not positive it's he," Neng said.

The inner door of the building had a security lock, but the glass was broken. Vang reached through and worked the latch. "Let's ask him," he said.

The staircase bisected apartments set front-and-back on either side. The carpeting on the risers was worn through to bare wood in the middle. There was no elevator. On the first landing, a big-bosomed, middle-aged black woman carrying two grocery sacks stuffed with clothing pushed past, giving them a narrow, red-eyed, suspicious look. A big irregular water stain covered the wall of the stairwell above the second floor, like an abstract mural.

Apartment 3 was in the rear on the left. The door rattled on its hinges when Vang knocked.

A watery voice called, "What do you want?"

Vang knocked again, not hard.

"Who is it, goddammit?" The voice was closer to the thin door.

Vang waited ten seconds and knocked again.

Nothing happened for a few moments. Then the door snapped open a few inches against the restraint of a chain.

Vang could see the middle third of a face in the narrow opening. The eyes were bloodshot, the skin pallid, the chin covered with a two-day growth of stubble, and the breath stank of stale alcohol. The eyes' pupils were dark and too shiny, almost malarial.

"Is your name Meeker?" Vang said.

"Who's asking?" the guy said slyly.

Vang stepped back and planted the sole of one shoe against the door, high up beside the chain. The bolts tore out of the soft wood and the door slammed inward, catching the man's shoulder. He stumbled back. Vang let the momentum of the kick take him through the door. Neng followed, and swung the door shut again. The loose chain rattled against the wood once and hung quiet.

The man stood off to one side, rubbing at his cheek with the edge of his hand. He wore greasy jeans, a white T-shirt with gray-stained armpits, and no shoes. He was very skinny, almost emaciated; his shirt hung on his shoulder blades as on a coat hanger. Above his right temple, a bandage held a wad of gauze over a one-inch shaved circle of scalp.

"Stay right where you are, please," Neng said. Vang went past the man and looked quickly around the little flat. Once it had probably been advertised as a "studio apartment." There was only this front room and, down a short hallway, a washroom with a shower stall.

A filthy, swaybacked single bed with rumpled sheets was pushed against the back wall, below an open window that looked across an alley to a back-porch clothesline. A torn-velveteen-covered armchair sat beside a cigarette-scarred coffee table occupied by a large glass ashtray overflowing with butts, a crumpled pack of Lucky Strikes, a pint bottle of Ten High bourbon, and a water tumbler with an inch of the amber liquor in it. A longitudinal rip like a knife slash split the shade of a floor lamp, and beneath the table lay a shiny hemp spiral-woven throw rug.

A half-counter separated a cramped pantry from the rest of the dim room. On its other side Vang found a chipped egg-yolk-smeared dish on a shaky-legged folding deal table, two straight-backed wooden chairs, an old round-shouldered refrigerator, a rust-stained porcelain sink with a dripping tap, and a countertop holding a two-burner hotplate and a grease-encrusted black cast-iron skillet. Roaches scuttled across the smeared tile floor.

The only wall decorations were pictures torn from magazines. The place smelled of rotting food, cigarette smoke, spilled booze, and a backed-up toilet.

The man laughed suddenly. "I had this hunch," he said. "Something told me: Expect company, clean up the joint." His hands shook when he dug a cigarette from the pack, and it took him two tries to light a match. "Now then," he said, "what the fuck are you doing busting in here?"

"Is your name Meeker?" Vang asked.

The man downed the whiskey in the tumbler and replaced it with another two inches. "How would it be," he said, "if I called a cop?"

Neng took two steps and a fistful of the front of the guy's dirty T-shirt. He slammed him hard against the wall. The guy did not react except to hold his glass out of the way and keep it upright. Neng lifted him to his toes; he seemed as light as a bird, as if his bones were hollow. "Is your name Meeker?" Neng said.

"It was," he said . "Once upon a time, in a galaxy far, far away." But then his eyes narrowed, and he looked at Neng as if seeing him for the first time. "I know you."

"From the hospital," Neng said.

"Uh-uh," Meeker said. "Somewhere else."

"It's a small world," Vang said.

Neng lowered Meeker to his feet. Meeker drank the bourbon in one long draft. Neng let him go. Meeker stared at him for a moment longer, as if expecting a trick, then began to move aimlessly around the little room. He was staggering a bit, like a battered fighter whose best chance of going the distance was to stay near the ropes and away from his opponent. "What do you want?" he muttered.

"Tell us a story, Meeker," Vang said softly. "Begin in June of 1975. We'd like to hear about the other two men on that monitor boat."

Meeker stared at the bottle on the coffee table as if afraid it might scamper off. "Five thousand bucks."

Vang backhanded Meeker across the face. The water tumbler flew out of his hand and over the counter and shattered against the refrigerator; a thin string of dark bourbon dribbled down its door. Meeker swayed. Vang grabbed his arm at the bicep. He felt bone below the thin layer of flesh.

"You listen to me," Vang said quietly. "I can kill you with my hands, right now." Meeker's breath revolted him.

Meeker smiled weakly. "Sure you can, only it won't do you a fuck of a lot of good, now, will it?"

"Were you one of the three men on that boat?"

"What boat was that?"

Vang swung Meeker around and folded his right fist over the forefinger and middle finger of Meeker's left hand, then slapped his left hand over Meeker's mouth. Vang held the fingers stiff and levered them over. Meeker closed his eyes and moaned. Vang released him. Meeker's two fingers were bent back, the bones snapped.

A fine sheen of sweat coated Meeker's forehead. He stuck the broken hand under his arm, wobbled to the couch, and sat. He was ashen, and Vang feared he might pass out from shock. But then Meeker grabbed the bottle with his good hand and chugged down an inch of the cheap bourbon. He coughed. "You motherfucking son of a bitch," he said to the bottle, low and not very vehemently. Vang waited while Meeker went on that way for perhaps thirty seconds, a low, mesmeric litany of the most vile obscenities.

When he was finished, he looked up at Neng. "You were there?"

Neng nodded.

"Sorry." Meeker smiled lopsidedly. "All you folks look alike to us."

"I was shot," Neng said.

"Not by me," Meeker said. He looked at Vang. "You finger-breaking bastard, you'd be killing an innocent man."

"That won't stop me," Vang said.

"I can believe that." He pulled his left hand from his armpit and examined it critically. "Christ, they're really starting to hurt." He reached for the bottle again.

Vang took it and stepped back.

Meeker surprised him. "That don't work so well on me," he said. "Back then, that business on the Mekong, I was a junkie for sure, but you know, I never took another hit after that day. So some good came out of it, huh?"

Vang set the bottle on the countertop. He had a hunch that Meeker wanted to talk. He had lived with this secret for nearly ten years. Vang turned away and looked over the tear sheets from newspapers and magazines Scotch-taped to the wall.

"So," Meeker said, "gimme back my goddamned bottle."

Vang was looking at an article from *Harper's* about the opium trade in the Golden Triangle of Indochina; there was an inset map of the area where Laos, Thailand, and Burma abutted. Behind him, Meeker said, "I was junked up all the time after I went back. A pack of hand-rolled cigarettes loaded with smoking opium cost like thirty-five cents on the street. A hit of Number Four white was two bucks in Bangkok. I was always buzzed out those days, and I was buzzed out when I hooked up with Scanlon."

Vang picked up the bottle and turned. "Where did you meet Scanlon?"

Meeker gave him a narrow, shrewd, alcoholic look. "You know Scanlon, huh?"

"Answer my question," Vang said.

"I met him in Bangkok."

"What was he doing in Bangkok?"

"I don't know. I had the idea he got around, scammed here and there. He had the best smoke and good white, and he paid me a couple bucks now and then. Three months I knew him, tops."

Vang stared at an article from *Ramparts*, torn and beginning to yellow, something about the CIA's involvement in drug traffic during the war, with head-and-shoulders photos of two alleged agents. Vang happened to know that one of them *was* CIA; the other was Military Intel. "Where is he now?" he asked casually.

"I don't know."

Vang turned and glared at Meeker.

"You want to break a couple more fingers, be my guest. The fact is, Scanlon didn't like the way I held up my end. He put me ashore at Nakhon Phanom that afternoon; told me if I ever mouthed off, he'd find me and kill me. I hitched a ride on a C-5A that was evacuating to Bangkok, and I never saw either of them again."

Vang examined another clipping on the wall. "Who was the third man?"

Meeker laughed. "You're looking at him."

Vang glanced at Neng. He came over to look.

It was a single page torn from a *Time* magazine dated three years earlier. The right-hand column was headlined: NEW FRENCH CONNECTION? and at its foot was a one-column mug-shot-type photo, slightly out of focus, of a Vietnamese identified as Nguyen Van Cao. According to the article, U.S. Drug Enforcement Administration officials had named him as head of a Vietnamese gang that had taken over a major part of the Paris link in the heroin chain that stretched from Southeast Asia to the streets of New York.

Vang said, "You had not seen this before?"

"No." Neng smiled ruefully. "We did not get *Time* in the refugee camp."

"Is this the third man?"

Neng bent closer to the picture. "I don't know." He shook his head. "It is possible. The face is thinner, but . . . It could be."

Vang put the bottle on the table in front of Meeker. "Are you certain Nguyen Van Cao was on the boat with you?"

"Nope." Meeker draped his good hand over the neck of the bottle. There were liver spots on his bony fingers. "I been staring at that picture for three years. I guess I've convinced myself by now." Suddenly he sounded weary.

"Have you had any contact with either of them?"

"Are you kidding? Jesus." Meeker put his broken hand between his legs and took a long gurgling drink.

"Where is Scanlon now?"

Meeker's eyes were moist, his skin ashen. "I'm hurting, man." His voice trembled.

Vang stood over him. "Do you know where Thomas Scanlon is?"

Meeker dragged himself to his feet. "Gotta get something." He wobbled past Vang to the bathroom.

"Leave that door open," Vang said.

"Fuck you," Meeker snapped, and slammed the door.

Vang sprang at the door, tried the knob. It was locked. He stepped back, crouched, and hit it with his shoulder, low and hard. The hinges groaned and the thin wood paneling cracked. Vang hit it again. The door crashed back on its hinges.

Meeker was squeezed up against the wall between the sink and toilet. Both porcelain bowls were stained with splotches of brown. Meeker held a nickel-plated snub-nosed .38 revolver on Vang.

"Easy." Meeker thumbed back the hammer. "Tell your buddy to stay put."

"Do as he says." Vang kept his eyes on Meeker.

"Good. Okay." The whites of Meeker's eyes were cross-hatched with broken capillaries. "So you want to know some things, you son of a bitch." His voice was thin and strained.

Vang shifted his weight to the balls of his feet.

"Right there is good." Meeker was pressed back against the wall as if trying to melt into it. "You move the least little bit, see what happens."

The little gun was steady in Meeker's uninjured right hand, but a muscle twitched spasmodically in his gaunt cheek. "You ever have nightmares?" He made a choking noise. "You ever dream of bullets tearing into men and women and children in the water, and Commie creeps on the bank watching like it was some kind of freak show?"

Vang watched the gun in Meeker's right hand.

"What do you see when you close your eyes?" Meeker wailed.

Neng was moving along the short corridor outside the bathroom. Meeker seemed not to hear him.

"If I drank enough," Meeker said, "I could convince myself sometimes: it maybe never happened, I was nodded up in Bangkok all along, made it up out of the smoke."

Meeker stabbed the gun in Vang's direction, the short wide barrel dead on his chest from four feet. "Ten years of convincing myself, and here you are, come to tell me just how goddamn real it all was. You want Scanlon, you bastard? Well, too goddamned bad."

Vang stepped to the right, feinted and dropped to a crouch, and started in under the gun.

Meeker snatched it clear, shoved the barrel into his mouth, and jerked the trigger.

The report was flat, not very loud. Meeker's eyes opened impossibly wide and his mouth puckered, as if he were sucking on the gun muzzle. There was a small splatter of red and gray on the dirty wall two inches above the back of his head.

Meeker's knees folded and he slid down the wall, leaving an irregular smear. He sat down with his legs spread like a doll's. The gun slipped out of his mouth and fell onto his lap. His head flopped forward and his chin rested on his chest. The bandage over his temple had shaken loose and hung from one adhesive side.

Neng came in the door and drew a quick breath. Vang stared down at Meeker's body and swore to himself.

In the other room, Vang memorized the date on the page torn from *Time* and left it where it was. He looked around the room, inventorying objects touched, then grabbed the bourbon bottle, dropped it out the window, and heard it shatter in the alley below. He used the sleeve of his jumpsuit on the bathroom doorknob and again to open the apartment door. Neng followed him out.

A fat man in a sleeveless T-shirt stood at the top of the stairs. He pointed a cigar at them and said, "Hold it right there."

Vang said, "Get out of my way." The fat man opened his mouth. Vang punched him in his soft gut, not very hard. The fat man grunted, dropped his cigar, and grabbed himself.

They went down the stairs quickly. The day was growing warmer, and the break dancers were sprawled on the stoop, drinking bottles of Coke. The little black kid was still at his post by the car, smiling with pride at his staunchness.

Dennison's Compound
March 3

The snow squall had come on quickly, violently, and from nowhere. An hour earlier, the pale noonday late-winter sun had been two-thirds of the way to overhead in the southern sky, floating alone and majestically in delicate chill blueness. But then the clouds had appeared, first as a low dark band over the ridge ten miles to the west, then as a gray blanket moving toward the compound and at the same time fanning out until the leading edge stretched from horizon to horizon. In fifteen minutes it domed the compound like a cloth draped over a parakeet's cage. The wind began to whine across the clearing perched on the mountain's south face, and all at once thick, opaque lashings of snow were swept before it, as if someone had knife-gutted a feather bed.

Dennison turned up the fleece-lined collar of his leather aviator's jacket. He stood well back under the roof of the porch that fronted his isolated mountain headquarters building, but gale-driven, ice-rimmed snowflakes shotgunned under the eaves to bite into the reddened flesh of his cheeks. Dennison's ears burned, and he slapped the jacket's pockets absently for his wool cap. It wasn't there. He swore softly and thought about going inside to look for it. He checked his watch—it was nearly one. She'd landed at the little municipal airport at Libby, forty air miles south, Dennison decided. There was no point in standing out in the storm. Dennison hunched his shoulders and turtled in his neck, and stayed where he was.

Ten minutes later the wind dropped somewhat. Off to Dennison's right, the western sky began to lighten. He relaxed his shoulders, brushed snow from his short dark hair, and stomped his boots on the porch planks. As he reached for the door latch, he heard the first faint whomp-a-whomp of the chopper.

Dennison went down the four steps and peered up into the shifting snowfall. The wind gusted, then ebbed; the snow might have been abating. The rhythmic beat of the Bell's twin turboshaft engines rose, and Dennison made out its forward lights. A knife-edged blast of wind drove a handful of snow into his face.

The chopper rose above the trees at the foot of the lawn, fifty yards to a side, that fronted the compound. The orange windsock mounted on a pole at the far side stood out as stiff as a pennant; near to the ground was a shear like a riptide. Dennison raised his hands to wave her off.

The wind went dead. The orange sock fell limp as a eunuch, and the snow stopped abruptly, as if someone had slammed a door. The gray clouds were whitening, and cracks in the sky to the west showed streaks of blue. The Bell Model 222 Executive skimmed the near trees. It hovered fifty feet off the ground while the tricycle landing gear unfolded from the truncated airfoils, then snow whirlpooled in the prop wash as it alighted in front of Dennison. The runners sank a couple of inches into the crusty spring snow that the fresh squall had left; the engine coughed and cut off, and the rotors feathered to a stop. There was a moment of stillness and silence before the front doors opened.

Miss Paradise wore a body-contoured black leather jumpsuit tucked into black cowhide Tony Lama boots, and tinted, teardrop aviator shades in a silver frame. The long fall of her platinum-blond hair was threaded through the vent of an adjustable cap with scrambled eggs on the brim and USS CORAL SEA—OV-4B on the crown. She stood six feet tall and had a figure that would make a Pope abdicate.

Vang climbed out through the passenger-side door, in a puffy Gore-Tex down jacket over wool slacks and hiking boots. He was bareheaded, and Dennison noticed that his close-cropped dark hair was flecked with gray. Dennison met him with an outstretched hand, and Vang took it.

Miss Paradise pinched Dennison's ass as she sauntered

past. "You should have waited until it passed by," Dennison said.

"Just a squall, boss dear." She kissed him quickly on the lips. Her breath misted, warm and fragrant. "We followed it in." She crossed herself solemnly. "God is my copilot." She gave Vang a sidelong grin. "You never lost faith, right, Vang?"

"Of course not," Vang said. "I may have lost a few years of my life, though."

Dennison had known this man for close to twenty years; despite Vang's bantering tone, he sensed his tension. "I've got a few items for you," Dennison said. "I'm afraid it's not much."

"I appreciate your help."

"Well, hell," Dennison smiled, "that's what we're here for."

Dennison racked a four-foot length of unsplit tamarack above the glowing embers in the big stone fireplace. He stood and dusted his hands together, and watched until the tamarack crackled and combusted. Sparks chased up the flue.

"If Nguyen is the same guy," Dennison said, "what do you want from him?"

"Reparations," Vang said.

Dennison smiled vaguely. He had first met Vang in the early sixties, when an Agency assignment took him up Route 7 to Muong Soui at the western edge of the Plain of Jars, where he was to consult with the Hmong general. They walked among the wooden stalls of the market, eating balls of sticky rice flavored with the pungent fermented fish sauce called *paddek*. Vang knew everyone's clan name, and he stopped frequently to murmur a few words—of greeting, inquiry, encouragement—to the women and children and old men in the little village square. There were no young men; they were in the field.

In the next dozen years, the Hmong would be literally decimated: one out of every ten would die. Men and youths would be killed in battle with NVA regulars, while women and children and the elderly would expire in the forced refugee evacuations from their highlands home: of exhaustion, of unfamiliar lowland diseases, or of despair.

Vang could not afford the luxury of despair. Dennison had felt split between the Agency and these people who were fighting their war for them. Vang, however, did not deal in abstracts. When he commanded, and later when he tried desperately to care for his people as the fighting became futile, the welfare of the Hmong was always his paramount concern.

In the United States, Vang's burden of responsibility remained weighty. The relocated Hmong needed support, both emotional and financial. Vang provided the first by his presence and example. For the second, he returned to the only profession he'd ever known: warrior. That's where Dennison came in.

Dennison and Miss Paradise had worked within the intelligence community at one time, until they decided there was nothing intelligent about rules that took the cuffs off the bad guys and put them on the cops. Ultimately, Dennison had come to the realization that the only way to deal with the rules was the way the other side did: ignore them.

Dennison had determined to play by one rule only: life on the edge was a mean dirty game, won by the toughest son of a bitch with the best guns.

Dennison's People, as his organization had come to be known in some circles, was ostensibly a profit-making enterprise; his fee was $250,000—and up. Dennison maintained a roster of professionals with the skills and guts to take on the dangerous jobs that the sanctioned authorities could not or would not touch.

You could hire Dennison—if you were walking the correct side of the street—but you could not buy him. To hire him cost you plenty, and the only thing you got for your money was results. You paid up front, in full, and there were no refunds. You had no say in how Dennison handled the job, and he decided when it was over.

You set Dennison loose, then got the hell out of the way.

Vang had been one of Dennison's first operatives, and he had never failed to earn his fee. And, though Vang had never discussed it, Dennison knew damned well that most of what he earned went anonymously to the community organizations the various Hmong communities had set up.

When Vang had called him the day before on the secure line, Dennison's feeling for the man had flared so intensely that he'd reacted with something like anger after hearing Vang's story. "Goddammit, Vang, whatever I can do for you, just ask."

"All right, Dennison," Vang said. "I want your help."

"You got it, pal," Dennison had snapped—and looked up to see Miss Paradise smiling at him indulgently.

Now she came through the heavy oak office door carrying a tray. She pushed the door shut with her foot, then set the tray on the sideboard and cleared a space in the jumble of papers, spine-up open books, computer printouts, photographs, and note-covered scraps mounded atop Dennison's heavy oak desk. She had changed into jeans and a wool sweater over a flannel shirt. She placed a glass mug of coffee laced with Bushmill's in the reclaimed territory and offered another mug of the Irish coffee to Vang, who sat in one of the four leather-upholstered armchairs facing Dennison's desk. Dennison lowered himself into the matching swivel chair behind his desk, then leaned forward and steepled his fingers to form a little shelter over his steaming mug.

"And Scanlon," Dennison said. "Do you want him as well?"

Vang raised a hand and gestured meaninglessly.

"Say you find him," Dennison pressed. "What then? More reparations?"

"We'll see," Vang said.

Dennison sipped his drink. Vang had not touched his. A resin-clotted knot in the log exploded and sent up a plume of sparks. Miss Paradise dug a hand under her sweater and came out with a soft pack of Marlboros.

After a while Vang said, "Let me tell you about the last days at Long Tieng."

Dennison leaned back in his swivel chair and clasped his hands over his flat stomach. His eyes were half-closed.

"While I got as many of my people out as I could," Vang

said, "my officers were drawing back to the base. Some had their families with them. The Americans were gone by then. The Pathet knew we were still on the base, but we had men and materiel, so in the beginning their squads skirted us on the way to Vientiane. But as soon as they took over, we learned from our people in the capital that we were their priority-one objective. We had a week, perhaps less."

Miss Paradise held an unlit cigarette between two fingers and rummaged under the mess on the desk.

Vang watched her for a moment. "I had a plane," he said, "a T-28. I could get out when I wished."

But he had not, Dennison knew, until he had done everything possible to evacuate those officers and the women and children with them.

"I managed to take care of most of them before I left," Vang said. "It was not always easy."

Miss Paradise found Dennison's heavy desk lighter and the ashtray under a six-month-old copy of *Smithsonian*. She set fire to the cigarette and blew out a smoke ring. "How did you pull it off?"

"One way and another," Vang said.

"Scanlon was involved," Dennison guessed. "The man who double-crossed you."

"The man who killed two dozen of my people," Vang said. He watched the smoke ring turn oblate and begin to dissipate. "We found an APC that was still operational and went down Route Thirteen. We met a squad of Pathet Lao on that leg, and another after we circled north of Vientiane and reached the river road. There was a firefight each time, and I did not lose a man. And then we rendezvoused with Scanlon."

Vang stood abruptly and went to the window. Dennison stared at his back. He thought he knew what was coming next, and did not like it.

"What happened after that," Vang said, staring at the snow. "It is my responsibility."

"The hell it is," Dennison said sharply, more angry than surprised.

Miss Paradise drew on her cigarette. "Tell us about it, Vang."

"I called Udorn to request an airlift," Vang said softly, watching the glass as if it were replaying his memories. "Peter was in Singapore, and I got an agent named Corwin. He said they were under firm orders not to breach Laotian airspace. I pleaded with him.

"A few hours later," Vang continued, "Corwin called back and told me he had set up a possible boatlift. One of their men would meet us on the Mekong east of Vientiane and take us downriver to a point from which we could reach the U.S. airbase at Ubon Ratchathani in Thailand."

"Not an agent?"

Vang shook his head. "A contract man."

"Scanlon," Miss Paradise said.

"Yes." Vang turned to her. "And I okayed the operation."

"That doesn't make it your fault."

"Wait a minute," Dennison cut in, before Vang could respond. "You must have tried to get to Scanlon afterward."

"Not for some time. For the last six months of 1975, I was more concerned with the living."

"We know about that," Miss Paradise said quietly. "We've been to war too."

"That's why I came to you first," Vang said.

"But eventually you must have talked to Peter," Dennison said.

"Of course." Vang looked at him. "And I found out why my officers and their wives and children died: bad timing, bad luck, and an honest mistake."

Vang sighed. "Twenty minutes after I radioed Udorn, Peter called. The agent Corwin did not tell him that I'd asked for a dust-off. The order against Laotian overflights had been in effect and observed for two weeks, and Corwin had no reason to think Peter might violate it. Besides, Peter was busy." Vang managed a smile. "The U.S. was losing the war, once and for all, in three countries at once. That kept him hoping."

Vang shook his head. "Corwin asked a contract man named Milton if he had anyone who could get my people out.

Earlier that same day, Milton had seen a man he knew slightly—Scanlon. Milton told Scanlon about the job, and Scanlon bid it at a thousand dollars a passenger. Milton told Corwin and Corwin told me. I accepted. It was a fair price, considering the risk."

"What you didn't know," Miss Paradise said, "was that it wasn't really a gamble."

"Correct," Vang agreed. "From the start, Scanlon meant to rob us—and then to kill us for the Pathet Lao."

"The bastard must have cleared plenty on the deal," Miss Paradise said.

"He also made friends within the Pathet," Dennison said thoughtfully. "Was Scanlon really on contract to the Agency?"

"At one time, yes," Vang said. "That was Corwin's honest mistake: he did not check Scanlon's file. Six months after we evacuated, I persuaded Peter to show me that file."

Dennison smiled slightly. He knew Peter Chamberlain well, had served under him at one point; he was a damned fine agent, one of the good guys. But he tried to go by the book when he could, and Vang had become the major thorn in his side. Now Vang's evidence of the CIA's involvement in the seamier sides of the war was resting in various safe-deposit boxes around the country. When Vang needed Agency information, he simply went to Chamberlain and threatened to release the material. And when Dennison needed something, Vang was his lever.

"Scanlon was a civilian, born in Tyler, Texas, who'd been in Southeast Asia since the late sixties," Vang said. "That was virtually all they had on his background."

"In those days, in that place," Dennison said, "the Agency ended up using some fairly unsavory characters."

"Scanlon was one," Vang said. "He did his first job in sixty-nine, and his last in seventy-two. The Binh Xuyen—the Saigon OrgCrime outfit—was fronting an opium-boiling plant for the VC, near the Y-Bridge in Cholon. Scanlon was part of the operation to shut it down, and he was given fifty thousand dollars buy money. The next day he disappeared."

"With the money."

"Of course. But he turned up again a week later, claimed he was unable to set up the buy, and gave back the Agency its fifty thousand."

"So where was he in the meantime?"

"He made the buy all right," Vang said. "Then he cut the stuff and turned it around for a hundred thousand dollars. The Agency got its money back, and Scanlon had a clean profit."

"Not so clean," Miss Paradise said. "Odds are that the smoking dope Scanlon sold was refined into Number Four—the crap that was hooking American G.I.s."

"A year after the Agency found out the truth and discharged him," Vang said, "there were rumors that Scanlon was involved in the drug trade on his own. There was a street war about that time, in which three Saigon gangs were ambushed and wiped out. Two were run by Americans."

Vang sat down again in the end armchair. "I bring it up to illustrate that Scanlon was never particular about whom he killed."

Dennison unclasped his hands and leaned forward in his chair. "So now you plan to kill him."

Vang's expression remained bland. "First I have to find him," he said. "A man who may have been Scanlon was spotted—by some of my people, in fact—in Luang Prabang, two months after the massacre. After that he seems to have disappeared."

"I tried to trace him through my contacts," Dennison said. "I didn't have much luck."

"He may be dead," Miss Paradise pointed out.

"I'd like to make certain," Vang said.

"And you think this Nguyen can tell you, one way or the other."

"I think that Scanlon's alive and Nguyen knows where he is."

"That's purely a hunch," Dennison challenged.

"All right."

"Well," Dennison sighed, "it's a good one." He lifted a pile of newspapers on a corner of his desk and pulled out a nine-by-twelve-inch manila envelope, removed a photograph, and handed it to Vang.

The photo was shadowy and foreshortened, as if it had been taken with a telephoto lens in poor light. In the foreground were half-a-dozen Asian men in uniform; one of them stood in front of a microphone, smiling and with both hands raised, as if acknowledging a crowd. In the background was an indistinct group of a dozen more people. The head and shoulders of one was circled. He was Occidental; the image was so small and the picture so poor that Vang could make out little more than the man's race. "Scanlon?" Vang murmured. He looked up. "How do you know?"

"Computerized enhancement and analysis," Miss Paradise said. "It comes up around a ninety-percent chance that it is Scanlon."

"When and where?" Vang waved the photo.

"Vientiane, summer 1981," Dennison said. "A government rally in That Luang Square. The picture was taken by an Argentine newsman who sold it to the Agency. He guessed that they might be curious about a guy who looked like an American. The Agency matched it up with Scanlon's file photo, and bingo."

Vang did not say anything for a full minute. Dennison wondered if his friend was moving toward the same conclusion as he. So far it was conjecture, but if Vang came to it independently . . .

"What can you tell me about Nguyen Van Cao?" Vang asked finally.

Dennison smiled. "Nguyen appears in Paris in 1979, claiming to be a one-time government official in the South on the run from the reds. But there's a rumor that he's one himself, an NVA regular assigned to deep-cover work in Saigon. In any case, he acts real capitalist. He buys a big house with grounds, and walls them up tighter than a tin can— security fence, guards, the whole nine yards. He gives a few newspaper interviews and says he fears assassination attempts. After that, he never comes out of his place, as far as anyone knows, and pretty soon the press loses interest."

"But not *la Sûreté*," Miss Paradise picked up. "Or Interpol or our DEA. Within a year after he moves to France, Nguyen has imported two dozen Vietnamese buddies, and not the kind of boys you'd invite to tea."

"Nguyen built a gang," Dennison said, "and started moving in on the heroin trade, not politely. He rocked the boat—there was a street war. Thirty men, almost all known narcotics dealers, died in eighteen months, but Nguyen won. Right now, the DEA thinks he may control as much as forty percent of the trade through France."

"Why haven't they stopped him?"

"The usual reasons," Dennison said. "Too little hard evidence and too much red tape. For what it was worth, they leaked some stuff to the press a few times—that's the origin of that page from *Time* that you Telefaxed to me—but nothing came of it."

Vang thought again for a few moments. "Where does he get his raw material?" he asked.

"Probably from the Golden Triangle—Burma, Thailand—"

"—and Laos," Vang finished. "Scanlon?"

The name hung in the air, drifting on the warm updrafts from the fire.

"Let's play with a scenario," Dennison said. "When the Pathet Lao took over in seventy-five, one of the first things they did was to lift the restrictions on the cultivation of opium poppies."

"They were a bit late," Vang murmured.

Dennison knew what he meant. The Hmong people had raised poppies for generations, primarily for medical and social use. The chain of events that made them become warriors began when their crops were burned and they were forced toward the lowlands. "Follow me," Dennison said. "You're the Pathet Lao right about then, and a man comes to you with a scheme."

"A man like Scanlon," Miss Paradise said.

"Scanlon shows you he's been around the country for a long time," Dennison said. "He gives his references, if you will. Anyway, he convinces you that he's a crook—but your kind of crook."

"And to show where his loyalties lie, he arranges the massacre of my officers."

"That's certainly possible," Dennison agreed. "In any case, he proposes a partnership with the new regime: He goes up north—into your territory, Vang—and takes over whatever growers are left."

"Mostly Hmong," Vang murmured.

Dennison nodded. "He uses money and muscle to appropriate the fields. Then, in exchange for noninterference from the government and army, he runs the entire operation, including export and refining."

"A franchise," Miss Paradise said. "Like a Burger King."

"Right—and the LPRP is the franchiser, for a regular cut of all receipts."

"Then for refining," Miss Paradise said, "the product goes to France—and his buddy Nguyen takes over."

"If Scanlon is in Laos, I can find him," Vang said. "With or without Nguyen."

"Maybe," Dennison said. "But I want Nguyen as well."

Vang looked at him curiously.

"You're on the payroll for this one, Vang."

"Are you taking over the operation?"

"Of course not. I see a job I'd like done, and since your interests run along the same channels . . ." Dennison took a gulp of his Irish coffee and sat back in his chair. "If I'm right, and if we can take out both Nguyen and Scanlon, we cripple a major segment of the heroin operation worldwide. I'm offering you the assignment, at your usual fee."

"Boss dear," Miss Paradise said in a cautionary tone. "This is supposed to be a self-supporting operation. There you go mortgaging the ranch again."

"I'm not too worried about the mortgage, my dear." Dennison smiled. "We've got no shortage of well-heeled clients these days. They can afford to pay the freight for the occasional *pro bono* chore."

"Have you been reading Marx again, boss?" Miss Paradise said.

Dennison ignored her. "What do you say, Vang? The mission is stop Nguyen, and Scanlon as well if he does turn out to be the Asian connection. Do we have a deal?"

"There's one more thing," Vang said slowly.

"I know," Dennison cut in. "Five hundred of your people are waiting in a camp outside Bangkok, and you need a couple of million dollars to repatriate them." Dennison grinned. "I haven't been snooping, but things do cross my desk."

Miss Paradise waved at the mess there. "Lots of things never complete the crossing," she said to Vang.

"Nguyen and Scanlon are murderers," Dennison said more seriously. "They deserve what's coming to them, and if you want to deliver, that's fine with me. But I also like your ideas on reparations."

"If our theory is correct, they should both be very rich men."

"Anything you can liberate, over my expenses, is yours, up to two million. We split the rest, fifty-fifty."

Vang nodded. "We have a deal."

"I'm glad to hear that," Dennison said, his smile returning.

"I see no point in waiting," Vang said. "What is our first step?"

Dennison leaned forward. "I'd say Paris."

Vang considered. "I could use a local contact."

Dennison smiled. "I have just the man."

BOOK TWO
Paris

Chapter Three

The man in the silk jacket leaned back and crossed his legs and made the ash glow at the tip of his cigar. The chair was covered in very dark brown leather and the antique desk it faced had a glass top and curled legs. The cigar was Cuban. The man in the silk jacket said, *"Qu'est-ce qui se passe?"*

There were five other men in the room. Two were Vietnamese, as was the man in the silk jacket. The third, an Occidental named Hugo Crain, was standing back near the door, regarding the backs of the fourth and fifth men. One wore a beret and a beard above a shabby cotton jacket and looked like a caricature of a Left Bank student in the sixties. His partner was balding and had a liver-sprung gut and a misshapen nose chased with broken veins that bespoke a long acquaintance with cheap wine. Both were somewhere in their thirties, and stood with hands behind their backs, wrists cuffed with disposable locking plastic straps.

"What happened, I think," Hugo Crain said, "is that these two guys lost their fucking minds."

The man in the silk jacket brought the leather chair forward and placed both palms flat on the glass desktop. Nguyen Van Cao was still a big man, unusually broad across the shoulders for a Vietnamese, with thick arms and a barrel chest. But his full-moon face had aged in the years since he'd left Indochina; the skin was neither as taut nor as deeply colored, and there were wrinkles below his eyes and at the corners of his mouth that threatened to collapse into dewlaps. He stared past the two Frenchmen at Crain, waiting for the story.

Hugo Crain flicked his eyes left and right, from one Vietnamese to the other. They were short, dark, neatly built men in their early thirties. One wore a Jean-Paul Belmondo sort of leather jacket that was not cut quite well enough to conceal the bulge under his left arm. The other wore his shoulder holster openly, over a plain gray sweatshirt; it held a Beretta 9mm automatic pistol.

Crain looked at the two Vietnamese again, more obviously. When Nguyen did not react, Crain said, "I don't like audiences. I get stage fright."

Nguyen smiled yellowly.

The man with the big gut moaned and said, "Get it done with." His face was greasy with sweat.

"Go have something to eat," Nguyen said. He was looking at the man with the big gut, but it was the Vietnamese in the leather jacket who replied.

"I'd like to hear this," he said.

"Go now." Nguyen spoke in a quiet, hard voice, and kept his eyes on the handcuffed men while the Vietnamese went out and shut the door to the office behind them.

Hugo Crain looked down at the richly woven Khotan carpet. "I like the way they talk to you," he said. "Nice. It shows a lot of respect."

"Not like you," Nguyen said, almost neutrally.

Crain smiled. "You know how it is."

"No." Nguyen's stare drilled into the two men. "But I would like to hear."

"There isn't much to tell," Crain said. "A couple hours ago"—Crain glanced at his watch—"they broke into our facility."

"Why?" Nguyen split a hard gaze between the men in cuffs.

"Monkey business." Crain shook his head, as if he could not fathom how anyone could be so cold stone dumb. "When our men got to them, they were about to start stuffing kilo-bags into a plastic garbage sack."

"Does that make sense?"

"Of course not," Crain snapped. "If you want explanations, ask them."

Nguyen stood. "Yes," he said slowly, as if Crain had suggested something that had not previously occurred to him. He pulled open the top drawer of the desk.

"They got in the back door," Crain said. "Someone took out one of the outside guards."

"Dead?" Nguyen asked politely, as if he might be asking for a match.

"Just bumped on the head. There were three chemists working at the time," Crain said. "The other guards were where they were supposed to be. They could not have been inside for more than thirty seconds when we stopped them."

"Someone told you a lie," Nguyen said with a smile.

"*C'est ca, c'est vraiment ca.*" The one in the beret nodded his head vigorously. "You understand."

Nguyen bent slightly and took a gun from a drawer, a Heckler & Koch Parabellum autoloader. "Let's go." He went past the two men and out of the office without looking at them again. He heard Hugo Crain say something in French, and their feet shuffling along the carpet.

Nguyen took the open-ironwork elevator down two levels. He crossed a concrete-walled basement storage space, unlocked a heavy metal-reinforced door, and flicked a wall switch. A ceiling fixture illuminated a bare, windowless room with two filing cabinets against one wall and four straight-backed wooden chairs against another. Nguyen stood with his back against the third wall, facing the door. Hugo Crain came in with the two men a few minutes later.

"Listen," said the man in the beret.

Nguyen inclined his head. Crain jerked the man in the beret over to the chairs and sat him down, then wrestled his pinned arms over the back of the chair. The man with the big gut stood waiting, as docile as a cow, until Crain pushed him into one of the chairs and yanked his arms behind him.

"I'm listening," Nguyen said. He crossed his arms over his chest, so the pistol pointed at the wall to one side.

"A guy told us that the heat was on your operation." The

man in the beret spoke fast, slangy French, and his words ran together. "He said that you feared a raid, and you had to pull out fast. He said there was two million dollars of powder left behind, two million easy."

"He was short by about eight million." Hugo Crain laughed.

Nguyen glared at him. The man in the beret looked from one of them to the other. "He said we'd get half," he said. "One million dollars."

"U.S.," the other man said.

"You believed him?" Nguyen asked softly.

The man in the beret shrugged.

"What was his name?"

"I don't know," the man in the beret said quickly.

Nguyen worked the slide of the pistol and pointed it at the man, holding it with both hands. The man's mouth opened and closed and opened again. Nguyen shot him there, so the bullet came out through the base of his brain and threw him back against the concrete wall.

The man with the big gut stared down at his partner. He was shaking and drooling.

"Why didn't you want the others to hear this?" Nguyen asked Hugo Crain in a conversational tone. The man with the big gut began to moan.

"I think something is going on." Crain was staring at the dead man. "Until we were sure . . ."

"All right." Nguyen pointed the pistol at the man with the big gut. "What was his name?"

"Swartz," the man barked, as willingly as a puppy. "His name was Swartz."

Nguyen shot him in the middle of the chest. The man's chair clattered back against the wall but did not go over. The man stared at Vang through dead open eyes for a few seconds, then toppled over sideways.

Nguyen looked at Crain. "Until you were sure of what?"

Before Crain could answer, Nguyen swung the muzzle of the H&K on him. Crain did not move.

Nguyen raised the gun and sighted down its length at the middle of Crain's chest.

"That is a very poor joke," Crain said.

Nguyen laughed. "I find it amusing enough."

Crain stared back. He could not keep his eyes from flitting between the gun muzzle and Nguyen's slack, smiling face.

"A joke," Nguyen went on thoughtfully. "Yes." He lowered the gun then and gestured with it. "But you see what could happen."

Chapter Four

Pigalle was no longer the nightlife haunt of the cognescenti that Toulouse-Lautrec had limned a century earlier. Sullen-faced whores lurked in dark doorways, and porno theaters competed with seedy by-the-hour hotels for sidewalk frontage. The black draperies masking the windows of the sex shops were in observance of the ordinances against overt grossness, but it might as well have been a sign of mourning.

The entry to the disco was a few steps below street level on a narrow street called Rue Germain Pilon, a couple of blocks east of the Moulin Rouge. A neon sign suspended no higher than six feet over the sidewalk identified it as HIMALAYA. The high-frequency track of some hard-rock composition drifted airily up to the pavement, but when Vang swung open the door, the music exploded in density and volume, so deep and throaty and incredibly loud that Vang felt his eardrums pulsate.

He was in a narrow foyer that ended at a stand-up desk and another door. The maître d' was a young man with pink hair. He wore it combed back, styled so that a lock fell across his forehead each time he moved. While he looked Vang over, he brushed the lock back into place with a self-consciously practiced gesture. The hair immediately fell back across his forehead. Vang wore a sweater and a sports coat against the evening chill of springtime Paris. The maître d' frowned and said, "*Oui?*" as if the word tasted sour.

"I'm a guest of Augustin Swartz," Vang said.

"How odd," the pink-haired boy drawled with bland rudeness. "I didn't know Augie liked Oriental food."

"Take me to him, please."

"And what was the name?"

Vang told him.

"I'll announce you." The pink-haired boy opened the door and said, "Wait here." Vang followed him through toward the pounding music. The maître d' deepened his frown, then threw a hip around, turned, and pushed through the crowd. A record ended and over its fade another began, full of thumping bass, so that the music felt to Vang as if it had taken on weight.

The room was long, narrow, high-ceilinged. It was oddly lit by green-, red-, and yellow-tinted bulbs recessed into portallike sockets. Some, mounted on motors, slowly panned the crowd; others blinked on and off at random intervals with no rhythmic relationship to the music.

A stainless-steel bar ran along one wall; tables lined the other. The ceiling was mirrored, and at first glance Vang thought the walls were as well, in a vain attempt to make the disco feel less claustrophobic. Then he realized that they were tinted glass partially masking the raised decks of other rooms on either side. Behind the glass, occupied tables overlooked the main room.

The tables surrounded a hardwood dance floor that gleamed in the colored light. At its far end, above the door through which the maître d' had disappeared, a doughy-faced woman sat inside a suspended glass cage, playing records and listlessly tapping out the beat on the console with a pencil. A few women danced with one another, but most of the customers were men.

A waiter materialized in front of Vang, his hips twitching to the music. Vang said, "Evian," and could barely hear his

own voice, but the waiter must have been a lip reader. He
lanced around behind the bar and came back with the bottle.
Vang dug a sheaf of bills from his inside jacket pocket and
unfolded it. The top note was a fifty-franc, which the waiter
snatched neatly with two fingers. It was a little steep for
mineral water, but Vang did not expect change and was not
disappointed. He had realized several hours earlier that the
City of Lights had grown meaner. . . .

Vang had not been in Paris since the summer of 1975,
when the CIA had flown him in from Bangkok after he'd
evacuated from Long Tieng. They'd put him on ice in an eight-
hundred-franc-per-day suite in the Crillon and pretended
there was a holdup in the endorsement of his U.S. passport;
actually, they were scrambling to figure a way to keep an eye
on him in the States. He'd had several weeks to wander the
streets and reacquaint himself with the city.

It was always changing. Not too long before, the Paris
skyline had been uniquely and timelessly European; now
thirty-story office towers stared down at scores of sixteen-story
high-rise apartment buildings, and elevated superhighways
cloverleafed around the city's perimeter. The quaint little
open-platform buses had been devoured by huge green
doubledeckers whose drivers' responsibilities were limited to
driving; surly abuse of the passengers was the sole province of
the conductors now. *Places* that Vang recalled as leafy squares
had been defoliated, bulldozed, paved, and painted into neat
stalls for commuters' autos.

That afternoon, Vang had strolled aimlessly along the
river, pursuing serenity in preparation for the savage night.
Near twilight he crossed the Pont d'Iéna and passed by
Gustave Eiffel's skeletal tower, and by full dark he found
himself at the end of the broad Parc du Champ de Mars, near
the old École Militaire. Napoleon's soldiers had drilled in the
park two centuries before, and those who came back from war
less than whole had retired to the Hôtel des Invalides a few
blocks away. It was a fit place for contemplation . . .

His time ran out there, in the shadow of the Invalide's
brilliant gilded dome. The third cab he flagged on the

Boulevard Saint Germain veered to the curb and screeched to
a stop. It was full dark now, and when the dome light of the
Citroën went on as Vang opened the door, he thought for a
moment there was already a passenger in the front seat. When
he got in, the "passenger" turned out to be a German
shepherd. The dog turned and stared balefully at Vang, its
tongue lolling. The driver merely glanced into the rear-view
mirror and said, "*Ou' est-ce que vous voulez aller?*"

Vang told him the Place Pigalle. During the jerky stop-
and-go thirty-minute trip through the snarled traffic and up
into Montmartre, the cabdriver explained that the animal was
trained to attack on command. Vang, who did not particularly
like dogs, kept one eye on the animal while the cabbie
described the three instances when he had sicced the dog on
passengers in the year and a half since he'd gotten him. Vang
would not believe the assortment of creeps, thugs, perverts,
and degenerates that one ran into in a single night, the cabbie
assured him. All his stories seemed to involve men with
larcenous notions and knives, and ended with the attacker
bleeding in the backseat, and the dog slavering and worrying
at his throat. The dog had pressed his tongue and teeth
against the windshield and slavered at Vang when he got out at
Pigalle.

Now the pink-haired maître d' of the Club Himalaya came
out of the door beneath the disc jockey's glass cage. He pointed
a finger at Vang and crooked it coyly in a summoning gesture.
Vang put the mostly full Evian on the bar as he passed, and the
bottle trembled, vibrating in sympathy with the pounding
music. A dancer grazed Vang's shoulder with his elbow and
spun angrily around. Vang pushed on through the knot of
gyrating men. A couple of them leered at him.

The pink-haired boy stepped aside, pointed upward, and
leaned very close to Vang. "The door on the right," the maître
d' said. Vang felt the warmth of the boy's breath in his ear. The
door shut behind him.

He went up uncarpeted stairs, then turned back down a
long corridor that was bare walled except for facing doors at
the end. He knocked on the one on the right. A voice inside

said, "Yes, what is it?" in English. Vang said his name and tried the knob. It turned. He pushed open the door and went in.

The man in the room looked much younger than Vang had anticipated, twenty-five at the most. He was small framed, thin, delicate featured, almost epicene; although he was several inches taller than Vang, they must have weighed about the same. He had fine blond hair parted in the middle and combed straight back, and sported a perfectly cut jacket over a silk shirt, its top three buttons undone to better show off his heavy gold neck chain. He wore a Patek Philippe watch with a gold band above his left hand, which held a long-stemmed champagne glass; and a gold signet ring on the fourth finger of his right hand, which held an ugly little .22 automatic pointed at Vang's middle.

"You forgot to wait for me to say, 'Come in,'" the young man said.

Vang shut the door behind him. The floor vibrated from the music below, but the sound was muffled, barely audible. The room was elegant for an office, with original oils in ornate frames on the walls, a three-stool wet bar set across one corner, a thick soft-looking sofa, and a small but intricate chandelier. A blotter-topped desk held a phone, an intercom, and a large glass ashtray on which HIMALAYA, against a stylized graphic of snow-covered mountains, was stenciled.

"You have some sort of identification," the man with the .22 said, not asking. "A business card, perhaps." He spoke English with the faintest trace of accent.

In the middle of the thick woven carpet a square had been cut out, perhaps six feet to a side, to bare a thick glass floor section. The man with the .22 stepped into its middle. Below his white patent-leather loafers, the lights and the dancers of the disco swirled and melded; part of the mirrored ceiling was a one-way window.

Vang raised his right hand to his breastbone and held it there.

"Slowly." The other man waved the .22, as if Vang might have forgotten about it. "Oh so very slowly."

Vang removed an envelope from his inside jacket pocket.
The other man took it, peered inside, and riffled the contents
with his thumb. "Benjamin Franklin has always been one of
my favorite presidents."

"Franklin was never president," Vang said.

"Is that so?" He continued to count the hundred-dollar
bills with his thumb.

"Twenty-five thousand," Vang said. "It's all there."

The other man threw the envelope on the desk. The pistol
disappeared under his left arm. "A glass of champagne,
perhaps?" He went to the bar, where a large green-tinted
bottle sat atilt in an ice-filled frosted brass bucket.

"Who is Augustin Swartz?"

"I am, in Paris." He removed the bottle. "You should try
some of this—it's Crémant de Cramont. Do you know it?"

"No."

"It is what is called a 'demi' champagne, halfway between
a full and a still vintage, just enough bubbles to add a bit of
sting, and a lovely bouquet." He sniffed the cork. "The
Mumm's people make it in very small batches. They rarely sell
it—it's generally a gift to their friends and better customers."
He poured. "I own this place."

"This is how you make your living?"

The man took a sip of the champagne, closing his eyes as if
external stimuli might sour the taste. "My name is Jonathan
Kay," he said, "and you know how I make my living." Kay
opened his eyes. He topped off his glass and filled a second
one. "Now do sit down, and we'll decide whom to kill."

Vang watched Jonathan Kay pace around the office,
crossing the glass square above the dancers' heads, stabbing a
finger in the air or waving a hand to emphasize a point, sipping
at his champagne. He had come highly recommended for the
job that Vang had to accomplish here.

"You know George?" Kay said.

"We've never met."

"But you know about him."

"Of course."

"George" had spent twenty years as a senior agent of the KGB, the Soviet intelligence agency. In those days he was Gregor Petrov, and during that long tenure he had erected one of the most efficient and wide-reaching networks of contacts in the annals of tradecraft. At that point the Russian administration underwent some major personnel and ideological changes, and Petrov was falsely accused of disloyalty. He spent the better part of the next year in a Siberian prison camp.

When his "rehabilitation" was completed and he was released, Petrov took the opportunity of his first foreign assignment to defect to the United States. He assumed the CIA would be happy to have him as a double, but instead they debriefed him, offered their best wishes and a rather small monthly retainer, and put him out to pasture and his own devices.

Dennison knew Petrov from his own days in the intelligence community; in following the strange twists and turns of the spook world, they had worked both as antagonists and as allies. But on the personal level they developed first a professional respect and later a warm friendship. It was Dennison who suggested that his one-time colleague maintain his vast network as a private enterprise. Now Gregor Petrov was George Petrie, U.S. citizen, resident of Manhattan's upper East Side, ostensibly occupied in writing his memoirs—and private spymaster. Dennison remained a steady customer.

Despite his age, Kay was a senior operative in the European section of Petrie's net. His personal life and even his nationality were ciphers; what mattered was that he was very goddamned good. Not long before, another of Dennison's People, ex-mafioso Matt Conte, had used Kay to help loosen the tongue of a very tough interrogation subject, when time was of the essence. Though Kay's method's strayed toward the brutal, they were inarguably effective. They got answers.

Kay perched his small rump on the edge of one of the bar stools. He folded his arms on his chest, so the champagne glass was a few inches below his vaguely aquiline nose. "I spoke to

George two days ago." He sniffed the champagne's bouquet. "Exactly what are you after?"

"Several items." Vang raised a forefinger. "I want to shut down Nguyen's operation—permanently. Nearly half the heroin on the U.S. streets come from that bastard. Some people think that's not right. I'm one of them."

"All right," Kay said neutrally. "And?"

Vang showed two fingers. "Second, I want to take whatever cash he has on hand. You can understand that."

"Money? Oh yes indeed," Kay said.

"Third, I want to talk to him."

"In regard to what?"

"A man named Scanlon—his supplier in the Golden Triangle, I believe."

"What do you want with this Scanlon?"

"The same thing I want with Nguyen."

Kay unfolded his arms. "I have more than, shall we say, a lay person's understanding of your friend Dennison's operation, and of his philosophical antipathy toward people like Nguyen and Scanlon. Whether you choose to believe it or not, my own feelings are not dissimilar."

"That's a relief," Vang said, deadpan.

Kay smiled politely. "Yet I wonder: why do I sense that you have a personal stake in all this?"

Vang nodded slowly. "Scanlon and Nguyen killed twenty-three of my people."

"War?"

"Murder."

"Ah," Kay said. "I must know one thing."

"All right."

Kay looked up. "Do you plan to kill Nguyen Van Cao?"

Vang returned the gaze for several moments. "I told you—I want to talk to him."

"But afterwards . . ." Kay smiled vaguely.

Vang said nothing.

"You see," Kay said, "you may have no choice." Kay reached inside his coat, the side opposite where the .22

rested. He took out a flat gold case, opened it like a small book, worried out a long brown-paper cigarette, and lit it with a matching gold lighter. "I want twenty-five thousand more when the job is completed." He blew out smoke. "To your satisfaction, of course," he added almost coyly.

Vang hesitated. "Agreed."

"You have the authority to make this agreement?"

"Kay," Vang said sharply, "are we doing business?"

Kay peered down through the one-way glass of the floor. On the dance floor below, two men were squaring off, faces contorted with anger, palms up and shoving, muscles throbbing along the sides of their necks: the preliminaries common the world over to mindless barroom havoc. The pink-haired waiter appeared between them, arms extended to either side like a traffic cop as he held the men apart. All three of them had their mouths open wide, but the triple-glazed sound-proofed glass turned the incident into an eerily soundless pantomime. The waiter grabbed one of the men by the upper arm hard enough to bring a wince of pain to his face. He walked him toward the door, out of Kay's and Vang's line of sight. The other men, and the few women, went back to their dancing.

Kay looked up, a bit bright-eyed. "Let me tell you about Nguyen," he said.

"That's why I'm here."

"Nguyen arrived in Paris with money and muscle—an imported army of Vietnamese. Some from the North, some of them collaborationist Southerners. All of them heavily involved in narcotics trafficking back home."

"Including Nguyen."

"Of course—it was the source of his seed money."

Kay stubbed out his cigarette. "One restless evening, a couple of months after he set up, Nguyen sent a squad of his men to a warehouse in the Algerian quarter of Marseille, off the Rue des Chaneliers. This particular warehouse happened to be a heroin refinery, the property of a Parisian named Eddie Picard. Nguyen appeared to know that Picard was doing an excellent business and that he would be in the factory on this particular night."

"Nguyen took it over?"

"Hardly." Kay seemed startled. "He tied up Picard and nineteen of his men and burned the place to the ground. Thereby not only eliminating a potential competitor, but also sending a less-than-subtle message to all the others. It worked quite well. He's controlled a large share of the business, without serious challenge, ever since."

"My information is that Nguyen never leaves his home."

"Your information is essentially correct." Kay went back to the bar. "Nguyen lives just outside the city limits, near Hauts-de-Seine. A rather nice neighborhood, actually—our Monsieur Nguyen has done well for himself. His estate is most of a city block, and I understand the house is sumptuous. It is certainly a fortress."

Kay's soft eyes were vaguely unfocused, as if he were looking over the setup as he described it, considering approaches. "The grounds are surrounded by a stone wall two feet thick and topped ever so discreetly with shards of glass and steel razor-wire barbs. That is merely to give potential visitors the right idea. His real defensive perimeter is much more sophisticated—surveillance microphones, infrared cameras, ground sensors, and at least a dozen guards on duty at all times."

"Just the same, we could get in," Vang said, thinking aloud. There were always ways. . . .

"Of course—creating an opportunity to ask your questions is simple. The difficulty lies in compelling him to answer, and truthfully." Kay's tone was didactic. "We must beard him in a venue of our choice. We want him naked and vulnerable and alone, convinced that we have all the time in the world and that he has no chance whatsoever of being rescued by any of his people."

"We want to scare him into running."

"With his cash on hand," Kay added. "Never lose sight of the money." He smiled. "We must convince him that his only chance is to take what he can carry, and flee."

"How do we do it?"

"I don't know," Kay said.

Vang had a sudden, unpleasant feeling that he was being strung along, toyed with. "Wait a minute," he began.

"I think I know how we can find out, however," Kay interrupted.

"I pride myself on my patience," Vang said in a tight voice. "But at this moment you are stretching it."

"I do apologize." Kay stared at Vang shrewdly. "As a matter of fact," he said finally, "I've already begun to work on your behalf."

Vang returned the hard gaze. "Can I trust you?"

"As long as I'm on your payroll."

"Tell me something," Vang said. "What do you believe in?"

Kay shook his head. "Let me tell you what I don't believe in. I don't judge people by appearance. The way I dress and act, this place"—Kay made a gesture that took in the room and the disco below—"I advise you not to attach a great deal of meaning to them. I like the protection of some camouflage, because I spend most of my time in the jungle, my friend.

"What do I believe in?" Kay echoed. "I believe in violence. I will not call it good, or bad, but I'll tell you one thing: it is real. And that is what we are talking about, isn't it? Scaring the truth out of people, or beating it out of them, and killing. Always the killing, somewhere in there. Let us be very honest about that, because for a while, starting right now, there is going to be a great deal of blood."

"Other people's," Vang said in a steady voice.

"That's right," Kay said in a hard tone that had nothing in common with his costume or manner. "Two men dead on behalf of your mission—so far."

"What are you talking about?"

"If we were going up against Nguyen—as George told me we would—I wanted him on edge as soon as possible. This morning two men and I went to burgle his refinery. I knocked out a guard, and they went in after his product."

"And?"

"They were caught, of course. Nguyen guards the place nearly as well as his home. I assume they were executed."

"You knew they would be."

"Oh yes," Kay said airily. "But I imagine it put Nguyen somewhat on edge."

"That's not how I operate," Vang said tightly.

Kay raised a long, slender finger. "Do you recall what I said about appearances? Several months back, the same two men, along with a third, named Jean-Paul, attempted to rob a refrigerated fur-storage facility on the Rue de Rivoli. They had some bad luck—a *flic* discovered them quite by accident. It was bad lucky all around—one of the two men killed the cop.

"Jean-Paul called them every type of idiot. He told them, quite correctly, that they would have to stand for the murder; he was not going to become a fugitive on a cop-killing charge. These two were not so stupid that they could not see that he was right, that someone had to take the blame. So they shot Jean-Paul in the leg, knocked him unconscious, pressed the gun into his hand, and took off. But of course the two were not so smart either, because they told several people the story."

"What happened to Jean-Paul?"

"The police found him there after a while and let him bleed to death."

"He was a friend of yours," Vang guessed.

"More than a friend." Kay looked away. "I did what was correct. That it may help our effort is merely a bonus. Do you object to my methods?"

"I'll tell you if I do," Vang said. "I'm sorry about your . . . about Jean-Paul."

"Thank you," Kay said stiffly. He took out another cigarette and stared at it without lighting it. "Now, assuming that this incident has made Nguyen at all nervous, we must follow up."

"Your plan."

"Yes." Kay rolled the cigarette between his thumb and forefinger. "Eddie Picard, the boss whom Nguyen murdered, had a lieutenant named Hugo Crain. Crain had the good fortune to be absent at the time of the attack. Instead of getting out of France as quickly as possible—that was probably his initial notion—Crain took a chance and contacted Nguyen. Crain convinced Nguyen that he could use someone familiar with the local operation and the various people involved in it, and offered to work for him. Nguyen was intelligent enough to see that Crain was right, and hired him."

"In the same capacity in which he had served under Picard?"

"Yes and no. Crain helped Nguyen pull a few smaller raids, consolidate his power. In exchange, Crain demanded a percentage deal of some sort—I'm not certain of the details. The rumor is that Crain holds something over Nguyen, information about his little escapades that could cause him a great deal of difficulty."

"Why hasn't Nguyen killed him?"

"I assume that Crain has worked it out so that whatever he has would be broadcast if he died. That's the way I'd do it," Kay said.

Vang sat back in his chair. Kay was a complex young man. Vang sensed that perhaps even his youth was a deception of sorts, another mask of appearance preserved through care, composure, and demeanor. Yet, he trusted the man. He was not sure he wished to be his friend, confidant, or even ally for very long—but he did trust him.

"I wonder," Vang said carefully, "exactly how much this Hugo Crain knows about the affairs of Nguyen Van Cao."

"Me too. I'm dying of curiosity." Kay stabbed the cigarette between his lips and finally used the lighter. He blew out smoke. "Let's go find out," he said.

Chapter Five

The city had closed the Rue Pot-de-Fer to vehicles since Vang's last visit. Now, a little after nine that evening, it was clogged with strolling Parisian *boulevardiers,* mostly couples, looking young and vital as they promenaded without haste or particular purpose, taking the fresh air of the early spring night, watching and being watched. Vang felt like an intruder, and pushed the notion from his mind: *Think always of purpose at these moments.* In the fact of imminent unpleasantness, the pleasant was invariably seductive, a temptation to be recognized and overcome.

"The food there is really rather good," Jonathan Kay murmured. "A man of taste, *nôtre ami* Monsieur Crain."

The trattoria was called Aubergerie Gigi. "Venetian style," Kay said. "The wines are a bit expensive for their labels, but one can make do." They stood back in the shadow of the awning fronting a darkened boutique directly across the narrow mall. "Showtime," Kay said in a harder voice. "Do try to hit your marks."

The first man wore a camel's-hair topcoat. He looked up and down the walkway as he held the door. The second man was taller, broader, and ten years older; he wore a dark suit and fedora, and held his coat over his arm. He was working on his molars with a toothpick.

"The boor with the toothpick," Kay said. "That's our man." A long black Lincoln Continental was parked at the foot of the mall. The driver was silhouetted behind the open window, from which cigarette smoke drifted. Kay walked in the other direction.

Hugo Crain parked the toothpick between two teeth and

shrugged into his coat. Vang went ahead of them toward the car, weaving among the strollers.

He paused at the sidewalk of the cross street. Crain and his bodyman sauntered toward him with the lethargy of the well fed. Ten steps behind, Kay turned and came up behind them.

Vang went around the rear of the car and leaned in the driver's window. He grabbed the man at the base of the neck below his left ear. The driver turned his head and opened his mouth and eyes very wide, then went limp. The cigarette fell into his lap and began to smolder.

Vang glanced across the roof of the car. Crain and his bodyman reached the sidewalk, and behind them Kay swung his left arm. The bodyman stumbled off the curb, half-twisted, and went down into the gutter. Crain stood still, his hands a little away from his sides.

Vang jerked open the car door and rolled the driver out into the street, stepped over him, and slid behind the wheel. He leaned back and pushed open the opposite rear door. Crain bent and entered, Kay's little .22 jabbed hard between two ribs. Crain turned a little and his hand moved. Kay tapped it with the shot-filled blackjack, and Crain jerked back. "All the way over, please," Kay said, and Crain moved into the corner behind Vang. Vang started the engine. Kay got in and closed the door, the gun on Crain's guts. Two women on the sidewalk stared at the Lincoln.

"*Écoute, fils de pute . . .*" Crain began.

Kay leaned toward him and raised the gun so that the muzzle was two feet from the bridge of Crain's nose. Crain shut his mouth.

"Neat, *n'est-ce pas?*" Kay grinned at Vang in the rear-view mirror. Vang put the big car into gear and pulled smoothly away from the curb.

They left the Lincoln along a dark narrow street a half-block past the Place Denfert-Rochereau, beneath one of the hostels of the Cité Universitaire, with the windows open and the key in the ignition. Kay got out. "Say *adieu* to your fine auto, Hugo," he said.

Crain ducked his head under the door sill and muttered something in a low hard voice as he got out. Kay stepped forward and kicked him hard in the stomach while Crain was still bent over. Crain moaned and grabbed at his gut. Kay stuck a handkerchief into Crain's mouth and tamped in several folds of the cloth.

Vang took one of Crain's arms, Kay the other. He kept the .22 jabbed up hard into Crain's kidney. A young couple, holding hands and carrying books under their arms, stopped under the streetlight up the sidewalk and stared.

"*Crise de foie.*" Kay smiled sympathetically, patting his own stomach. The boy urged the girl off quickly in the other direction.

A taxi cruised by, only its parking lights on. Crain gasped, trying to draw sufficient air into his lungs. Vang held him close against the brick wall of an unmarked building. Its door was set flush with the sidewalk. Kay produced a small ring of keys, picked one, and used it on the dead-bolt lock.

It opened on a closet-sized foyer, empty except for a padlocked cabinet mounted on the left-hand wall. Kay opened it with another key and handed two five-cell steel flashlights to Vang.

The inner door wasn't locked. Behind it was a narrow dark corridor with brick walls.

"Walk," Kay snapped to Crain.

"*Minute.*" Crain sneered at Kay. "*Espèces de conards. Qu'est-ce . . .*" he started to mutter.

Kay hit him in the mouth. Teeth snapped, and immediately Crain was drooling blood. He drew a gurgling breath and expelled a choking cough. The blackjack was in Kay's left hand, the dark leather casing wet and shiny.

Crain spit on the stone floor and coughed some more. When he was finished, Kay reached out with the barrel of his little gun and lifted Crain's chin, almost tenderly. "You see, Hugo?" he said, in the tone of a rueful but firm parent explaining to a child why he must be punished. "Not a word, unless you are asked to speak. You do understand, don't you?"

Crain wiped spittle and blood from his lantern-shaped jaw.

"Don't you?" Kay pressed. His tone was low and sweet and venomous.

Crain nodded.

"Let's go." Kay glanced past Crain. Vang nodded. Methodology was not the issue here. He passed Kay one of the flashlights.

Another locked door at the end of the passageway opened on a staircase leading down to a storage basement. Cardboard cartons and wooden boxes were piled to within a few feet of the plank ceiling.

With the beam of his flash, Kay picked out a crate the size of a refrigerator standing against the wall near a corner. "Hugo," he said. "Do me the kindness of moving that carton, *s'il vous plaît*."

This time Crain did as he was told without mouthing off.

The large crate masked another padlocked door. Kay unlocked it and pulled it open on inky darkness.

Kay suddenly moved very quickly and said, "In you go, Hugo." He planted a palm between Crain's shoulder blades and shoved him through the door. They heard him stumble, fall, then cry out in pain and fear.

Vang flicked on his flashlight. Beyond the door was another descending stairway. Despite himself, Vang felt a little ragged at Kay's relentlessness.

"Listen, my friend," Kay said in a tight voice. "The chain to Scanlon begins with this man. He's tough and he's mean, and not likely to fold up like a morningglory at sunset. It's not enough that we scare him."

In the darkness below, Crain was muttering a string of filth.

"He must be desperate," Kay said. "So pained and panicked he'd do anything to save his stinking life. He'll try to guess what we're after, answer questions we don't even ask, and that's how we want him. Do you understand?"

"Yes," Vang said.

"Remind yourself always: Crain is a killer," Kay said. "He is your key to Nguyen, and Nguyen is the key to Scanlon." He gestured toward the darkness below. "This is necessary. This is justice."

"Do you wonder—?"

"No," Kay interrupted. "Not at a time like this."

They found Crain on his hands and knees at the foot of the staircase. He squinted up into the light. His face was cut, and blood was smeared across his cheek. "*Vous êtes vraiment dingues,*" he muttered, with something like grudging admiration.

"Of course we are crazy," Kay agreed pleasantly. "Remember that at all times." He jerked Crain to his feet, holding his elbow. Crain swayed slightly.

There was a scraping sound coming directly toward them along the stone floor. Vang swept the flash's beam in its direction. A rat froze in the light for a moment and stared into it through red eyes before skittering off. Vang felt a breath of cool breeze stirring a thick, stale, musty smell. He raised the light and swept it along the far wall.

Vang drew a quick breath. "Jesus Christ," he gasped.

Bones were piled waist-high as far as the flash could illuminate—human bones: femurs, tibiae, flat triangular scapulae; and skulls, set upright in a row atop each skeletal haystack. On the opposite side of the passage, shelving was mounted, lined with pile after pile of the same white bones. Here and there, low-ceilinged winding tunnels snaked off into the darkness, each lined with more bones.

"The Catacombs," Kay announced. "The largest ossuary in the world—the mortal remains of nearly four million lost souls repose here. Isn't that correct, Hugo? You are the native."

Crain stared with loathing at Kay.

Kay slapped Crain's face lightly. "I asked you a question, Hugo. I asked if I was correct about the Catacombs."

"*Oui,*" Crain muttered.

"You must learn, Hugo," Kay said, in his patient didactic

tone. "Each time I ask you a question, you must answer correctly. Otherwise I will hurt you. Do you understand?"

Crain grunted.

Kay tapped the side of Crain's head with the flashlight. "Do you understand?" he said again.

"Yes."

"Marvelous," Kay said. "Now then, forward march."

Vang doubted that he could find his way out by himself. Kay had led them to a low-ceilinged alcove littered with odd bones and partial skeletons, somewhere at the end of a maze of indistinguishable passages. An intricate spiderweb, nearly a meter wide, hung from one corner. The walls were covered with spray-painted declarations of love and loyalty, and a brassiere lay atop some old, crumpled sheets of newspaper.

Kay stood in one corner, stripped down to his shirt-sleeves, the silk dirty and stained dark with splotches of Hugo Crain's blood, and torn in the front where Crain had managed to claw it. Kay's face was slick with sweat and contorted into an awful grimace. Vang stared: the effete Dr. Disco had metamorphosed into Mr. Hyde.

But so far it had worked; that was the important point.

Crain lay sprawled on his back on a pile of bones. He was naked, his clothes puddled in a corner. His nose was smashed all over the middle of his bruised, swollen face, and his eyes were tiny slits between puffs of bloated tissue, so that he was effectively blinded. Dark round burn scars acned his chest, and one of his feet was turned at an unlikely angle, where his ankle was broken.

"Benoit," Crain muttered in a low, bubbly voice. "Benoit was no good, you know that. We had to kill him, you understand. Maybe we should not have cut him like that, but we did have to kill him, is that not right?"

Kay looked at Vang. "Go ahead."

Suddenly Vang wanted to finish this as quickly as possible. He smelled the mildewed bones and Crain's blood, and felt nauseated and claustrophobic. He wiped the blood from

Crain's eyes with his handkerchief and pulled up his face.
"Shut up," Vang snapped.

Crain tried to open his eyes. "Who is it? Who are you?"

"Listen!" Vang breathed fetid air through his mouth. "Do
you know the name Thomas Scanlon?"

"Scanlon . . ."

"Answer him," Kay barked.

"I can handle this," Vang said, sharper than he meant to.

Kay spun abruptly on his heels and moved back into the
dimness.

"Where is Thomas Scanlon?" Vang asked.

Crain turned his mutilated face toward the sound of Vang's
voice, and smiled. It was horrible to see. "I know who he is."
Crain's tone was childlike, the smile almost beatific. *Brain
damage*, Vang thought. *Damn it . . .*

"I saw him," Crain murmured.

"Where?"

"He came once, and I stayed and watched," Crain said in
his child's singsong voice. He began to giggle.

Vang grabbed Crain's shoulders and shook him. His head
flopped back and fourth and he went on giggling. Vang slapped
his face three times, not hard.

Kay leaned over Vang and hit Crain, crisply, brutally.
Crain stopped giggling.

"That's enough," Vang said to Kay.

"You must understand pain," Kay said, very nasty at this
moment. "You must know exactly how much to apply."

"I said that's enough."

Crain rolled his head on his neck and began talking in a
strange, high, rhythmic voice, like a ventriloquist's dummy.
"After he blew up Eddie's place, Nguyen got ready. I was with
him. He pushed too hard. There was going to be a war in the
street, and everyone would lose. Scanlon came to Paris. He
told Nguyen to stop."

"Where did Scanlon come from?" Vang said.

Crain smiled up at him. His eyes were completely closed
now.

"Where did Scanlon come from?" Vang shook Crain again.

"Dunno." Crain shook his head. "Dunno," he said again, and his eyes turned up in his head.

Kay said, "He's finished."

Vang straightened. Kay had gone through another instant transformation: he stood calmly, his face wiped clean, breathing normally. "It does not work unless he believes," Kay explained quietly. "He had to think I was crazy enough to do anything to him."

"You convinced me," Vang said raggedly.

Kay worked the slide of the .22, bent, and leveled it on Crain.

"Wait a minute," Vang said.

"No." Kay shook his head. "I have to operate around here. I cannot afford to let him live." Kay looked a little weary now. "Another thing: the one time I was talked into letting one of these"—he jutted his chin toward Crain—"live, he came back and almost killed a good man—your friend Matthew Conte. We learned our lesson."

A trickle of blood oozed from the corner of Crain's mouth. Vang closed his eyes, started to turn away, then stopped himself. He watched Kay bend over and shoot Crain in the side of the head. The .22 did not make very much noise, but its report echoed down the passageway. Crain twitched and lay still. Blood ran down the ridge of bone under his ear and plopped in big drops from its end.

Kay stood up, stretched his neck, closed his eyes, and let out a shuddering sigh. He pocketed the gun, bent, and got Crain's corpse under one arm. "Help me, please," he said, grunting. "*Mon ami* Hugo must do us one last favor."

Chapter Six

Vang flipped open the cover of a spiral-bound pocket notebook, speared it with the beam of a pencil flash, and punched the number written there on the keypad of the cellular mobile phone. This number rang only in Nguyen's private study, according to Hugo Crain. Jonathan Kay stared through the windshield of the black van and whistled tonelessly. He wore a black leather jacket, matching gloves, and untinted rimless glasses.

The suburb of Hauts-de-Seine was separated from the city by the twenty-two hundred acres of the Bois de Boulogne, and by the abrupt horseshoe meander in the course of the sinuous Seine that sent the river on a 180-degree turn to the north. This neighborhood was all high shrubbery, elaborate wrought-iron fences, and an occasional gate revealing a glimpse of a long private drive curving through manicured grounds. The mansions themselves, beyond a roof eave, a bit of chimney, were hidden from the casual eye. "One can always tell the truly elegant neighborhoods," Kay had remarked as they drove through the empty lamp-lit streets. "The residents are more interested in privacy than ostentation."

The van was now parked at the end of a tree-lined street; branches arced over the pavement like the swords of an honor guard. Fifty meters back, a barred iron gate interrupted the unbroken line of a high stone wall.

"Get him," Vang said into the phone in Vietnamese. He waited a moment. "Nguyen . . . Sure, sure, old men need their sleep." Vang laughed unpleasantly. "Never mind who I am. Hugo Crain is waiting at the front gate—someone should take care of him . . . yeah, before he starts to smell." Vang listened. "He can't—not anymore." Vang laughed again and thumbed the disconnect.

At three in the morning the street was quiet, peaceful—except for the body of Hugo Crain lying in a limp pile on the sidewalk a few meters from the gate. A phone rang, and Vang imagined a guard startled awake, wondering if he was in trouble. . . .

The gate swung inward two minutes later. Three men exited, one fully dressed, the other two in trousers and T-shirts. All three were Vietnamese, and each carried a handgun. The guard rolled Crain over and gawked down at his broken, blood-caked face.

"One is probably saying, 'What do we do with him?'" Kay laughed, watching through the windshield. "Now they're all going to shrug." A moment later they did. Vang had to admit to himself that it was funny, the universal pantomime of distress at finding a corpse in the street in front of their secure compound in this wealthy district of Paris at this awful hour. "Now someone is going to say, 'We can't leave him here'—ah, there they go," Kay said. The three men wrestled the awkward bulk of Hugo Crain through the open gates, his heels dragging on the pavement. The iron bars swung shut.

"A hundred, hundred and twenty-five meters to the house," Kay said, figuring in his head. "They won't be moving too quickly—the late Hugo nearly outweighs the three of them." He took a small metal box, the size of a transistor radio, from his jacket pocket, then leaned out the van window and extended a whip antenna from the box. "Halfway there," Kay said softly. He flipped up a plastic lid that covered a toggle switch, then pointed the antenna in the general direction of the gate. "We don't wish to make too great a mess—yet. . . ."

He flipped up the toggle. "Surprise, Monsieur Nguyen," Kay murmured.

The silent night was punctured by a dull muffled explosion, and a moment later torn by a long terrified scream.

Kay telescoped the antenna back into the box, dropped it between the bucket seats, levered the van into gear, and pulled it quietly around. He went by the gate slowly, headlights off.

The plastic charge had been strapped to Hugo Crain's stomach, and the detonation had torn his body in half. His torso lay a meter from his legs, which were joined at the crotch by a strip of meaty flesh. Two of the Vietnamese appeared dead: one's throat had been split open by the force, a great wash of blood under his chin; the other lay armless. The guard was moving, but one leg was mangled and useless.

Lights came on behind the house's curtained windows as the van moved on.

"It going to be a long night for everyone," Vang said wryly.

Kay nodded. "We'd best get on with our part of it," he said.

The transformation of opium into morphine, and then into heroin, is, in terms of yield, one of the more efficient among the processes involving plant products for human consumption. It requires ten pounds of potatoes to produce a fifth of hundred-proof vodka, and a gallon of pure maple syrup is the product of forty to fifty gallons of maple sap. A ton of coca leaves produces a mere fifteen pounds of cocaine hydrochloride, itself rarely more than eighty-percent pure.

Compare heroin: While ten pounds of raw opium yields only one pound of morphine, that morphine can, if properly treated, produce slightly *more* than its weight in ninety-nine-percent-pure heroin. But because heroin is analgesically ten times as powerful as morphine, there is roughly a one-to-one correlation between the sap of the *Papaver somniferum* poppy and its deadly distillate, refined heroin.

Morphine can be, and often is, extracted from opium in or near the field. The opium is dissolved in water heated in an oil drum over an open fire, ordinary lime fertilizer is added to precipitate gross organic waste, and the morphine base suspends in the chalky surface portion of the water.

After filtering removes residual waste, the solution is reheated, and concentrated ammonia is added. Chunky gray-white kernels appear when the solution is filtered once more. The kernels are morphine.

The chemicals required to convert morphine to heroin make the process more dangerous, although the procedures are within the capabilities of any alumnus of a high-school chemistry lab. Equal parts of morphine and acetic anhydride are heated to 185 degrees Fahrenheit for six hours in a glass or enamel container, producing a solution of crude diacetylmorphine. Diacetylmorphine is the chemical name for heroin; the latter term was a trademark of the Bayer company, which first marketed heroin commercially in 1898 in its line of medicinal painkillers.

The diacetylmorphine solution is treated with dilute chloroform, which precipitates impurities, then with sodium carbonate, which causes heroin particles to solidify and sink. The particles are filtered under pressure, then added to a fresh solution of alcohol and activated charcoal. When the alcohol is evaporated, granules of Number 3 heroin remain at the bottom of the flask.

Number 3 heroin is typically forty to sixty percent pure and is generally smoked by itself or with tobacco. If prepared carelessly, it can contain enough residual acids to cause fatal liver failure in as little as a year of chronic use. Most heroin sold outside the United States and Europe is Number 3.

The last stage of purification requires ether and hydrochloric acid, the former highly flammable, the latter highly corrosive. Number 3 heroin is redissolved in alcohol, and the two unstable reagents are added. The tiny white flakes that form, when filtered under pressure by a suction pump and then dried, are eighty- to ninety-nine-percent-pure heroin.

If some trouble is involved, the economy of the trade makes it worthwhile. Ten kilograms of raw opium is worth $500 to the grower. The kilo of crude morphine it yields brings $4,000 in Paris. In turn, the kilo of Number 4 heroin into which the morphine is refined wholesales for $25,000 at its U.S. port of entry, and retails for $225,000 on the city streets. The markup between grower and consumer is 45,000 percent.

None of the manufacturing steps is prohibitively complex,

although each requires some care and attention to detail. All the chemicals used are all licit, and the equipment—primarily burners, glass vessels, and filter paper—is rudimentary. A serviceable heroin lab will fit into a bathroom.

Nguyen Van Cao's lab was quite a bit larger; no surprise, since it produced ten thousand of the twenty-five thousand kilograms of near-pure heroin that was imported to supply the addicts of the United States each year. The lab was in the northeastern corner of the city, in La Villete in the Nineteenth Arrondissement. Once, this area was the center for the city's slaughterhouses; but now, from within the camouflage of one of the old abattoirs, a different, slower sort of slaughter emanated.

At the moment, no refining was taking place, due to a temporary glut on the market; the next big shipment was not scheduled for several days, and its quota had been filled. But five hundred kilos of refined product, worth ten million dollars on the New York docks, was stored inside at that moment, guarded by ten armed men on duty at all times. All were North Vietnamese, like Nguyen. Hugo Crain had told them all this, after he'd given them the phone number and before he'd died.

Vang despised them; they had adopted the same law of the jungle as that under which they had operated in Southeast Asia. He knew this sort of Communist, had battled them from the first days of the Ho Chi Minh Trail's invasion of Hmong country. They styled themselves freedom fighters, but they were merely vicious, rapacious hoodlums. As soon as they drove the Hmong from the highlands, they took over the opium crop and sold it to the heroin traffickers. They were war profiteers and war criminals then; they were no different now, except that they could not hide behind the tenuous justification they had had when the war was raging.

But they were also damned good. That was one of the reasons why Vang had planned the operation for the early-morning hours, when the human biological clock was running down, and ambuscade came as a lethally unpleasant surprise.

Vang crouched behind a cross-hatched stack of creosote-scented railroad ties, thirty meters from the rear of the mothballed slaughterhouse. The narrow, two-story, peak-roofed building was about a hundred feet long and twenty wide, undistinguised from the dozen or so other abattoirs lined in two rows. A railroad spur had run behind Vang's position, but now the right-of-way was bare earth, the rails torn up for salvage. To one side and between Vang and the building, an empty fenced stockyard ended in a chute that climbed to an overhead-pulley-operated sliding door between the roof's eaves; the door was boarded up.

The two-way radio in Vang's jacket whispered static for three seconds, the volume cranked down. In the elementary code they had worked out, one long was a query: Had Vang found his man?

Vang keyed the transmit button, one short—"Not yet"—and saw the Vietnamese come around the corner. The Vietnamese played the beam of his flashlight over the double door, then tried its locked latch: the somnabulistic routine of the night watchman everywhere.

Vang pressed the transceiver speaker hard against his chest and keyed one long: Have you found yours?

He felt the vibration of the speaker—two short buzzes: Yes. Kay paused, then transmitted a long once more.

Vang keyed two shorts: Got him now.

The Vietnamese guard spun around abruptly and peered into the darkness toward Vang's position, the flash tracking onto him. Now there was a pistol in his other hand. The man had heard something, or sensed something—Vang wasted no more than a fraction of a second considering the why of it. He got a shoulder under one of the ties and levered it off the pile. It thudded into the cinders. The beam of light stopped, then backtracked toward the noise.

Vang moved out in a flanking maneuver. He carried a silenced Uzi that Kay had produced from a cabinet in the back of the van. It turned out to be a mobile arsenal: more of the Uzis, handguns, extra clips, as well as the C-4 plastic explosive and remote detonator they had wired to Hugo Crain's corpse for the first step in terrorizing Nguyen. Vang had not asked

where this material came from. In the international shadow
world, weapons were always available for the right price, and
the illicit arms merchants of the world did not generally
demand character references from their customers.

The guard circled around toward the fallen railroad tie,
while Vang eased along the opposite side of the pile. The
mission was breaking down to steps, and this one was for
Dennison. Stopping Nguyen and his men was not enough;
they had to blow his entire operation into pieces too small for
anyone to pick up.

Ten feet away, across the log cabin of ties, the guard bent
out of Vang's view. Vang moved noiselessly to the front of the
stack.

Within the shadow along the side of the building,
someone worked the slide of an automatic pistol. Vang swung
the Uzi in that direction, spotted a Vietnamese on one knee
with a handgun extended in both hands, and saw a muzzle
flash but heard no report.

Vang swung the gun back, spotted his man atop the pile,
and aimed up at him from three feet away. Vang squeezed the
Uzi's grip safety and stitched a silent four-shot burst across the
guard's chest.

The other guard lay face down in the dirt within the
shadow of the abattoir. Kay straddled the body, the muzzle of
his Uzi pointed at the back of the dead man's head. Over his
shoulder, Kay carried a hard-cased leather satchel about the
size of a camera bag.

"Sorry," Kay whispered as he came up. "I didn't want to
take him near the front door. Best not to cause any overt
ruckus."

"Not yet," Vang agreed. "But soon . . ."

"Did you spot any other outside men?"

"We're clear so far. Can we get in?"

Kay pointed at the boarded-up trapdoor at the end of the
stock chute. "That used to open on a chain-drive track running
the length of the killing floor—they'd meat-hook the rough-
dressed animals or the split sides on it, transport them to

another door at the far end, and pulley them down to vans. Apparently they use that door—it's not sealed, in any case."

Vang considered for a moment. "Lead the way."

They went up the cattle chute on rubber soles. Vang held the guns while Kay pulled himself up on one side of the sloped roof, then handed them up and followed. They went down its shingled length on fingers and toes, testing each step for footing and creaking noise. The moon had set an hour earlier, and wisps of clouds chased among the stars, their glow diluted by the city lights.

A triangular mounting bracket for a block-and-tackle protruded from the front eave like a ship's figurehead. Kay set his Uzi carefully against a chimney flue and gestured for Vang to do the same. From a pocket of his leather jacket Kay removed what looked like a case of electric drill bits, but the lengths of tempered steel racked inside were thinner, more delicate. Kay selected three, parking two of them between his teeth.

"I've never really liked heights," Kay said, his lips an inch from Vang's ear. "So please don't drop me." He lay out on his stomach. Vang braced himself and held Kay's ankles as the other man squirmed over the brink headfirst. Vang heard the faint mouselike scraping of one of the pick locks, a pause, then more scraping. A door hinge squeaked; Kay stiffened. Ten seconds passed in silence. Kay's torso rose above the roof's edge. He flashed Vang a thumbs-up and grabbed the mounting bracket. Vang released his ankles, and Kay swung over the edge and out of sight.

Vang anchored to the chimney pipe with one hand and held out the two Uzis with the other. He felt Kay take the guns. For a moment after that, Vang was suspended awkwardly, stretched with one hand gripping the pipe, the other the bracket. He released the pipe, dropped off the roof, then pendulumed through the door before he got his other hand on the bracket and his feet inside. Kay snatched at his belt and drew him through the opening.

They were perched on a platform about a yard square, bisected by the pulley that was one terminus of the motor-driven transport chain. The chain ran along the roof's peak to the sealed door at the far end, then looped down along a track running about six feet above the floor. Spike-pointed meat hooks hung from the chain at ten-foot intervals. A metal ladder bolted to the wall beside the main front door descended from the platform.

Only every other light in the middle of three rows of fixtures was lit, casting eerie, diffuse illumination over the slaughterhouse's warehouse-sized interior. The rough concrete floor was stained wine red by the strata of decades of animal blood, and deeper-colored gutters ran along the walls. Two big table bandsaws stood silently at either side. What had been the killing floor was now an assembly line of long narrow tables holding beakers, flasks, wire stands, and burners. At the far end was a bank of close-set halide drying lights over sheets of filter paper. Red-painted industrial barrels marked ETHER—INFLAMMABLE were stacked three-high along the wall to the right.

Kay pointed to the opposite side. "Ten?"

"Unless Crain was lying to us," Vang said.

A line of small rooms was partitioned along one side of the open space. The one closest to their position was a roofless equipment enclosure, with some kind of circuit board, or control panel, mounted on its outer wall. A vented door opened on a smaller room, and past it was what must once have been the supervisor's office; its panoramic glass windows afforded a full view of the operations area. The other three doors were set in blank walls, so that their occupants did not have to spend their days typing or ledger-keeping in sight of cows and pigs being sledgehammered.

Kay was pointing at the large-windowed office. Three more Vietnamese were inside, each jacketless, each carrying a sidearm in shoulder leather. Two faced each other across a desk. A gooseneck lamp illuminated a telephone and a layout of some kind of game tiles. While Vang and Kay watched, the third man rolled up one sleeve and tied off his arm above the bicep with a length of rubber tubing. A syringe lay on his end of the desk. He added water to a spoon with an eye dropper and began to heat the underside of the spoon with a plastic disposable lighter.

"It would be nice to know if they have colleagues waiting around," Kay whispered. "Wait or go?"

Vang glanced at his watch: it was a little past three-thirty. "We've got to flush Nguyen before dawn."

Kay nodded. "Fine. How do you wish to play it?"

"As neatly as possible," Vang murmured.

Kay went down the ladder three minutes later. Vang watched him and the men in the office, his Uzi charged and ready. Kay made the concrete floor, edged along the wall past the storage room and the vented door, paused beside the window with his Uzi up next to his ear, and glanced up at Vang.

Vang showed Kay his hand, palm up, fingers spread: five seconds. Kay nodded, then turned, his weight forward on the balls of his feet.

Behind him, the vented door opened and a fourth Vietnamese came out hitching up his pants. From inside the room came the sigh of a toilet tank refilling.

The guard slapped for the gun under his arm, and Vang stroked the trigger of the Uzi. It was a low-percentage shot with a silenced weapon at that range, and though Vang aimed for the middle of the man's trunk, he got him in the shoulder.

The guard released the butt of his holstered gun. He staggered back, then forward, and opened and closed his mouth like a mime doing a drunk. Kay turned, watched helplessly from a few meters away as the guy took another step forward and reached for one of the tables to steady himself. A ten-liter Pyrex flask sat atop the center of a wire rack.

Vang fired again. The slug punched the guy back, but then he spun like a hamstrung ballerina, caught the edge of the table with his hip, and slumped out of sight.

The flask teetered on its stand like a mis-hit tenpin. Vang realized he was holding his breath.

Kay stood pressed against the wall with his mouth half-open.

The flask fell over on its side, rolled across the table and off the edge, and shattered on the concrete floor.

The crash exploded the silence, and the play went to hell.

The two men at the desk grabbed their guns as they came to their feet. Kay stepped out in front of the window and it dissolved in a spray of 9mm lead. The two gunmen dived to either side as the window imploded, but the doper had his hands full: he was just squeezing down the plunger of the syringe, mainlining the heroin into a bulging vein.

Slugs cut across his neck, and he was dead before the drug rush could hit. He went over backward, the needle dangling from the pallid flesh of his arm.

By the time his partners could get off return fire, Kay was moving toward the control panel. Vang slid down the ladder's rails, thinking: *Four men still unaccounted for . . .*

Kay unscrewed the silencer, dropped it into his pocket, and tossed a quick burst toward the office to keep the men pinned inside. Now that the plan was blown wide open, noise worked for them. It added to the confusion, and kept Nguyen's Vietnamese from getting a good idea of what they were up against.

Vang reached the floor and ducked behind the cover of the line of tables, then moved down them to flank the other side of the office. Kay was carrying plastique in his satchel, and if they could keep them pinned a minute longer . . .

Behind him, Kay hollered, "Down!"

Vang flopped to the floor and a shot whistled a foot above his head. Under the table he saw Kay's legs below the control panel, and everything came to life at once. Lights flared overhead, an electric motor hummed, and one of the big bandsaws began a mean, plaintive whine. Directly above Vang, the chain creaked and moved.

Vang rolled under the table and came up like a base runner sliding into second. One of the missing Vietnamese stood spread-legged at the end of the tables. He saw Vang and tracked his pistol on him as Vang brought up his Uzi.

One of the meat hooks swung on the chain drive and slammed into the back of the guy's head. He sprawled forward, and more glassware shattered under his deadweight. Vang ducked out of the way as the icepick-sharp hook trolleyed past him.

In a few moments the empty silent refinery had become a garishly lit chaos. From inside the office, the pinned guards threw out irregular shots while the bandsaw whined.

Kay dropped an empty clip from his Uzi and seated a full one. "Five seconds to come out, *mes amis*. We have grenades." He pulled back the cocking handle. Vang moved up on the other side of the broken picture window.

"Tell them," Kay said.

"Two seconds left," Vang called out in Vietnamese.

"Your time is up," someone said in Vang's ear—and a gun barrel jabbed into his ribs. "Drop it."

Vang dropped the Uzi.

"Put your gun on the table," the missing guard said to Kay.

Kay watched expressionlessly. The Vietnamese behind Vang called out, "I've got them."

They were dead the moment Kay was disarmed. From the corner of his eye, Vang saw the two men rise slowly from behind the desk, guns up.

"Do it," the man behind Vang ordered.

Vang blinked at Kay.

Kay bent from the waist, gently lay his Uzi on the floor—

Vang leaped and back-kicked with both feet, catching the man hard in his shins. A shot crackled above him. Vang twisted in the air, came down on his back, and arced up again, catching the man's wrist with the point of his boot. Bone snapped, and the guy let out a womanish scream and dropped the gun.

Kay went down on one knee and snatched up his Uzi as the other two men came charging out of the office. Kay fired and one man spun and flopped belly-down over the jagged glass shards remaining in the windowsill. The second man threw his empty gun at Kay's head, missed, and dived, arms outspread. The crown of his head rammed Kay in the stomach and drove him back. The edge of the table caught him painfully across the kidneys. Kay let go of the Uzi and went down under the guy's weight.

Vang leaped to his feet. The other man was facing him in a semicrouch, his legs set, his good hand out and ready. His broken wrist was bent at a right angle and must have hurt badly, but the man showed no sign of pain. He knew a thing or two about discipline and martial arts, Vang realized.

The other man feinted to the right, jabbed with his good hand in a second feint, and punched out a lightning kick that caught Vang in the side of the jaw, very hard. Vang hit the table with his hip and grabbed at it, but the table went over, spilling a wave of glass across the concrete. Vang managed to remain on his feet. The other guy started past him toward his buddy, atop Kay.

Vang lunged for him. The guy sidestepped and clipped Vang behind the ear with the back of his hand. Vang's knees were loose and did not work quite right as he went for the guy once more. A bulk loomed in front of him, and at the last moment Vang ducked away as the sharp point of a meat hook swung past his face. A buzzing noise was centered in his head.

Kay was pinned; the Vietnamese was his equal in weight and had superior leverage. He cupped his palm under the guy's chin and pushed. Both men had an arm outstretched, fingertips inches short of the fallen Uzi, but neither could quite reach it without letting the other get control.

Vang saw them as if through a veil, blinked blood out of his eyes, and willed the buzzing to stop. He was still on his feet, circling as the other man closed on him again. The other man was grinning.

Vang expected another feint, but the guy came in low and straight. Vang moved to parry, and the guy's shoulder caught him in the gut and carried him back. The guy's arms were around him, and Vang felt the hard edge of another table. The buzzing in his head grew louder.

The other guy bent him backward, and Vang understood that the buzzing was not in his head after all.

His ear was pressed against cold flat metal, and the whizzing blade of the bandsaw was six inches from his chin. The other man replanted his feet and twisted Vang toward it, turning his body and pulling his jaw up to expose his neck. . . .

On the floor, Kay got his head turned and spotted Vang bent over the table saw. The man atop him felt Kay's weight shift, and lurched for the Uzi and got his fist around its barrel.

Kay drove his fist into the middle of the man's face. He let go of the Uzi and reared back, and Kay arched his back and rolled free. The other man threw an arm out at the Uzi. Kay grabbed his belt and climbed onto the guy's back.

Vang drew up a leg, found a few inches of leverage, and got his knee between the guy's legs. It was not hard enough to hurt him, but it did surprise him, and the guy eased the pressure for a moment. Past his head, Vang saw one of the meat hooks swaying from the chain.

Vang snapped an elbow into the guy's jaw, and when he instinctively pulled back, Vang grabbed his broken wrist and twisted. The man yowled with excruciating pain.

Vang braced himself against the table saw and slammed both feet into the man's gut, a jackhammer blow. The man flung both hands wide and left his feet, flying backward as if hit by a hurricane gust.

The point of the meat hook caught him in the back of the neck, a half-inch above the end of his spine. His weight and the momentum of Vang's kick drove it through his throat, so six inches of glistening wet red metal spike protruded like a unicorn's horn from his Adam's apple.

The Vietnamese's body floated past Vang, the toes of his shoes dangling a few inches above the floor. The chain angled upward, and the corpse rose toward the upper door.

"For Christ's sake," Kay grunted. Vang blinked and turned.

But Kay did not really need assistance. He had his man by the calves, and as he tried to reel in the Uzi, Kay climbed up to straddle him. The man got both hands on the Uzi and clawed for the trigger. Kay swiped at his own boot and there was a little snicking noise. A long thin blade materialized out of Kay's fist.

He drove the steel into the guy's kidney overhand. The guy's entire body bowed as if he had been electrocuted. Kay flipped the blade to underhand and drew it across the front of the guy's throat. Blood spilled out beneath him.

Vang hit buttons on the control panel under the chain motor and the bandsaw fell silent. Kay wiped his knife on the back of the Vietnamese's shirt. Vang stared up at the other man's body, slumped on the pulley platform. Blood dripped from his shoes. It was an awful way to die, Vang thought . . . nearly as bad as the bandsaw. . . .

"Did I save your life, or did you save mine?" Kay stood. "I wasn't able to pay complete attention, there at the end." He glanced up at the body on the meat hook, and Vang thought he saw Kay shudder. Kay was careful not to look at it again.

Kay retrieved his leather satchel from under the table and took it into the office. He swept broken glass from the desktop, took a screwdriver from the satchel, and began to work on the base of the telephone. Vang checked the other rooms and found the first two dark and empty. In the third were sacks, some big enough to have contained fifty pounds of Gold Medal, others merely Baggies. Vang tore one open, rubbed a pinch of the white powder between his fingertips, then dabbed a tiny bit on the tip of his tongue. It tasted bitter, uncut. By eyeball estimate, all five hundred kilos were in the room.

Kay came out of the office and said, "Help me, please," businesslike. Vang followed him to the other side of the long room, ducking under one of the hooks. "Four of those should do." Kay indicated the barrel of ether. "Space them." Vang placed two at intervals along the table. When he went back for the other two, Kay was splashing the contents of two gallon jugs of alcohol over the wreckage of the office. Vang set out the cans, and Kay went into the storeroom with more alcohol. "You can open those cans now, I would think," he said when he came out. As soon as Vang did, the ether's thick, doughy smell began to fill the room.

Kay slid the front door open a few feet, then glanced back with a satisfied look. "Not so neat as it might have been," he decided. The scattered corpses and fresh blood made it appear that the abattoir might be back in business. "But it will do, I should think." Kay dusted his hands together. "Anything else?"

"I'll get back," Vang said.

Kay nodded agreement. "I don't think Nguyen will spook this easily, but you had best be on site."

"Give me twenty minutes."

"Luck." Kay offered a hand.

Vang shook it, glancing past him at the now-silent meat saw. "So far," he said, "it is running with us."

Chapter Seven

Nguyen Van Cao leaned forward in the leather desk chair and said, "Who the hell are they?"

The other man held the curtains open far enough for a limited view out the front window of the second-floor office. Two of the men were basket-carrying a large plastic garbage sack around toward the back of the mansion. In the crushed-stone driveway where Hugo Crain had lain in pieces were one large dark satin and several small splotches. "More to the point," he said, "what are they after?" He was a compact, slim-waisted Vietnamese named Truong.

The phone rang.

Nguyen stared at it. Designed in the antique style, the earpiece hung from the forks of the microphone. It rang again. Nguyen glanced at the clock: it was 3:58. The phone rang a third time.

Nguyen snatched up the receiver. "Yes?"

"Unfortunate, what happened to Hugo," the caller said in Vietnamese. "I hate to see a man go all to pieces."

"Dammit, what do you want?"

"I want you, Nguyen. Come out, come out." The voice was singsong, mad and maddening. "I see you, right now."

Nguyen clamped a hand over the mouthpiece. "Get some men out front, with guns," he said to Truong. "Look for strange vehicles, anything out-of-place. Search the grounds." Into the phone he said, "Listen, whoever you are. Let's discuss—"

"Too late," the voice interrupted.

"Don't hang up!"

"I almost forgot." Now the voice was as smooth as glass. "Your refinery . . ."

"What about it?"

"Why not find out?"

"Damn you, you son of a pig—"

"You shouldn't have said that."

The line went dead.

Nguyen stared at the receiver for a moment, then slammed it down. He glared at Truong. "They're bluffing, dammit."

Truong considered alternatives, keeping his face expressionless. "Still, we'd better check with the soldiers at the refinery."

"What for? This is garbage, bluster." Nguyen's hand was still on the phone. "All right." He picked up the earpiece again, shoved it at Truong, then turned the phone so that the dial faced him. "It can't do any harm."

Truong hesitated for a moment, then began to dial.

Kay was checking his watch and almost didn't see the old woman.

He stood in the shadow of a rusty boxcar in the railyard across the cobblestone street from Nguyen's refinery. A 125cc Honda was propped on a kickstand beside him. The woman wore a man's dirty suitcoat and a babushka and carried a cloth shopping bag. She walked with her head down, in small steps and without picking her feet more than an inch off the ground, and was shuffling toward the refinery.

Kay eased out of the shadow, whistling so that he would not startle her, and said, "*Bonsoir, p'tite mère.* Where are you going?"

The woman turned and stared at him through too-wide eyes. She was somewhat older than fifty and had bristling gray hair as stiff as a wire brush.

Kay touched her arm with his fingertips, murmuring meaningless soothing noises, as if he were addressing a skittish horse. He could scent her vague madness. "Come with me a moment, little mother." He took her arm, and despite the coat his fingertips met around her bony bicep. He drew her back toward the boxcar and she let him, neither assisting nor resisting.

Kay lifted her chin and lay a finger against his lips. "Listen, Mother," he whispered. "Listen for a telephone bell."

The woman's eyes glowed. An automobile came into earshot, and then a late-model Saab clattered slowly over the cobblestones and pulled to a smooth stop in front of the abattoir door. Kay kept one eye on the woman; he did not want to frighten her, but he had to be ready to clamp a hand over her mouth if she made a sound.

The Saab's doors butterflied open, and Vietnamese thugs exited from either side of the car. The doors slammed. One man clanked a keyring and went to the sliding door, but the driver stopped to light a cigarette, and so he lived.

The other man slid the door open a few feet, and at that moment the ring of a telephone cut the silence. The man frowned and turned to say something to the driver.

The plastique made a deep dull thud when the phone's clapper triggered its detonator, but a second later the ether fumes went with a sharp, hard crack that ripped a jagged hole through the abattoir's shingled roof. Flames spewed into the night like lava, and shards of red-hot metal rained from the sky.

The man at the door took two steps backward, and another secondary blew. The front door ripped off its track and fire washed from the entry. The driver turned and took off at a dead run, and the other man followed. The back of his jacket

was flaming. He called to the driver. The driver never looked
back.

Another hole exploded in the roof and a huge mushroom
of white powder billowed into the night.

The Vietnamese flopped to the ground and rolled over,
but everything he wore was burning now. He was still alive,
though barely, when the fire detonated the cartridges in the
gun under his arm, exploding the clip and blowing a hole
through his heart.

The old woman was whimpering like a pup. Kay pulled
her to him, feeling how tiny, bony, fragile she was. The
refinery roof buckled and sagged. Kay watched the destruction
and crooned to the terrified woman.

Of everything this night, he felt worst for her, but he
could take no more time with her. He found money in the
pocket of his leather jacket and peeled off a bill. The woman
took it and held on to his hand, snuffling—and then saw it was
a five-hundred-franc note. "*Merci, merci beaucoup, monsieur.
Dieu vous protége.*" Kay pried himself loose after a bit and
climbed onto the Honda.

Nguyen jiggled the fork of the telephone, the receiver to
his ear. He heard silence peppered with static, and then the
dial tone.

Truong was watching him. Nguyen glowered back, then
went to the window to be doing something. The outside lights
had been doused, but thick starlight washed over the lawn.
Nguyen let the curtains fall together. "How many men on the
grounds right now?" he asked, not looking around.

"Fourteen," Truong said. "They've all been awakened and
put on patrol."

Nguyen turned and glared at Truong for a moment, as if
this were all his doing. Behind the desk was a small closet, on
its floor an assortment of hand luggage. Nguyen selected a
leather carry-on bag, hoisted it onto the desk, and opened the
two clasps. Across the room, a delicate oil of a ballerina hid a
recessed safe. "Get the cars ready," Nguyen said. He began
working the safe's dial.

Truong was startled. "Which one?"

"All three." Nguyen set the last number of the combination, worked the L-bar latch, and swung the laminated steel down and outward. Currency—mostly U.S. dollars—was banded and stacked on two shelves. Nguyen began to transfer the packets to the suitcase, overlapping them like bricks.

"You have decided to leave here?" Truong asked.

"I am preparing for that possibility."

"As chief of security," Truong said, "I suggest you are safest here." Truong paused, choosing his words with care. "The business with Crain was perhaps meant to suggest that these people—whoever they are—can get to us within our own walls. It's a trick, and a cheap one at that. Otherwise, they are all threat and bluff."

"We will see." Nguyen continued emptying the safe.

The phone rang. Nguyen went stiff, one arm elbow-deep in the strongbox. He jerked it out as if it were snakebit, dropped a handful of hundred-dollar bills on the glass desktop, and snatched up the earpiece of the phone.

The voice at the other end was already chattering in quick, frightened Vietnamese. "Shut up," Nguyen snapped. The other speaker drew a quick sharp breath, as if his face had been slapped. "Now tell it," Nguyen said.

Nguyen's expression grew increasingly dark as he listened. After thirty seconds, he hung up, cutting off the caller in mid-sentence. Nguyen glared at Truong. "Threat and bluff?" he said in a low, insinuating voice.

"What happened?"

"That was Ky. Someone blew up the warehouse."

"Was there much damage?"

"It was leveled."

"What about the men?"

Nguyen slammed his fist into the desktop. "Fuck the men," he snapped. "Ten million dollars' worth of product was destroyed." He drew himself up, squared his shoulders, and struggled visibly for self-control. "Do you still believe we are safest if we stay here?"

"Where would we be safer?"

"Call the heliport."

"And where are we going?"

"Nowhere," Nguyen said. "Yet."

The phone rang.

Vang swung open the double back doors and helped Jonathan Kay wrestle the Honda inside. The van was parked on a pleasant, quiet, tree-lined side street a few blocks from Nguyen's estate. Kay secured the bike, and was climbing into the driver's seat as Vang finished dialing the mobile phone. Vang listened, then glanced at Kay and nodded.

"Once more," Nguyen's voice barked. "What do you want?"

"I want you," Vang said.

"You're with Marchand, aren't you?" Nguyen said. "You tell that bastard—"

Van cupped his palm over the mouthpiece and said, "Who is Marchand?"

"Next to Eddie Picard," Kay said, "the largest of the traffickers whom Nguyen put out of business. Marchand gave up peacefully—after Nguyen's Vietnamese cadres killed seven of his men—but I understand that lately Marchand has been making noises about moving back in."

On the phone, Nguyen was blustering out some kind of threat. "You've got one chance to live," Vang cut in. "Walk out of there, right now, alone."

Nguyen spit out an obscenity.

Vang hung up. Kay gave him an interrogatory look.

"He's still skeptical," Vang said.

Kay smiled. He moved between the seats into the van's cargo area. One wall was lined with floor-to-ceiling metal lockers. Kay fished out keys and unlocked the second one.

He returned carrying identical weapons, stocked, two and a half feet long, looking something like single-barrel sawed-off shotguns. "That should make him a believer," Vang murmured.

"It should make him wet himself." Kay was hardly the stylized posuer whom Vang had first encountered in the Himalaya disco. He was on the jag now, at work and all business.

"We want him to run," Vang reminded him.

"Then we'd best hurry him along." Kay checked his watch. "An hour to dawn." Kay showed him what appeared to be an oversized bullet or an undersized artillery shell, an inch and a half in caliber, about twice as long. "We might possibly soften them up a tad."

Kay cracked the breech of the grenade launcher, seated the green-and-gold high-explosive round against the extractor ring, snapped it shut, and handed it to Vang. It was an M79, one of the most versatile and reliable weapons of those the United States had supplied to his forces during the secret war, designed to throw a grenade up to 400 meters, with point-target accuracy to 150.

Kay loaded his M79 with an incendiary cartridge. "Most animals fear fire," he said. "Let us see what sort of animal our Nguyen is." He passed three extra HE rounds to Vang, who dropped them in his jacket pocket.

"And when he runs . . . ?"

Kay chuckled. "Then we bring out the real firepower."

Vang returned the smile. "I don't suppose you're carrying any small nuclear devices back there."

"Oh no," Kay said gaily. "I've always found that sort of excessiveness perfectly tacky."

Kay started the engine, the M79 lying across his lap. "I imagine Nguyen has heard the bad news about his factory by now." The van eased forward, lights out. "No doubt he will be extremely angry, and at least a bit nervous." Kay smiled into the darkness. "But that isn't enough, is it?"

"I want the bastard." Vang was beginning to appreciate Kay's special genius for cutting through to the point. Vang was damned glad the man was on his side.

"You want the bastard frightened mindless." Kay raised a finger professorially. "The sole purpose of terrorism is to terrorize. I do not think Nguyen is terrorized yet. But soon . . ."

Kay turned left, pulled over near the end of the block. "Around that corner," he said, pointing ahead with his chin. "Expect men at the gates." He turned on the headlights. "Ready for action?"

"Certainly." Vang pushed the M79's safety lever forward past the *F* on the receiver. The van moved around the corner.

The gates of Nguyen's estate were in the middle of the block on Vang's side. Kay slowed to about five miles per hour and drew abreast of the entryway. Vang spotted three men and their guns behind the gate's bars; they were staring out at the vehicle, itching to open fire but held back by the chance that here was merely a citizen passing by on legitimate early-morning business.

Kay rested the phone's handset against the wheel and punched up Nguyen's number.

Vang rolled down the window and rested the M79's barrel on the sill. The men were framed in the sight, realization dawning on their faces. . . .

Vang stroked the launcher's trigger. The HE round arced across the street and into the middle of the gate, twisting the metal bars into a grotesque parody of modern art—and the men into flesh-torn corpses.

Kay said, "Go." Vang threw open the door, seating another grenade as he stepped down.

Nguyen came on the phone with a curse. Vang moved closer to the gate, adjusting the sight up another fifty meters. Into the phone, Kay said, "Here comes number two, my dear."

A ragged, roughly round hole split the middle of the gate. Two men with automatic rifles were dogtrotting down the drive. One started to bring up his weapon, and Vang spun behind the protection of the wall. A burst of autofire sprayed out the gate.

Vang butted the stock of the M79 against his thigh, counted three beats, and twisted into the open, unloosing the second grenade.

The two gunners dived in opposite directions and tried to burrow into the lawn. The grenade passed ten feet above them and hit a few yards short of the house's front door, fountaining a spray of grass and dirt and spring blossoms into the air. Muzzle flashes lit a ground-floor window, and in the room above it a lamp winked out.

In the van, Kay said into the phone, "Better check under the desk." He laughed at the notion that Nguyen might actually be peering frantically under the desk at that moment. "Just kidding," Kay said in a nasty thin voice. "Here comes the rest of the gag."

Beside the gate, Vang loaded a third HE round. He glanced back in time to see Kay hang up the phone and slide out the open passenger door, carrying his M79.

Vang worked numbers in his mind, estimating distance, readjusted the sights once more. Kay was in position now on the other side of the gate. Vang brought the M79 up to his shoulder, drew a breath, held it, and moved out.

He tracked onto the open window and fired. There was the boom and flash and whistle of the flying grenade, and a brief counterpoint of off-the-mark autofire.

The grenade hurtled through the window and detonated with a dull, foundation-rattling thump. Plaster dust billowed out through the opening, then there was the sharper crash of a ceiling caving in, and then men screaming.

Kay murmured, "Coup de grace time," and fired.

The guy was good. The incendiary grenade tore over the fine manicured lawn of the stately Hauts-de-Seine mansion and into the front door, splintered it to kindling, and ripped on into the front room, splashing white phosphorus everywhere. Something came out of the glowing doorway—something human-shaped and enveloped in flames.

In the few seconds it took Vang and Kay to get back to the van, fire shot from the door and window, climbing up the front wall. . . .

Kay snatched up the phone and dialed. When he heard the click of Nguyen picking up, he murmured in his most unctuous voice, coy and mean at the same time, "Monsieur Nguyen—are you dead yet?" Kay passed the phone to Vang without waiting for an answer.

"Nguyen!"

"Yes."

"Get out," Vang snapped. "Just get out. Take nothing— go, right this moment. I will give you five minutes' safe conduct. Do you understand me?"

"Yes."

Vang slammed down the phone. "I think we have him," he said grimly.

"Not yet," Kay smiled, "but soon."

Truong was holding a handkerchief to his mouth and nose when he came into the office. "Ready."

One of the blasts had shattered the French doors, and the draft was sucking tendrils of smoke into the office. Nguyen squeezed down on the bulging leather suitcase with the heel of one hand and managed to close the latches. The Heckler & Koch Parabellum went into his coat pocket.

Another explosion, dull and ponderous, shook the mansion like an earthquake. A crack chased up the wood paneling on one wall, then opened several inches wide. "The oil burner," Truong guessed. "Come—we have little time."

"The cars . . . ?"

"All set. Let's go."

Nguyen rechecked the safe, but it was empty except for a few loose bills, scattered like scrap paper.

The fire had climbed to the landing of the front staircase. Truong took Nguyen's elbow and led him to the other end of the corridor. The staircase there went down to a service kitchen, and from it a passageway opened onto an electric-lit, three-car garage. Smoke drifted up against its ceiling.

The Lincoln Continentals were black and late model and backed in to face the closed doors. Two were factory length, the third custom extended by three feet in the middle. Eight Vietnamese stood around them, looking tired and uncertain. Each held an automatic rifle at parade rest and ready to go.

Truong opened the front door of the oversized limo for Nguyen, then slid behind the wheel. The eight soldiers split four and four between the other cars. Nguyen glanced left and right through the tinted glass, then said, "Go."

The ceiling lights blinked out and the garage doors swung up and outward. The limo on the left pulled out, then Nguyen's car, with the third car bringing up the rear, moving swiftly, smoothly, in a tight caravan.

The driveway curved around the house, then straightened toward the mangled gate. Nguyen clutched the case, unconsciously worrying the leather with his fingers, staring into the taillights of the lead car. Flames rocketed into the night sky as they came abreast of the house.

"It does not matter," Nguyen said aloud.

Truong shot a glance at him.

"They cannot touch us. We are safe now." Nguyen sounded like a child at night in a cemetery, declaring that spooks did not exist.

Truong made a gesture that took in the mess that one hour earlier was the elegant estate. "Safer," he said woodenly.

"Yes," Nguyen said. "Absolutely."

Truong did not reply. Nguyen balanced the case on his knees and stared at the gate as they approached.

Kay said, "Here we go."

Sirens whined, momentarily faint and faraway, then quickly grew louder. It was 4:34; the first grenade had gone in six minutes earlier.

Kay was pointing up the street at the mangled barred gate. The two panels began to open outward, but the one on the right ground to a stop after moving a few feet.

A moment later the fender of the first limo plowed into it. The gate slammed back against the high wall and one of its hinges tore loose. The car's grille and headlight appeared undamaged. It swung left, followed immediately by the extended limo and the tail car.

Two fire trucks rounded the far corner, sirens wailing and

lights blinking and spinning. Vang saw men in black slickers in the cab as the first truck veered through the shattered gate.

Kay floored the van, cut across the second fire truck's tail, and took the corner with tires squealing. The taillights of the third car were fifty meters ahead, and Kay let it keep that lead. "Did you note how those cars handled?" he asked.

"Something about the suspension." Vang did not take his eyes from the taillights. "They seem to be riding low."

"Because each is carrying about a half-ton of armor plate," Kay said. "Assume bulletproof glass as well." The three cars turned left onto a divided boulevard. "Our Nguyen must feel secure at last. Let's disburden him of his misconception."

Vang stared straight ahead. The three limos cruised under the spreading maples at a steady forty kilometers per hour, then turned right again. Kay followed them across the Pont de Puteaux, the length of the Île de Puteaux bisecting the smooth wide Seine to either side.

"Any idea where he's going?" Vang asked.

"It depends how scared he is—and how far away he wants to get."

"And how quickly."

Kay nodded. "I'm assuming he has an aircraft of some kind. I doubt if they transport their product by bribing young air hostesses."

"Which airport?"

Kay frowned. "Bourget and Roissy are in the other direction. Orly is possible, although it doesn't handle that much general aviation. There's the Aerodrome de Villacoublay, near Versailles. . . . Hello!" Kay said suddenly.

Ahead of them, the taillights of the last Lincoln swung ponderously right into the dark greenery of the Bois de Boulogne, then veered left past the Bagatelle's miniature château.

"Can we take them here in the park?"

"I can't think of a better place." Kay fished the keys from his jacket pocket, selected one. "Why don't you fetch the heavy artillery—the cabinet at the far end."

Vang climbed between the seats, unlocked the cabinet, and drew a quick breath. "Jesus, Kay, you must have some excellent sources."

"We do what we can," Kay said from up front.

In the cabinet were two gray plastic tubes, each with a ridge along the top and a darker gray label near the business end reading U.S. ARMY—M72 Light Anti-tank Weapons, five pounds of launcher and rocket with enough punch to knock over a house.

The van swerved left. Kay said, "Trouble. I believe we've been spotted." Vang grabbed the LAWs and edged up front, stashing one of the tubes under the seat.

The tail car had split off onto a narrow lane, and now it spun around in a lawn-gouging U-turn. The four armored doors opened and gun barrels bristled above them.

Kay snapped, "Get down!" and the van's windshield imploded. Bits of glass snowflaked down on the back of Vang's neck.

"Goddammit," Kay said. "Now I am genuinely angry."

"We've no time to waste here," Vang said, and moved to the back door. He popped the safety pins as he stepped out, and the launcher's end covers fell away. Vang untelescoped the plastic tube to its full length of three feet, automatically cocking the firing mechanism. He unfolded the front leaf sight and shouldered the tube, supporting it with his left hand, his right resting atop the firing bar.

Vang stepped into the open. In the frame of the sight's window he saw the wide smiling front grille of the Lincoln Continental, two of the gunmen tracking on him.

Vang depressed the bar. The firing mechanism kicked and shot flame from the back end of the tube, and the twenty-inch rocket, no bigger than a hobbyist's toy, oozed from the tube, no toy after all. . . .

The Lincoln's hidden steel sheathing was designed to stop the most powerful small-arms round. The LAW's rocket was designed to penetrate one foot of solid armor plate.

It slammed into the front of the Lincoln like a fist into a

face, cored through into the cast iron of the engine block, and blew. The fore end of the car bucked three feet and hung impossibly for a moment, like a wild mustang pawing the air in anger and panic. The engine and body and glass and grille and bumper became a tearing cloud of shrapnel, and the four gunmen simply dematerialized, in the moment before the gas tank became a secondary and the entire vehicle was bathed in greasy flame.

Vang tossed away the plastic tube. It rolled to a stop against a sign reading, GARDEZ VOTRE VILLE PROPRE.

Kay threw open the passenger door and Vang dived in as the van's oversized tires tore ruts in the lawn. The whole episode had taken perhaps ten seconds. Cool night air came through the shattered windshield.

The van lurched southbound onto the Allée de la Reine Marguerite. The first faint glow of dawn was visible across the city to the east. "Damn it," Vang muttered—and spotted the other two limos a couple of hundred meters ahead.

"They're spooked," Kay said.

"They should be," Vang said. "Catch them."

Kay shot him a glance. "I don't intend to let him off the hook now."

"What the hell . . . ?" Up ahead, the taillights veered to the left and winked out of sight.

"You'd best be ready to use that other LAW," Kay snapped in a low tight voice. "Hold on."

Kay cranked the wheel and the van careered up on two wheels, settled with a teeth-cracking bounce, and shot into a narrow park lane. Kay stood on the accelerator, lurched over a little rise, and locked the brakes. The tires traced lines of rubber on the pavement.

"Go," Kay said. Vang was already out the door with the second LAW.

He had the two limos in sight, racing hard down a wider avenue that opened on the Boulevard Suchet at the eastern edge of the park. If they made it they would be instantly swallowed by the traffic of the awakening city. The road where Vang stood ran parallel to the lane, on the other side of an open meadow.

A one-lane bridge with gingerbread skirts crossed a finger lake. The two Lincolns bore down on it.

Vang dropped to one knee, figuring wind, trajectory, range, lead time. The bridge was somewhere around two hundred meters distant, a good fifty meters farther than the LAW's rating for a moving target. But Vang saw only the elementary puzzle in logistics: take out the lead car, and Nguyen was out of soldiers and boxed in tight.

From the corner of his eye, Vang watched the two limos race toward the bridge—one hundred meters, seventy-five, fifty—he hit the LAW's trigger.

The missile rocketed over the park, backflash splashing a rain of sparks onto the dark green grass.

The rocket clipped the top of the first car's armored trunk and skipped off like a flat stone on water. It dropped into the lake, its momentum spent. The rear end of the car slewed around on the narrow bridge and swept through the baroque-carved rails. Wood splintered and the car hung there for a long moment, teetered excruciatingly, and went over. It flipped and splashed roof-first into the lake. Three seconds later, the rocket shell went, geysering a plume of water into the air. The bridge was not touched.

The extended Lincoln shot across its span, slowed as it made the park entrance, turned left, and disappeared down the boulevard.

"Let's move," Kay said behind Vang.

Vang threw the tube aside with vast disgust. "We won't catch him." A knot of frustration and anger clutched the middle of his chest: a decade to find the butcher, finally getting close enough almost to reach out and get his hands around his throat. . . .

"No," Kay spat, "but we might find out where he is going."

The van lurched down the rise and across the lawn. The

headlights pinned a man to the ground where he had been sleeping under a panel of cardboard carton. He sat up, staring into the beams like a jacked deer. Kay pulled on the wheel, and the front tires missed the vagrant by a few inches.

Kay slid to a stop at the bridge, leaned across Vang to take a flashlight and a Colt .45 automatic pistol from the jockey box.

The Lincoln had fallen very close to the armor-piercing rocket in the moment before it exploded. The car lay upside down, the top few feet of roof submerged and the chassis and the four tires sticking up into the air like the legs of a dead animal in a cartoon. The rear of the car was crumpled forward into the passenger compartment.

Vang and Kay scrambled down the bank and splashed into the water. Where unreinforced car doors would have sprung, the armored version had buckled. Nothing moved. Kay flicked on the flash and played its beam over the interior.

The men on the passenger side, front and back, were dead, their various parts pressed between the folds of the thick-gauge metal like flowers between the pages of an unabridged dictionary. The one in front sat open-eyed, both hands crabbed around the sheet of armor that had crushed his thorax flat, frozen in the last futile position of instinct. The man behind him had died more quickly. His head lay at a ninety-degree angle on his shoulder. A bit of rocket sharpnel had cut halfway through his neck and remained embebbed in what was left. The other man in the back had been pinned underwater; only the back of his jacket, inflated by an air pocket, was visible above the surface.

"Dammit," Vang said, softly and fervently.

"I'm sorry," Kay said.

The man in the driver's seat moaned.

Kay splashed around the car's hood. The driver's-side door had sprung outward about a foot. Kay pocketed the flash as Vang splashed up behind him. They got fingers around the edge of the door and pulled in unison on Kay's count. The first time, the door did not give more than a couple of inches; on the second, it popped open another foot.

The driver slumped on the ceiling of the turtled car, his back against the seat hanging above him, his head above the lapping water. He did not appear badly hurt, but when they tried to pull him clear he let out a blood-chilling scream. Kay clapped a hand over his mouth and they tried it again. The guy moaned and passed out. They slid his limp body out into the gasoline-slicked water and wrestled him up onto the steep bank.

Kay ran the flashlight beam over the man. Vang dropped to one knee and slapped his face three times, not hard. The man's eyes fluttered open. Vang said in Vietnamese, "Where is Nguyen going?"

The man stared back from eyes wet with pain and terror. His skin in the flash's beam was the color of eggshell. They saw the blood now, soaking the middle of his jacket.

The Vietnamese opened and closed his mouth and opened it again. "Help me." His voice was as tight as wire.

Kay plucked at the wet cloth, and got the front of the jacket open.

Vang choked back rising bile. The driver's gut had been ripped open: a gash ran from navel to breastbone, and from it spilled ropy gray entrails greasy with blood. The driver clamped his hand over the opening, as if trying to keep everything where it belonged.

Kay leaned over him. *"Où est-ce qu'il va? Reponds, bon Dieu!"*

"Will you help me?"

The smell of the man's innards was obscene, nauseating, and Kay gagged. He glanced at Vang, and his face was white. Kay pressed the muzzle of the .45 against the man's forehead. "Answer me."

"I will," the thug said—except that he was no longer a thug, merely a pathetic dying animal. "But you must promise to help me. . . ."

In Kay's face Vang saw something for the first time, something beyond ruthless androgyny to feeling, even pity. Vang said, "We will help you. First answer my question."

"Issy," the Vietnamese got out past the pain. "The Heliport de Paris."

Kay nodded. "Nearby—a couple of kilometers." He shrugged—and slapped the gun across the man's sweat greased face. "Tell the truth, damn you."

"I swear," the Vietnamese said. "The Heliport—"

Kay lay the muzzle against the man's temple and fired. The body twitched and lay still.

"He would not have lived." Vang stood.

"Of course not." But Kay sounded a little ragged now, and when he rose it was unsteadily.

"It was an act of mercy," Vang said.

"We do not have time for an elegy." Kay sounded angry. He turned and scrambled up the bank.

Vang followed, and reached the top in time to see a Corsican kid step out from behind the van's open driver's-side door. He had the keys in one hand and a stiletto in the other. The punk grinned and waved the knife.

Kay pulled out the .45 and leveled it on him. The punk stopped grinning. Kay went around the door, grabbed the punk's knife wrist, and twisted it hard. The knife dropped to the grass and Kay stabbed the gun into the punk's face.

This had gone too quickly, and all wrong, for the punk. His eyes rolled up in his head and he fainted. Kay threw him aside like a dirty shirt.

Behind the wheel, Kay drew a deep breath. "I hate to see this city change," he muttered. He looked at Vang. "I remember when this park was safe after dark."

The extended limo screeched to the curb in front of the small general-aviation building at the Heliport de Paris. A chainlink fence flanked the structure on either side, masking off a tarmac apron on which several dozen small choppers were parked. Truong came quickly around the front of the car and held the door for Nguyen. Nguyen was carrying the leather suitcase.

Truong tried the door, rattled it hard when it would not

yield. The open lobby area inside was empty. Truong slammed the heel of his hand against the door's glass. A yawning night watchman approached out of the dimness. He peered out at them, then pointed to his bare wrist, shook his head, and held up five fingers, as if this were a game of charades.

Truong checked his watch: 4:55.

"The fool," Nguyen snapped. He fumbled the suitcase to his left hand, dug out the H&K with his right, and laid the muzzle against the glass across from the watchman's nose.

The watchman opened his mouth wide, stepped back, turned, and fled. Nguyen swore and fired. Cracks radiated from the hole and the door shook, but it remained entire. Nguyen clubbed the pistol and slammed the butt into the window. The butt bounced back.

Truong said, "Let me." He stepped forward and planted his foot over the hole, putting his weight behind it. Spears of glass split free and shattered on the tiled floor inside. To Nguyen, everything seemed to take an awfully long time, as if the air had thickened. . . .

"Let's go," Truong said. "Careful of the glass." He ducked through first, then offered a hand to his boss.

Nguyen ignored it. A point of glass grazed the back of Nguyen's hand as he went through. "Move it," he snapped at Truong, sucking at the thin line of blood.

"How can they find us now?" Truong said, less than cordially.

"How could they blow up my refinery and my house?" Nguyen snapped, petulant. "How could they kill so many of my men—my countrymen." The patriotism struck Truong as misplaced and mistimed, but he said nothing. Dammit, he was wondering the same things. How the hell could their world have been turned inside out in three ungodly hours on an early-spring morning in Paris?

Nguyen clutched the suitcase to his chest and followed Truong across the empty lobby, their heels echoing on the tiles. The watchman was cowering behind the window of an office to one side: an odd duck in a khaki uniform, no hat, skinny, with a fringe of hair around his bald pate—an old ex-soldier pensioner, Nguyen thought absently. The door opening on the apron was not locked.

The chopper was a Hughes 300, a little two-seater bubble-front that looked like a crouching fat man. It was always kept serviced, fueled, and ready to fly; Nguyen had not survived this long without learning the wisdom of maintaining a fallback for just this kind of emergency. The Hughes was parked off by itself, because Nguyen leased six berths, and the privilege of easy access and instant takeoff.

The fallback lay three refueling hops to the southeast, on the coast of Sicily near Palermo. There, some noncompeting Mafia colleagues would honor a long-standing reciprocal deal for sanctuary while more carefully laid plans were made. Seeing the chopper cheered Nguyen. He was carrying several million dollars, and he was alive—which put him several million ahead of most of his men. But recruitment was never a problem. . . .

Truong settled into the pilot's seat and began to flip switches. Nguyen watched the fuel gauge rise to Full. Truong reached for the ignition switch, but his hand stopped halfway there. "What the hell . . ." he muttered.

The old watchman was running across the apron toward them, toting a double-barreled shotgun—a fowling piece, for Chrissake. He looked like he was charging the Huns at Arles.

Behind him, from the other side of the terminal, tires squealed on pavement.

The van shot around the curve of the road toward the building.

Vang said, "There!" and pointed through the chainlink to where the Hughes sat, its point lights glowing in the dawn.

Kay said, "Hold on to your privates," and spun the wheel.

The grille of the van tore into the middle of a section of chainlink at high speed. Vang ducked as fence wire whipped through the shattered windshield, then fell away. The rest of the fence dragged behind, sending up a rooster tail of sparks.

Kay slalomed past three corporate choppers, then hit the open tarmac and was in the clear, bearing down on Nguyen's Hughes. Its rotor began to turn.

The watchman stood ten meters in front of the bubble, aiming the shotgun like a white hunter standing his ground in the face of a charging rhino. Nguyen hung out the passenger door, holding a pistol. They turned at the same time and stared at the van.

Kay charged the chopper.

The watchman spun around and fired both barrels. The buckshot loads passed harmlessly over the van's open windshield. The watchman dropped the scattergun and ran for it.

The rotor came to speed and the chopper began to lift off.

Kay cut the wheel and the van went into a sideways slide. It was starting to go over when the edge of the roof clipped one of the chopper's skids. The van jolted, settled back on four wheels, and slowed.

Vang leaned through the broken windshield in time to see the chopper list wildly, hold for a moment, right itself unsteadily—

Kay hit the gas hard enough to throw Vang back in his seat, and went at the chopper again.

Nguyen leaned out the open door and fired. The underpowered chopper slewed as the van clipped it again. It wavered, the engine laboring, then settled reluctantly back to the tarmac.

The van swung around again in a controlled four-wheel drift and came at it. Vang glanced at Kay: they were both determined to finish this, here and now. No more cat and mouse, no more games.

The van crunched into the chopper and the bubble crushed like eggshell. Vang flung himself sideways in the seat as the glass washed over him. When he sat up, Truong's face was a yard in front of him. The Vietnamese was pinned to his seat by the van's weight, and blood bubbled from his mouth.

Nguyen rolled out the door and came up on one knee with the automatic.

But Vang and Kay were out by then and behind the van's doors. Kay had the Colt out now as he circled behind the van and around the chopper. It was over, and twenty seconds later Nguyen knew it. Vang heard Kay say, "Do not move. That is the first thing."

The leather case had broken open. Nguyen knelt over the spilled money like a votary. Kay stood behind him, his gun in the back of Nguyen's neck. Nguyen let his weapon drop from his fingers.

He looked up at Vang as he approached. He stared blackly for a long moment, then lowered his head again, slow and deliberate, and spit on Vang's shoes. "A Hmong," Nguyen sneered. "My humiliation is complete."

"Not yet," Vang said.

Without taking his eyes from Nguyen, Vang bent and picked up his H&K. He lay the gun muzzle under Nguyen's nose and rose to full height again, levering Nguyen's head backward until Nguyen was bent like a bow, and the gun barrel was aimed up his nostrils.

"Where is Thomas Scanlon?" Vang said in a soft, even voice.

Washington, D.C.
March 6

Miss Paradise wore a severely tailored dark serge dress with flaring pointed lapels, pearl buttons, and stylized padded shoulders. She would have looked something like Joan Crawford in *Mildred Pierce*, except that she had six inches on Crawford, and a figure that was long and lithe instead of chunky and mannish. She sat in a black-enameled captain's chair, crossed her legs, and pulled the hem of her dress over her nylon-sheathed knees. The Yale College seal was stenciled on the back of the chair's crosspiece, above the motto: LUX ET VERITAS. Dennison stood behind her, both hands braced on the chair, vaguely aware of her fresh scent as he peered blackly across the desk at Peter Chamberlain.

"Goddammit, Peter," Dennison said. "Have you looked at the report?"

"Of course," Chamberlain said smoothly. He was in his forties, tall and lean with superb posture. His blond hair was freshly trimmed, and his charcoal-gray suit and eggshell-blue shirt were perfectly cut and unwrinkled. In the twenty years Dennison had known the man, he had never seen him ruffled, emotionally or physically—not behind a broad oak desk in the eighties, nor in the midst of a midnight firefight in the hill country north of the Plain of Jars in the sixties.

They'd once been colleagues and had always remained friends. But at this moment Dennison was perfectly prepared to throttle his old buddy if Chamberlain did not come through.

Miss Paradise sensed his mood. "Peter, you can't have it all your way." She smiled brightly at him, then cocked her head and gave Dennison a wink. "Vang did you a favor, and he's asking one in return."

Chamberlain picked up a neatly stapled set of papers. "He didn't bother to be very subtle, did he?" He let the report drop on the desktop. "A mansion in a ritzy neighborhood, an old slaughterhouse, a couple of limos, a chopper—not to mention a corner of the Paris Heliport—all blown to hell. Bodies lying around like popcorn boxes after a double feature."

"Only bad guys," Miss Paradise pointed out. "No civilian even had a hair mussed."

"And what's the bottom line, Peter?" Dennison rapped. "The biggest heroin pusher in France—the middle man in the major Golden Triangle connection—is out of business for good."

"Did Vang have to kill Nguyen?"

"Why, is he an old buddy of yours?" It was a nasty crack, but the hell with it, Dennison thought. Vang's report had left

Dennison feeling a little raw. Dennison cared for no man more than Vang, and his friend was going through serious hell this time around.

Nguyen did not yield his answers easily, Vang had told Dennison over a secure line. The threat of death was useless, and Nguyen turned out to have an astonishing tolerance for pain. He made them work for each answer, and by then Vang and Kay had spent too long a night elbow-deep in blood. They were gut-sick of it, but they concentrated on what they had to do, and after a time the Vietnamese was dead and they had their answers.

"I shot him in the head, Dennison," Vang had said on the safe phone. "By that point it had nothing to do with the murders he'd committed, not with Scanlon—it was not about justice or vengeance. He gave me what I wanted, and then he said, 'Finish it, please.' I shot him in the head."

Dennison asked, "Are you all right? Do you want someone else to take over?"

"No," Vang said evenly. "We do not have time. Scanlon might spook. . . ." Static etched the pause. "But I could use some assistance."

Nguyen had been carrying nearly $3 million, U.S. Dennison had rigged a contingency, and all Vang had to do was deliver the cash to a diplomatic attaché at the U.S. embassy on Avenue Gabriel, a man named Mahoney who owed Dennison a favor. Mahoney agreed to get the money out of the country by diplomatic pouch.

In the elegant, subdued Washington office Dennison said, "Yeah, Peter, he had to kill him."

"Someone will take his place," Chamberlain said with exasperating equanimity.

"All right—we'll go in and blow away the new guy for you, soon as he's up and running. I'll give you an I.O.U. In the meantime, you've got to run some interference for us."

"Do I?" Chamberlain said blandly.

"You're goddamned right." Dennison straightened and turned his back, pacing the length of the office.

On the official lists, Peter Chamberlain was carried as deputy assistant secretary of state for Intelligence Affairs, and his office was on the third floor of the State Department building on C Street. In fact, Chamberlain was serving his twenty-second year as a senior agent of the Central Intelligence Agency, even if he was assigned to ride a desk. His job was to buffer the Company from bothersome or nosy members of Congress or the Cabinet. From its origins nearly four decades earlier, the Agency had generally regarded elected officials and bureaucrats as pains in the ass. Peter Chamberlain, with his Ivy League smoothness, experience, and considered judgment, was the perfect foil for keeping them out of the Agency's business and hair.

Dennison paused at the door, admiring the thickly varnished finish over its solid oak. The carpet was as lush as a putting green.

"Our friends in Paris were not pleased at first," Chamberlain said to Dennison's back. "They thought we were behind the operation, and they resented the interference, not to mention a certain lack of finesse."

"If the Agency had run this one," Dennison said nastily, "the main problem would be a certain lack of results."

"Now, boys," Miss Paradise cut in. She recrossed her legs, patting her skirt. That grabbed Chamberlain's attention for a moment. "Boss dear, come over here and sit down," she said in a firm maternal tone.

Dennison calmed himself. Sure, the Agency could at times be impotent—that's why he'd left it to start his own "agency." But it wasn't entirely fair to tar Peter with that same brush. In the field, where they worked side by side, Dennison could not have asked for a more competent, loyal, and courageous partner. Peter had earned whatever he had now—the hard way.

Dennison slumped into the chair next to Miss Paradise. "Sorry about that last crack, Peter," Dennison said. "But let's stop chasing our own tails. You wanted Nguyen stopped, and Vang did him for you. Messy or not—and cleanliness isn't next to godliness in my book—it won't kick back on you, or on us. You've got no beef."

"I'll grant that," Chamberlain conceded.

"Thank you, Peter," Miss Paradise said gravely. She shot a sly grin in Dennison's direction.

"And you're right," Dennison continued. "Someone else *will* step into Nguyen's shoes—unless we cut the shit off at its source."

"Nguyen's Asia connection," Miss Paradise said.

"Thomas Scanlon."

"That's right."

Chamberlain frowned. "We're not the DEA."

"We're on the same team," Miss Paradise said. "All of us."

"Damn right." Dennison stared at Chamberlain. "But this time, there's more to it than that."

"Is there?"

"You know there is, Peter," Dennison said fervently. "You know what Scanlon did to Vang's people."

Chamberlain raised his eyebrows. It was as close as he came to appearing startled, Dennison knew. "It was a stupid mistake."

"It sure as hell was," Dennison said. "And I don't mean Scanlon."

"What are you talking about, Dennison?" Chamberlain asked. Even Miss Paradise was watching him curiously.

"I'm talking about fifteen years of secret war, Peter. I'm talking about dropping two-thirds of a ton of bombs for every man, woman, and child in Laos, my friend. That was *our* war, yours and mine and the rest of the spooks. Vang is my friend, and we used him and his people, and when we decided that we'd been screwing around to no good purpose long enough, we walked out and left Vang holding the shit end of the stick. You ever think about that, Peter?"

"More than you might realize," Chamberlain murmured.

Dennison stared at him and shook his head. When he continued, it was in a quieter voice. "We thought we were doing the right thing. We thought we were fighting godless

Commies who threatened truth, justice, and the American way."

"We made a mistake."

"Yeah," Dennison said bitterly. "We sure as hell did."

"You never told me," Chamberlain said, with dawning comprehension. "That was why the two of you quit the Agency, wasn't it?"

"One of the reasons," Miss Paradise confirmed.

"I'm not making accusations," Dennison said reasonably. "Against you, or against myself. We did our damnedest, Peter, all three of us. You were always the straightest guy in Southeast Asia, pal." Dennison managed a grin. "Straighter than I was, as far as the rule book went. That's why Vang came to you when he was ready to do a little horsetrading."

"Or blackmail," Chamberlain said. "Not to put too fine an edge on it."

"Come on, Peter. We break our word to the guy, cut off the airstrikes, pull out every last plane except the T-28s we gave the Lao, and leave him and a couple of thousand of his people sitting in Long Tieng, defenseless as decoys on a duck pond. We say, 'Hey, thanks for fighting the bad guys for us for the last dozen years, but we've sort of lost interest now. Adiós, and watch your ass.'"

"Is that how it was?"

"If you can't remember, ask Vang." Dennison shrugged. "He trusts you, Peter. You should be pleased."

"It's your honest face, Peter," Miss Paradise said with a smile. "Considering that the rest of the CIA, not to mention the DIA and the U.S. Air Force, screwed him royally."

"The point is, Peter, we owe him."

"Why us?"

"Because we're in a position to pay him back."

Chamberlain stared across the fine wide desk, regarding Dennison and Miss Paradise through clear blue eyes. He did not move for thirty seconds. Then he sighed and stabbed the intercom button on his desk phone, said, "Freda, would you come in here for a moment," and stood.

Chamberlain's secretary was about fifty, a big-boned horse-faced woman with severe, chiseled, craggy features. She wore a dress almost identical to Miss Paradise's. Dennison groaned inwardly; Miss Paradise's costume was Freda's idea of contemporary office wear. Freda stood inside the door and glared at Miss Paradise through small red eyes.

Chamberlain cleared his throat. "Freda, would you—ah, entertain our guests for a few minutes."

"Yes, sir." Freda had a voice like a sack of ball bearings.

Chamberlain went out. Freda stood behind the desk, folded her arms, and stared at them with stoppered fury. Dennison realized that the woman must have weighed as much as he, though she was not fat.

"What a lovely outfit," Miss Paradise piped up.

Freda ignored her. She stared at Dennison as if daring him to laugh. He struggled not to and sat straight as a schoolboy. Freda said not another word, simply stood looking from one of them to the other like a teacher supervising afterschool detention.

Chamberlain returned in a couple of minutes toting a manila folder. "Thank you, Freda," he said. She favored each of them, including Chamberlain, with one last scowl, then frumped out of there.

"I think she's sweet on you, Peter," Miss Paradise said, as the office door swung silently shut. "While you were gone, she told us she wants to be the mother of your son."

"How's that?" Chamberlain looked startled. "Oh, a joke. I get it." He rummaged through the folder, which was about a half-inch thick. "Let me tell you some more about our friend Thomas Scanlon."

Chamberlain selected a typewritten sheet. "His father owned a crop duster, and Scanlon soloed for the first time when he was fourteen."

"Following in the old man's footsteps?"

"That's right. The father used the duster to fly marijuana in from Mexico, and Scanlon took to it right away."

"How did he get from Texas to 'Nam?"

"We're not sure. He never served. Maybe he figured out that the real Wild West was in the mysterious Orient." Chamberlain turned the page over. "He was nineteen when he showed up, in his twenties when he worked for us. In between, he apparently tried pimping, pushing, and possibly contract murder. After the incident with Vang's officers, he was positively tagged twice in the next six months, both times in Vientiane. There were unconfirmed sightings in Ho Chi Minh City, and with the Vietnamese military command in Kampuchea."

"That isn't out of your official files, is it," Dennison said. "How do you know?"

Dennison grinned sheepishly.

"One of your people updates us on your computer access code," Miss Paradise said. "When I tapped in and queried for Scanlon, I drew a virtual blank."

"Care to tell me who my stoolie is?"

"He's a patriot," Miss Paradise said. "And no."

Chamberlain sighed. "Okay, you're right. Scanlon's file was pulled during the Pentagon Papers business. The director didn't want any record that we'd been involved with a scumbag like Scanlon."

"But instead of destroying the file, you transferred it to your personal collection."

"Yes," Chamberlain said with some pugnacity. "Because I had a stake in getting the bastard." His voice rose. "Dammit, I gave my word to Vang. I said I'd do my best to get them out."

"You did, Peter. And Vang knows it."

"The point is, I know how Vang feels." Chamberlain cut himself off, sat straighter in the desk chair. "I'm human, you know."

"That's what I keep telling the boss," Miss Paradise said lightly. "I think I've almost got him convinced."

"Okay," Chamberlain said more calmly. "Sure I'd like to see Nguyen's Asia connection stopped cold—and I'd also like to see Vang accomplish . . . whatever he feels he has to." He closed the folder. "Is Scanlon still in Laos?"

"According to Nguyen."

"Where?"

"You don't want to know, Peter. You're sticking your neck out too far already."

"That's for damn sure. All right, what do you want?"

"The Agency is still running the station at Udorn, correct?"

"We remain on cordial terms with Thailand, yes," Chamberlain said warily.

"I'll bet you've got a man across the Mekong in Vientiane, too," Dennison said.

"That information is classified."

"Right. Forget it. All we want you to do is arm Vang and get him into Laos."

Chamberlain opened and closed his mouth.

"You won't have to cross any borders," Miss Paradise said. "Just drop him somewhere on the frontier where the traffic is sparse."

Chamberlain found his voice. "That may not be possible."

"Yeah," Dennison said, "it is. And it will get you Scanlon."

"Is that guaranteed?" Chamberlain said sardonically.

"I'm risking a man, aren't I?" Dennison did not like voicing it that way. He was sending Vang in cold, without much more than his skill and courage and expertise to see him through against a damned powerful foe. It was the risk Dennison's People took each time they moved out on assignment, and the responsibility rested solely on Dennison's shoulders. He knew what had to be done, and how to do it. He knew it all—except how it would get to him if one of his People were taken down. . . .

"You'll do it, Peter," Dennison said.

Chamberlain stared at him. He understood; whatever his team, he knew whom to bet on. "Yes," he said, eyes down. "Yes, of course."

BOOK THREE
Laos

Chapter Eight

In the rainy season, when the highlands of northern Laos are draped in mile-high clouds and drifting elusive mist, they recall Chinese drawings rendered in delicate pen strokes on scrolls of rice paper. Rugged ridgelines cut by fantastically carved peaks wind in rough parallel like relief lines on a topographic map. Erosion has gouged caves and craters in the porous limestone bedrock, breaking it down into friable soil. The opium poppy, a fastidious plant that demands sweet soil and a temperate climate at least three thousand feet above sea level, finds northern Laos a most salubrious home.

Poppy farming is a labor-intensive, year-round endeavor that begins in March or April, when growers begin clearing new fields by chopping down saplings and brush with iron-bitted axes. For larger trees, a faller balances on a thin notched pole to scale the first twenty feet of the trunk, where he cuts away the top of the tree. When done precisely, the falling treetop will take out a number of smaller trees.

The slash is left to dry for a month and is then burned off, blanketing the plot with ash rich in phosphate, calcium, potassium, and other fertilizing nutrients. If the land is left fallow, these minerals will be leached out during the rains, but the most common food crop—dryland rice—does not mature until November, two months after poppies must be planted. So, most cultivators plant a hearty mountain corn that keeps the soil free of weeds, provides fodder for domestic animals, and matures by August.

At the beginning of September, the soil is turned with a heavy triangular hoe, chopped fine, and smoothed with bamboo brooms. The tiny poppy seeds are sown broadcast. They are white and blue and yellow and black, and those not planted are ground for cooking oil. These are the same edible seeds that garnish bagels and kaiser rolls, and of the more than fifty varieties of poppies, only the *Papaver somniferum* produces them. However, because the poppy sap turns inert before the plant goes to seed, those who enjoy a roll with a meal are spared the embarrassment of dropping into a nod during the soup course.

In November, the six-inch-high plants are thinned to six inches apart. Tobacco, beans, and spinach are planted among them, adding minerals to the soil and supplementing the village's diet. In late December the poppies are thinned a second time; the leaves that fringe the base of those shoots that are uprooted are eaten as salad greens. The vegetables interplanted with the poppies mature in January.

The poppy blooms during the next month. Its flower, bright red or pink, white or blue or even mauve, is shaped something like a tulip and sits atop a rigid, reed-straight, pale-green stem the thickness of a pencil. The flower's perfume is unsubtle, and to some people malodorous.

As the plant reaches full maturity, the petals drop away to expose the pod, a bluish-green bulb about the size of a bird's egg, crowned with a little mouth fringed with tiny petals. To extract the fraction of a gram of fluid contained within, the bulb is tapped, like a Vermont sugar maple or a Malaysian rubber tree. Precisely choosing the correct night on which to cut the pods requires experience and cultivator's savvy. Too soon, and the sap is runny and dribbles to the ground where it is lost; too late, and the alkaloid in the sap will have become codeine, only one-sixth as potent as morphine.

In the cool of late afternoon on the correct day, the grower cups the bulb in one hand and with a three-bladed knife incises shallow, parallel longitudinal slits exactly three-quarters of the way around the pod. Early the next morning, before the sun dries the sap, a gatherer, traditionally a woman, scrapes the surface of the bulb with a flexible rectangular blade, collecting the resin which has oozed from the slits during the night and depositing it in a small copper cup hanging from the belt around her blue cotton wrap.

The cut pod emits narcotic fumes so potent that babies, riding their mothers' backs during harvest, have died in their sleep of drug overdoses. So children are not allowed to help with the harvest until they are tall enough to breath above the fumes.

Some mountain people chew the dark sticky sap, biting off hunks as one might do with a chaw of tobacco. Raw opium tastes like licorice, and is the best cure for the symptoms of dysentery.

When the harvest is complete, the opium is shaped into bricks, wrapped by the kilogram in banana leaves, and tied with string. Each family with a share places a small brick in the center of the exhausted field as an offering to the *phi*, and after that no one is allowed in the field for fifteen days, so the *phi* can smoke the gift in peace.

The rest of the wrapped bricks of crude opium are stowed in wicker containers for the pack trip out of the highlands. Every couple of weeks during the growing season, the opium broker visits the village. He burns a pinch on foil, watching the color and intensity of the flame to judge the morphine content. Depending on the result, each kilo brings between forty and sixty dollars to the grower.

In crude jungle compounds, the opium will be reduced to morphine nuggets. Some time after that, in laboratories in Beirut, Aleppo, and Rome, in Brussels, Amsterdam, Madrid, and Zurich, in a dozen places each in France and Turkey, the morphine will become heroin.

In most human bodies, the heroin will produce a feeling of well-being, warmth, and euphoria, although a significant number of first-time users complain of depression, nausea, or tachycardia. In every case, repeated use produces an addiction characterized by an overwhelming psychological and physiological craving. It can be overcome either by extraordinary willpower and the grit to withstand the most unpleasant physical reactions, or by taking more heroin. Because few addicts are able to complete the first course, there is a steady and dependent market for the drug. At whim, the seller may raise the price, dilute the potency, even temporarily reduce availability, without affecting his trade.

He can make his customers leap through flaming hoops or slaver like Pavlov's dogs. Heroin addiction is that way.

Thomas Scanlon's dark hair was flecked with gray now, and he wore it long and full and flowing to his shoulders, bound by a headband fashioned from a madras neckerchief. His stomach was still flat and hard, his carriage strong and erect; somewhere in his forties, he remained a tough, fit, clear-eyed specimen.

Scanlon unfolded the small blade from a Swiss army knife and used its point to remove the tiny milky drop of fluid pearled at the bottom of the shallow gash in the poppy bulb. "I'm starting to get good at this, Pao," Scanlon said in his soft Texas-flavored English. "Five years, you get the knack. If I ever need work, you think I can handle the fields?"

Scanlon shot a grin at the Hmong; he was about twenty, with dark straight hair and hard eyes. Pao looked past Scanlon at the Hmong man who had come to the village with him: about ten years Pao's senior, in khaki fatigues with no insignia, a peaked cap, carrying a Russian-made AK-47 assault rifle.

The woman said to Scanlon, "I would like to see you in the fields—deep beneath them."

Scanlon laughed. "What I like about your sister, Pao," he said, talking as if she were not there, "is her mouth. You know what I mean?" he added nastily.

Pao shrugged. "Someday I think she will kill you."

"You never know, son," Scanlon said blithely. His right hand rested casually on the butt of the Colt Python .357 Magnum riding webbing on his right hip. "But in the meantime," Scanlon said, "cool it, sis."

The woman started to say something. Pao held her arm, not roughly, and said her name: "Tsia."

"What you do or say does not touch me," the woman said to Scanlon. She had high regal cheekbones and smooth, light brown skin, and was slim and high-breasted in a plain black blouse and long skirt. "When my body is with you, my mind and my soul are in another place. You are lying with the dead."

Scanlon fingered the tip of his bushy salt-and-pepper mustache. "Yeah, I thought you were losing your enthusiasm, the last time. Course, you take what you can get, is what I figure. So be ready—tomorrow night, same time. Vongsaly will be down to get you."

"Vongsaly!" Tsia spit the name at the AK-toting bodyguard like a malediction.

"Where was your village?" Pao said to Vongsaly in Hmong. "How do *your* people live today, while you turn your fellow tribesmen into *kha*?"

Vongsaly looked away. "Let's go," he said to Scanlon. "We are finished here."

Scanlon gave no indication that he had heard. He proffered the drop of sap on the tip of the pocketknife. "You know what that is, Pao?" Scanlon said.

Pao did not bother to respond. Tsia divided her outraged gaze between Scanlon and Vongsaly.

"That's power, son," Scanlon said. "You talk about your *phi*—right here we got God in a drop of dope."

"How nice for you," Tsia snarled.

"That's right, lady. And I couldn't've done it without you, my humble Hmong niggers. You folks damn-sure know how to raise this shit, and I know how to turn it into gold. You and me—hands across the sea."

The field stood above the village on a broad, gently sloping plain that climbed a plateau below the ridgeline. Some of the larger trees along its edge showed fire scars. About three hundred meters to a side, a good ten hectares, the field faced south into the sun, and in the light of a winter day it was an undulating sea of delicate green stalks.

Pao and Tsia knew of over two hundred similar fields of varying sizes in the district, all under the control of Thomas Scanlon.

About fifty air kilometers away, the Mekong River began a giant S-curve that took it due north for a couple of dozen kilometers before it turned south toward the sea once more.

The river formed the western frontier of Laos, and at the head of the big meander, where the river's course was bisected by the common border of Burma and Thailand, was the symbolic center of the Golden Triangle. Around it, in an area about the size of Colorado, seventy percent of the world's opium was grown.

In Burma, the trade was controlled by Shan rebels and Lahu tribesmen banded under whichever warlord provided the best weapons. In northern Thailand, ethnic Lao who had fled the Communist takeover maintained an uneasy opium alliance with the remnants and descendents of Kuomintang troops driven out of Yunnan Province by the Chinese People's Liberation Army nearly four decades earlier.

In the northwestern corner of Laos, Thomas Scanlon ruled the opium roost.

"Guess we'll be running along, son," Scanlon said to Pao at the edge of the sloping field. "You and your sister might as well see us off—I like having you close by when I'm in the neighborhood."

A narrow trail through the coarse *tranh* grass led down to the village. Vongsaly stayed behind them, the AK-47 pointing off to one side, but ready all the same. Scanlon wiped the knifeblade on a handkerchief, refolded it.

"You care nothing for our people," Pao said. "I understand that."

"Good for you," Scanlon said.

It was pointless, but Pao went on. "What about the ones who end up tormented by the heroin you sell? Your countrymen?"

Scanlon laughed. "You're a hoot, son. You still got a soft spot for the old U.S.A., even after the way we ran out on you."

"I was not here at the end of the war."

"You were off getting educated," Scanlon snorted. "'Course, if you'd learned anything, you wouldn't have come back." He gestured at the village. "Lovely place, son."

Phu Nam Kok hamlet was spread out below them on a rocky bench above the Tha River, which flowed into the Mekong ten kilometers downstream. Its two hundred Hmong residents lived in three dozen houses of brown lumber rough-planed in a portable mill, some roofed with a thatch of dried leaves of areca palms or banana trees, others with corrugated tin. Chickens and piglets scratched in the brown dirt; mountain ponies were stalked in the square, and four water buffalo were penned near the edge of town above the river.

Pao looked down on the place where he and his sister had been born. The village was living its second life; its first had ended fifteen years earlier, when the American bombing forced evacuation. The women and children and old people had been sent to the refugee camps in the lowlands; most of the men had stayed to fight the Communists. It was bad for them all, and it had gotten worse after the Communists won.

Four years later, the people of Phu Nam Kok were suddenly repatriated to their Houakhong Province homes and put to work resurrecting opium cultivation.

The Hmong did not tolerate the smoking of opium except among the elderly or the terminally ill, although they had grown the poppies as a cash crop for over a century. To the Hmong, opium was a currency. In poor growing seasons it bought food; in times of Communist invasion, it bought guns.

Pao shook his head. There was no explaining to someone like Scanlon. As they approached the clutch of houses, the faint smell of roasting meat rose toward them. Scanlon's helicopter, a Hughes 500M Defender painted in green-and-buff cammie, was parked in a clearing above the village square. UNITED STATES ARMY was stenciled on the rotor cowling, and U.S. 518 on the tail. Mounted at the nose was a 30mm Chain Gun, and two TOW missles were racked under each stabilizer wing.

Scanlon took Pao's arm. "But you're smart enough to know which way the wind blows, college boy."

Scanlon jerked Pao around to face him. Tsia leaped toward Scanlon, her hand crabbing at his face. Almost casually, half-looking, Scanlon backhanded her across the side of the head. She stumbled away and went down on one knee.

Pao stared into Scanlon's face, a few inches from his. "I've got two dozen armed men up at my place," Scanlon said in a low thick voice. "I've got the People's Revolutionary party"—Scanlon barked a short hard laugh—"in my hip pocket, 'cause they can finance one fuck of a good revolution on a fifty-percent cut of my trade, which is what I pay them, month in and month out."

Scanlon kneaded Pao's bicep beneath his hard fingers. "What have you got, Pao? You ain't got shit."

Tsia picked herself up and said something hard and mean in Hmong. Vongsaly reddened and looked away.

"You're the headman," Scanlon said to Pao. "If something happens to the people here, it'll be your fault. It's real simple—even a gook can understand." Scanlon's hand on Pao's arm was trembling a bit. "You cross me once, son, and I'm going to walk into the center of town here, pick the first five people I see, and shoot them dead. You cross me again, I'll kill five more. And so on, as many as it takes. If I have to wipe out every goddamned one of you, I'll do it, and Vientiane will send up another couple hundred to work the fields in your place.

"You want to remember," Scanlon said, "the Commies got no use for Hmong. You-all were a real pain in their ass during the war, and Commies got long memories. What you call your sense of history."

Tsia swore, "You son of a dog."

"Shut up," Scanlon said, without looking at her. "You're disposable, son," he told Pao. "I can kill as many of you as I want, and when the soldiers come through they won't say a damn thing. You can pile up the bodies like a roadblock, and they'll pretend not to see them. You understand what I'm telling you?"

Pao stared back rigidly.

"You understand, you cocky son of a bitch?"

Pao spit in Scanlon's face.

For a moment Scanlon did not move. Pao watched his spittle drool down to the point of Scanlon's chin, a few inches away.

Scanlon eased Pao back without releasing him. Scanlon's face was twisted in a horrid rictus. Scanlon drew the Colt Python, his hand moving slowly, deliberately—

Scanlon whipped the revolver forehanded across Pao's face. The gun sight raked a long thin gash in Pao's cheek along the jawline. Scanlon hit him again in the side of the head, and Pao went down, blood dripping from the point of his chin.

Tsia screamed and lunged for Scanlon. Vongsaly stepped between them, cross-blocking with the AK. Tsia grappled at his face. Vongsaly levered her back and jabbed the gun barrel into her stomach.

Scanlon kicked Pao twice in the ribs, swinging his leg rhythmically. Pao moaned, rolled over, and lay still.

"All right." Scanlon stepped back. "Okay." He stared down at Pao, then at Tsia. He shook his head. "I'll see you tomorrow." Scanlon pushed past her and went down toward the chopper.

Vongsaly circled around Tsia, holding her at bay with the rifle barrel. "Quisling," Tsia said. "Father-killer." Vongsaly backed away, turned, and half-ran to the Hughes. Scanlon fired the engine, and the rotor began to spin.

Tsia knelt by her brother, wiping dirt from the cut on his face. The chopper lifted from the clearing, spun on its shaft, and turned north along the course of the Tha River. Tsia watched it until it disappeared over the ridgeline, her body quaking with loathing.

"LBFMs," Scanlon said into the intercom mike, jinking the chopper to the left as he followed the path of the river valley below. "That's what the Air America pilots called the country girls who went down to Vientiane seeking fame, fortune, and U.S. dollars."

"LBFMs?" Vongsaly echoed.

"Little Brown Fucking Machines." Scanlon laughed. He shot a crude grin at his Hmong lieutenant, but Vongsaly was staring straight ahead. "Something wrong with you, Vong? You look like you just had your first blow job and decided you didn't like the taste."

Vongsaly looked at him. "Do you have to talk like that? The woman, Tsia—"

"For Chrissake," Scanlon broke in. "What's your problem—she *your* sister too?"

"I went to school with her older brothers. When we were very young."

"Where are the older brothers now, pal?" Scanlon answered his own question: "They're deader than last week, right? They got their asses shot off fighting for the good guys, while you were across the frontier in Chiang Mai hiring your gun to the KMT's opium-protection racket."

"I went to war."

"Yeah—for cash on the line." Scanlon barked a laugh into the intercom. "Don't get me wrong, Vong. I like to see a little healthy greed in my soldiers. But don't start whining to me about 'your' people, and what 'I'm' doing to them, okay? You're a deserter, son, not to mention a hypocrite. Nothing wrong with that—nothing right, neither. The main thing you want to keep in mind at all times is you are working for me now. Well hey." Scanlon pointed down through the glass at his right knee. "Lookee what I see."

A gravel road paralleled the Tha along a little bench a few meters above the river's surface. The water ran clear and swift at this time of the year, but a month or so from now, when the rains came, it would turn brown with mud and roil up to bite chunks out of the side of the narrow roadbed. The wall of the river valley rose abruptly above the road on either side to ridges of jagged limestone karsts.

Below them the canyon was a couple of hundred feet deep. An open Jeep was moving slowly up the track, lurching over potholes and ruts. Scanlon worked the controls and the chopper eased down between the lush valley walls. Now they could make out four men in tan uniforms in the rig. It bucked to a stop at the sound of the approaching chopper. All four men looked up, and the one in the right front seat waved. Scanlon waggled the rotor in reply.

"Kay Soong," Vongsaly said.

"Yeah." Scanlon grinned. "Let's give that son a thrill."

Vongsaly gulped but said nothing. Scanlon pulled the nose of the bird up and out of the valley. He circled to the right above rolling hilltop ridgeline, climbed five hundred feet, then swung back toward the valley. "Keep your asshole puckered, Vong," Scanlon said into the mike.

The chopper banked and dived hard.

"What . . . ?" Vongsaly closed one eye and braced himself.

"Bombs away," Scanlon said. He reached to the control panel, flipped up the red cap over one firing button, and stabbed it with his forefinger.

A quick sizzling noise sounded from the left side of the Hughes, followed by a whistle. With a back burst of white smoke, a TOW missile stabbed from its tube, trailing thin wire guide.

Vongsaly gaped at the tracker sight: the cross wires were centered dead on the Jeep.

The four men scrambled out of the Jeep and ran for it. One slipped at the edge of the cutbank and slid down a mud chute into the river.

Scanlon edged the tracker up at the last instant.

The missile slammed into the limestone wall five meters above the road. Rock and dirt geysered out and rained down on the Jeep, concealing it in a cloud of smoke and dust.

Scanlon pulled up over the valley and descended toward the Jeep. The prop wash blew aside the dust. A limestone boulder blocked the rig. Two of the men were down the road, pulling their buddy from the drink. The fourth, a ball-shaped little guy, was picking himself up where he had fallen on his face in front of the rig, brushing dust from his uniform. No one looked hurt.

Scanlon threw a selector switch on the radio control. "This is the fucking U.S. Air Force." Scanlon's voice boomed from the speaker mounted under the TOW's nose sight. "We got you covered, you godless Commie bastards."

The chubby man was shaking his fist and screaming.

"Think he's pissed off?" Scanlon asked.

Vongsaly did not answer. He was having trouble keeping his breakfast down.

"You turning into a candy-ass, son?" Scanlon laughed. He was having a fine time.

The chubby man fumbled an automatic rifle from the back of the Jeep, butted it against his shoulder, and sighted up at the chopper.

"Whoops," Scanlon said casually. He yanked the control back to the left, and the chopper rose sharply.

A burst of autofire sniped below the chopper's skids. Scanlon juked in the other direction, then looked down in time to see the gunner rip out the empty clip and fling it into the river.

Vongsaly moaned and swallowed as the chopper slewed back down between the steep valley walls. Scanlon flicked on the loudspeaker again. "Hey, back off, Kay," his amplified voice boomed. "Can't you boys take a joke?"

Kay waved his arms, shouting orders. Kay's three men heaved at the boulder. It dropped over the cutbank and splashed into the river. Kay was signaling the men back into the Jeep.

"See you at the compound, Kay," Scanlon broadcast. He pulled the chopper up in a radical ascent, skimming within a few feet of the karst as they shot over it. Scanlon leered across at Vongsaly. "Some fun, eh, kid?"

Vongsaly clapped one hand over his mouth and wrestled open his door with the other. He just managed to lean out against the restraint of his seatbelt before spewing into the valley below.

Scanlon's chopper climbed out of the river valley and came in from the south. Here the ridgeline widened into an oblong summit with steep scree-slope sides rising toward a roughly cone-shaped hilltop that must once have towered several hundred meters over the surrounding high country.

But at some point the top of the little mountain had been sheared cleanly off. The result looked strikingly like a volcano, the steep outer sides ending abruptly in a jagged knife-edge arête rimming an irregular bowl formation, or rather two overlapping bowls set in a roughly hourglass-shaped formation. It was as big as a village—two hundred meters long through the hourglass's "waist," a hundred wide at each of the bulges.

There were no volcanoes in these parts. The overlapping bowls were craters, a common geological formation in northern Laos; the three million tons of bombs the United States had dropped during ten years of secret war had produced more profound and rapid topological changes than millenia of natural phenomena.

Here the bombs had literally blown the top off the mountain. For most of the circumference, the sides were near-vertical limestone scarp, ten meters high on average and not yet much eroded. The defoliating agents that followed the bombing had withered most of the thick forest cover, but by now some grasses and low shrubs were regaining root-hold.

The inadvertent result was a virtually impregnable natural fortress. The bowls' figure-8, set perpendicular to the river's course, was invisible from below. The loose gravel on the outer slope made it a technical climb calling for ropes, hardware, and enough time to make any invader a sitting duck on the open face. The only possible exposure was at the "top" end of the hourglass, the end farther from the river, where a limestone dome rose above the depression. But fifty yards farther on, it too dropped precipitously to the thick forest floor.

A small stream flowed down the wall of the near bowl, meandered across its grassy floor, and disappeared through an underground channel to reappear as a thin cascade rippling down the canyon wall to the river. A double tire track ran back along it, through the high narrow hole-in-the-wall cut, and into the far bowl. The track was faint enough to be invisible from the air unless you were looking for it.

Four men armed with automatic rifles were stationed atop the rim of the double bowl at intervals, where they commanded a panoramic view for miles in any direction. The guard on the south gave the chopper a languid salute as it came overhead.

"If the Hmong had had a base like this," Scanlon said on

the chopper intercom, "they'd've been safe as lambs. The NVA would have had to drop a nuke in their laps to flush them."

"We had such places," Vongsaly said.

"I thought you were out of town when that shit came down."

"My people, I mean. They had bases in the mountains around the Plain, just as strong as this."

"Yeah?" Scanlon said nastily. "Then why didn't they win, son?"

"You know why: the Americans ran out."

"Well," Scanlon said. "I'm back now."

"Our luck," Vongsaly murmured.

"Don't be a whiner," Scanlon said. "Sometimes I don't know why I took you in, Vong. Must be I got a soft spot in my heart for guys who will sell out their own people cheap."

Vongsaly's mouth clapped shut like a garden gate.

A catwalk, camouflaged with brush, was mounted atop the limestone rim girding the crater. Besides providing a patrol platform, it canopied the entrances to the caverns and tunnels carved into the rock walls, hiding them from aerial observation. Electrical wire was strung along the wall below the canopy, and a diesel generator hummed from somewhere inside.

Scanlon set the chopper down in the far bowl, near the waist of the figure-8 and about opposite the high round dome at the far end. As the skids settled into the grass and the rotor began to feather to a stop, a couple of men in coveralls came out from under the catwalk.

A door was set into the rock here, twenty feet high and three times as wide, with a metal control box mounted beside it, wires ducting from its top up to the main circuit. One of the mechanics worked a switch, and the big wooden door, painted the buff brown of the limestone cliffs, swung up and outward. The other mechanic backed a 4WD Jeep up to the chopper and hooked it up to the hitch. A second Hughes was hangared inside.

Scanlon came around to the chopper's passenger door. "Didn't mean to get your cookies scrambled, Vong," he said.

The gag on Kay Soong and his men had brightened Scanlon's mood. "I purely love putting that bird through the drill." Scanlon shook his head nostalgically. "When Saigon went, they were dumping these babies off carrier decks into the sea so they wouldn't fall into the wrong hands. I figured, hell, they're tossing them out, I'll take a couple."

Vongsaly climbed out, a little shaky. The 4WD strained against the hitch and the chopper eased after it, skidding smoothly into the hangar. The rotor cleared the top by about three meters.

"Let's go meet Kay," Scanlon said. "Hope he's not real pissed off."

At the end of the bowl above the river valley, where the little creek seemed to disappear into solid rock, a clump of scrub juniper hid the mouth of a narrow tunnel. Scanlon ducked inside. Years before, using carefully placed C-4–shaped charges, he had widened the natural outlet channel to about five feet in diameter; indirect sunlight illuminated it from the far end, perhaps ten meters down. Scanlon and Vongsaly emerged around another thicket of thorny bushes.

That put them on a little flat-rock platform overlooking the river road a hundred meters below. At this point the Tha jogged upstream to the right, and from the point of the elbow a footpath switchbacked up along the steep face. The path was narrow, faintly worn, and washed out in places, nearly indistinguishable from the natural erosion ruts, and difficult to spot even from the road unless you knew which landmarks to look for.

Twenty meters below the hidden tunnel mouth, where the slope steepened almost to vertical, the visible path ended at a boulder. There a ladder was bolted to the chalky rock, climbing to the tiny platform at the tunnel mouth, which was hidden by hedges of brush.

"Right on time," Scanlon said. Motor noise grew louder, and the open-topped Jeep came into sight around a bend and pulled to a stop below them. The rig and its occupants were dusted with white crushed limestone; one of the men in the back was still dripping river water.

"Hey there, Kay," Scanlon called. "How was the trip?"

The chubby man looked up. "You are a *macha macha* bastard, you know that, Scanlon?"

"Don't be that way. Come on up."

Kay barked orders. One of his soldiers hoisted his rifle from the Jeep and assumed a casual approximation of an on-guard position. The other two crouched and lit cigarettes. They were kids, too young to have seen real action and, like soldiers in any army, most happy when goldbricking.

Scanlon had heard the rumors: some diehard Hmong, armed by the Chicoms, were still raiding north and east of the Plain of Jars. But any violent skirmishes here in the Golden Triangle involved neither politics nor government troops, merely greed.

Scanlon's competitors across the border in Burma or far northern Thailand were always looking for ways to expand their opium territory, but he lost no sleep worrying about them. He had settled the issue for good soon after he'd taken over the province.

That first spring, as Scanlon's initial crop was being harvested, a Burmese named U Aung had gotten the bright idea of muscling in. A couple of years earlier, some reporter for the Bangkok *Post* had referred to him as an "Opium Warlord," and the poor son of a bitch must have believed his own notices.

Scanlon watched Kay Soong labor up the steep path. Kay was as round-faced as a Buddha and had little banty-rooster legs. Before he made the first switchback, he was panting like a steam engine. Scanlon grinned down at the fat little bastard.

U Aung, the Burmese, had had more ambition than savvy, and he was a piker to boot. The merc army he'd bought himself, fifty or sixty men, had come cheap, and U had ended up with what he paid for: thugs who hung around the Irrawaddy waterfront at the foot of C Road in Mandalay; a few ethnic Lahu from the north region, where banditry was an accepted social tradition; and a half-dozen Hmong and Yao who had crossed the Mekong for greener and less bomb-pocked pastures as the secret war on the Laos side grew too close for comfort. U Aung piled his boys into a ragtag convoy of vehicles—a couple of old ZIL-151 Russian-made canvas-topped 6x6s for the troops, and a Toyota Land Cruiser as a command car. Instead of spending a couple of bucks on Armalites or, better yet, Russian AKs, U picked up an assortment of Chicom crap: Type 56-1 assault rifles, a couple of K-50M submachine guns, and a 75mm recoilless rifle that he tripod mounted on the back of one of the ZIL trucks.

Scanlon was billeting about two dozen men then, as now, and U Aung figured that three-to-one were winning odds. What he didn't know about were the two armed choppers and the stockpile of seventy-five TOWs and twenty Stinger missiles to make them talk loud and clear. The first load of antitank rockets took out the recoilless. After that it was too easy, so Scanlon limited himself to the 30mm Chain Gun for the survivors, to keep it sporting. It was still a turkey shoot.

Scanlon's men found U Aung hiding behind a thorn bush, all scratched up but mostly whole. Scanlon shot him in both knees. An Agency guy in Saigon had told him once that it was as good as cutting off a guy's balls; being crippled for life took the starch right out of the old pecker. So some good had come out of it after all: U went back to Burma and told the other guys that the Yankee bastard was crazy and also goddamned hard to touch, and no one had made trouble in the years since.

You did what you had to, Scanlon reflected as he watched Kay Soong scrambling up the path; with thugs like Aung, or with the "revolutionaries" down in Vientiane—the boys with Commie hearts and capitalist minds. Bombs or bribes, depending on the circumstances; now there was a metaphor for Southeast Asia. Kay was on the ladder now, gasping as though he might die. Scanlon gave him a hand up the last few steps.

"Listen, Kay, I was just kidding around."

"Some fine joke."

"Come have a drink. You bring the mail?"

Kay took a large manila envelope from inside his blouse. "You bring my money?"

"*Macha macha* money, son," Scanlon said. "You're gonna retire rich. Come on—show you how bad I feel about dirtying up your dress tans, I'll break out the good scotch—not that swill I used to give Piang." Piang had preceded Kay as regional commander in Houakhong Province, but he'd turned out to be such an innovative little bandit that a year ago the party had promoted him down to Luang Prabang, where they could keep a closer eye on him.

Scanlon patted Kay's little round gut. "You got a touch of Dunlop's disease there, son." Kay looked at him blankly. "That's when your belly done-lops over your belt." Neither Kay nor Vongsaly got it, though Kay smiled hollowly. Kay smiled a lot, like a nervous tick. You looked at his mug, you thought you were dealing with a feeb'. But Scanlon reminded himself that the grinning son of a bitch was his partner—or at least was the bagman for his real partners, down in Vientiane.

Kay waddled like a sailor on shore leave as he followed Scanlon back through the tunnel. While they crossed the first bowl and went through the waist, Kay studied Scanlon's sentries as if reviewing the troops. "You still recruit Hmong, I see," Kay said, as if Vongsaly were deaf.

"Sure—some of my best friends are Hmong."

"But I also observe some Laotians. That is good, using true revolutionaries."

"Kay, you're so full of shit," Scanlon said, laughing. "These guys are hoodlums, as you damned well know." The gooks loved to play these games.

"Perhaps they are refugees," Kay said slyly.

Scanlon gave him a narrow look. It was Kay's turn to laugh.

Scanlon sighed. "Sure, Kay, I'm the refugees' best pal."

"You are a freedom force of one, Thomas Scanlon." Kay peered through his own perpetual grin. "CIA, perhaps?"

"Nope, sorry," Scanlon said solemnly. "The CIA quit this war a long time ago. Just us renegades now."

"So glad to hear it," Kay murmured.

Nearly a dozen tunnels radiated from the far bowl like bicycle spokes. Scanlon led Kay to the adit opposite the waist of the double-bowl hourglass, at the foot of the big domed formation. He had not invited Kay inside his personal quarters before, and the Laotian hesitated at the doorway. "The Hmong . . ."

"Don't be narrow-minded, son."

"I do not like being outnumbered."

"You don't trust me." Scanlon pretended to be hurt.

"Only a bear hides in a cave."

"What's that, an old Commie proverb?" Scanlon shrugged. "Suit yourself. We can talk out here in the dust and sun, or we can drink some scotch."

"All right," Kay decided.

It never hurt to show a new guy around the compound; it gave them an idea what they'd be up against if they tried any strongarm tactics. Whatever Kay's men knew about war came out of comic books; Scanlon's mercs, on the other hand, were veterans of the real thing. Sure, most of them had fought for whoever paid best, but they'd fought. . . .

Anyway, Scanlon didn't get that many chances to show the place off. Folks didn't come calling that often, except for Tsia.

The craters from which he'd fashioned this headquarters redoubt dated back to the earliest days of the bombing, before most of it was concentrated on the Plain of Jars and the Commie-controlled "thumb" jutting into North Vietnam to the east. Everyone knew it was a waste of good bombs. They blew the shit out of the Laotian leg of the Trail and the Pathet headquarters at Sam Neua, the country ended up looking like a moonscape, and the Commies went right on, same as always.

Scanlon knew that area well; he had moved in during '74 and '75 to arrange liberation, transport, and delivery of U.S. vehicles, weapons, and other material left behind when the CIA hauled ass and left the Laotians to the Commies.

The Commies were great customers. They took all the G.I. shit he could steal, and they paid top dollar, cash on the barrelhead.

But over here in the west, it was less a war and more a pissin' match between the Pathet and their Red Chinese allies on one side, and the Meo tribesmen and their fellow mercs—Yao, Lahu, a few Kuomintang Chinese—on the other. They took turns occupying Houakhong Province, but they got into real scraps only toward the end of the dry season in February or March, when the poppies were flowing. Both sides had always financed a major part of their war efforts with the profits from whatever opium they could steal.

Each had occasionally holed up in this same double crater, and the various regular units, guerrillas, and random marauders passing through had dug in, expanded, and improved the real estate. Scanlon had added the final touches.

The steel-reinforced door protecting Scanlon's quarters stood at the end of twenty meters of dim, rough-cut tunnel. He worked a key in the lock. The door opened silently on well-oiled hinges to a bare anteroom with a TV camera mounted in one corner of the ceiling, within a box of bulletproof glass. The camera faced a second door with both a dead-bolt key lock and a combination dial.

Scanlon pulled it open and swept Kay in with an exaggerated gesture of hospitality. The main living area was a square room a good forty feet to a side; the effect was of space and, surprisingly, of airiness and light: the domed ceiling, rising to an apex thirty feet above the center of the floor, opened at the top in a chimney skylight to admit fresh air and sunshine.

A bench a couple of meters wide rimmed the room, around a central area like a sunken conversation pit, furnished with modern-style chairs, sofas, and lamps. Scanlon threw the manila envelope on a long glass-topped coffee table. "Take a load off your feet, Kay."

The room's design countered potential claustrophobia. The walls were hung with silk drapery here, heavy brocades there; the floors were completely carpeted with thick oriental rugs. Yards of high bookcases full of leather-bound volumes rose on one side. A wet bar sat across from it. In the far wall, another steel door hid Scanlon's personal quarters.

"We'll have a taste o' the heather," Scanlon said. He produced a bottle of Glenfiddich, dropped ice cubes from a half-sized refrigerator into crystal glasses, and splashed a generous tot of the unblended scotch into each. Kay, looking slightly uncomfortable in a low-slung armless chair, coolly accepted his drink, grinning his grin. In a gold humidor on the table he found an assortment of American cigarettes. Kay selected a Salem methol and lit up with a matching table lighter.

"I keep Salems around for sentimental reasons," Scanlon said. "I hear Ho smoked them."

Kay puckered up his smile like a politician about to kiss a baby. "You are an admirer of Comrade Ho?"

"I am an admirer of shrewd operators."

Scanlon carried his drink to the other side of the room, where a finely wrought hardwood cabinet stood six feet tall and twice as wide, faced by an upholstered swivel chair. Scanlon used another key, then swung open wide double doors.

On the left was a control panel and communications center. One video monitor showed the camera's view of the anteroom, another a bird's-eye view of the compound from a camera mounted on the hilltop above their heads. An international-band radio receiver and two receivers with antenna rotor controls were fronted by a fold-down shelf. Scanlon worked a switch: a motor rumbled and a metal plate slid closed across the skylight opening. An air-conditioner automatically came on.

The other side was strictly for pleasure. Set in racks were a large-screen TV, a video recorder, and a fully equipped stereo system, with hundreds of records. Scanlon set one on the turntable and flicked on the amp; the strains of Wagner's *Siegfried Idyll* welled up.

The adjacent cabinet was about the same size, but its double doors were steel. Scanlon punched a number into a keypad, and a numerical display above it glowed red. Scanlon pulled the doors open with a flourish.

It was a small armory: Kay saw automatic rifles, handguns, a grenade launcher, passive light-amplifying night-vision viewers, the works. Scanlon smiled smugly. He wanted Kay to report all this to his bosses in Vientiane, so that no one would get any stupid notions. Symbiosis—that was the key to everyone doing just fine, thank you.

"What do you think, Kay?"

Kay smiled his smile. "It is very nice," he said. "For a cave."

Cocky bastard, Scanlon thought. "Only one thing impresses you, pal." Scanlon opened the other door. At first Kay saw only a blank rock wall, but then he realized that a door was set flush into it. Scanlon worked a combination dial, cranked two handles in opposite directions, and pulled laminated steel doors outward. Scanlon took out a cheap fake-leather briefcase, toted it down into the pit, and set it in front of Kay.

Kay smiled and raised the lid. The briefcase was packed to the gunwales with U.S. hundred-dollar bills.

"There goes the revolutionary government's hard-currency problem for another month." Scanlon raised his drink. "Here's to crime."

Kay was smiling at the money like a charmed snake. He picked up his glass and sucked at it, unaware that it was empty.

Scanlon slapped the case shut and picked it up. The show was over, and Scanlon was tired of Kay's smirk. "Vong will see you out, son," Scanlon said, and carried the case over to the tunnel doorway, where he gave it to Vongsaly. Kay scampered after it, as if afraid it would get away. He did not bother to say so-long.

The hell with him; it had been a long day and now it was R&R time. Scanlon took a fresh drink and the manila envelope with his mail, and sprawled on a sofa, his boots propped on the armrest. Inside the envelope he found a note from Vientiane confirming receipt of the last payment, along with a couple of newspapers. The most recent was a four-day-old Bangkok *Post*. Peace talks were stalled in Europe, terrorists were setting car bombs in the Middle East, and the military had taken over a government in South America—the usual crap. Scanlon took a slug of scotch and turned the page.

He almost choked on the whiskey. "Son of a bitch," he murmured fervently.

On page 3, a two-column headline over an article perhaps ten paragraphs long, and set unobtrusively beneath the fold, read: VIETNAMESE DRUG KING MURDERED IN PARIS.

* * *

Scanlon shut off the radiotelephone and slumped in the swivel chair. It was late afternoon now; he'd waited several hours before his contact in Bangkok got back to him with the rest of the story:

Five and a half days earlier, some son of a bitch had wiped out the entire Paris end of his operation, where fully eighty percent of his product was handled under the personal direction of his old comrade-in-arms Nguyen Van Cao. Scanlon's refinery, the home in Hauts-de-Seine he owned in Nguyen's name, and his chopper were destroyed, and Nguyen, Hugo Crain, Truong, and about a dozen Vietnamese gun cocks were dead.

Scanlon crossed to the bar and refilled his glass, took it down into the pit, and lowered himself thoughtfully into an aluminum-and-canvas armchair. All the furnishings had been floated up the Mekong on bamboo rafts, then heli-lifted or ported overland by locals the rest of the way. All of his operation—including Paris—had been assembled the same meticulous way.

And now some son of a bitch had destroyed it in one night.

Scanlon remembered one of his daddy's old sayings: *No use crying over spilled milk—it could have been whiskey.* Scanlon managed to smile—and, hell, his daddy had never been half the crook he was now.

Nguyen was no loss. The guy was good, but Scanlon had never let himself forget that Nguyen had played both ends against the middle during the war. You could never really trust a double-crosser; that's why Scanlon had set it up so that Hugo Crain reported everything to him—and let Nguyen know it. Otherwise, the Vietnamese would have tried to take over the first chance he saw.

As for the operation, it could be rebuilt. It would cost some time and effort, but so did anything worthwhile.

Scanlon unfolded himself from the chair and went to the safe. From an interior drawer he took two bankbooks, the old-fashioned kind that were issued for accounts in precomputer days.

The kind that were still issued to savers who valued their privacy and did not trust the security of elctronic data storage. The kind issued by banks in Zurich, Algiers, and a few other places.

Each had a marble-grained cover with a number embossed on it: nine digits on the Zurich bank, seven on the State Bank of Algeria. The entries inside were handwritten.

The last notation in the first bankbook showed a balance of a bit less than two million dollars; in the other, just over three million. The old retirement fund wasn't doing too badly. . . .

Scanlon put the bankbooks back where they belonged. He was smiling when he returned to his drink. There were ways; Paris did not have to mean that much. But then his smile faded, because there was one damned good question remaining, and it had to be answered sooner or later:

Who the fuck was behind this shit?

A rival gang was possible, but why now? Nguyen had been operating for years without interference or serious challenge. Besides, he and Hugo Crain both had stoolies and contacts all over the Paris underworld, well-paid rats who had never failed to alert the organization to potential trouble. It would have been pretty near impossible to subvert them all at once. Anyway, no one went in for wholesale slaughter anymore; it riled the cops. Gangsters in this day and age had more subtle methods. . . .

So it had to be something not directly related to a takeover. Hell, Nguyen had plenty of enemies. The corrupt son of a bitch had been ripping off people indiscriminately from the earliest days of the war; he had a finger in every pie, from the whorehouses at Cam Ranh Bay to the casinos he co-owned with the Chinese in Cholon and the currency and precious metals his boys smuggled north up the Ho Chi Minh Trail. He'd browned off enough people to form a small army—and it must have taken a small army to come down on him like they had.

Sure, Scanlon thought with some relief, old enemies made the most sense. Except that there was a third possibility, and Scanlon liked it least of all:

What if whoever dropped the shitstorm on Nguyen was really after him?—and didn't care how many people he had to step on to find him?

Jesus, Scanlon thought, *if that was the deal, the bastard must be pretty goddamned pissed off.*

And pretty goddamned good.

Chapter Nine

The JetRanger's pilot was a cowboy named Donahue, a good-looking blond kid in a well-worn leather jacket, teardrop Ray-Bans, and elephant-hide Tony Lamas. "Land of a Million Elephants, right?" Donahue said, pointing into the darkness off the right skid, toward Laotian territory. "I figure one of them could spare a patch of leather."

Vang had been in the air for most of the past twelve hours. A Thai in civvies met his commercial flight when it landed at Don Muang airport in Bangkok, and escorted him to an unmarked C-130. The Thai never said a word after they'd exchanged identifications.

The C-130 had no doubt flown for Airborne Control Command during the war. When the American bombing was at full force, an ACC C-130 was in the air over Laos twenty-four hours a day, coordinating targeting and delivery. This one was loaded with supplies for the base at Udorn, just across the Mekong from Vientiane; Vang passed the flight in a jumpseat between a half-dozen racked kegs of Budweiser and a crate of *Playboy* magazines.

The C-130 landed at Udorn at three in the morning, and as soon as the door was cracked, an Agency officer named Bailey came aboard to scowl at Vang. Bailey was a middle-aged black man, balding and sour-tempered. "The pilot's orders are to fly you up north and haul his tail the hell out," Bailey said in the Jeep, grinding the gears. "Don't try to get him balled up in anything else." The JetRanger was waiting in the dark at the far end of the runway. "What I hate," Bailey said, "is orders from home: some VIP is coming, and kiss his ass and have one of the boys chauffeur him anywhere the hell he wants. Get up in the middle of the night, and say 'Yes, sir' and 'No, sir' and 'Good luck, sir,' and don't ask any questions, like a good field nigger. You know what the hell I mean?"

"No," Vang said. By then they were at the idling JetRanger. Vang said thanks and grabbed his gear from the back. "Well, drag my dick in the dirt," Bailey said to his back.

Donahue, on the other hand, was all cheer, an open-faced kid in his late twenties, one of the postwar hands; the Agency must have stolen him from the navy or air force right out of flight school. Ten minutes from Udorn, Vang tuned out the kid's well-modulated monologue and dozed off. An hour later, Donahue said, "Coming in, sir," and Vang was instantly awake.

The chopper skimmed the treetops canopying the jungle. The moon was down, but the starry dry-season sky illuminated hilly terrain cut by valley streams. At eleven o'clock, a clearing bloomed along the side of a south-facing slope. It looked like neither a natural formation nor a slash-and-burn garden plot.

"You see those patches all along this side of the river," Donahue said. "Old war wounds, napalm or defols, I guess. According to the older guys, the Agency used them as staging areas for infiltrating mercs across the river." Donahue looked across at Vang. "I guess you know about that, sir."

It seemed a paradox, having to sneak back into one's own country. On the other hand, the Hmong never felt themselves of Laos, any more than they had considered themselves of China two centuries earlier. The high-country homeland of the "free men" was theirs not by national boundary but by industry, a willingness to live where others would not, and the hereditary right of eminent domain. Ethnic Lao discrimination against the Hmong was a constant. Today the only "free men" were the guerrillas in the northeastern hills. The remainder of the Hmong still in Laos were interned in "refugee" camps near the Vientiane Delta, or otherwise oppressed.

Among the latter, according to Nguyen Van Cao's dying words in Paris, were Thomas Scanlon's slaves.

Donahue swung the JetRanger around above a flat spot on the denuded slope and brought it down in an elegantly gentle landing. "Over that ridgeline," Donahue said, "and then about three klics down the stream on the other side, and you'll hit the Mekong. The Tha comes in two klics upstream from there." Donahue rummaged between the seats. "You want to see a chart?"

Vang shook his head. "I know where I'm going." He stared through the windshield and did not unbuckle his belt.

He was not a Laotian, yet he had grown up there, in highland country like this, and he had been exiled for over ten years. He remembered the last days, and flying down from his Long Tieng base to the capital to get some reassurance from the CIA agent in place. Instead, he was wished good luck. Good luck, and goodbye.

"Listen," Donahue said. "I'm willing to break ranks if you need a lift to the interior."

Vang looked at him. "I beg your pardon."

"They don't tell me shit," Donahue said. He dug a pack of Winstons from his jacket and offered one to Vang. Vang shook his head no thanks. "All I know is you've got some guns with you, and once I drop you off my job is over."

Donahue dragged on his cigarette. "The rest I've got to guess: you're crossing the frontier and you're on your own." Donahue smiled. "Like you didn't get a good enough fucking-over the last go-around, they've got to fuck you over once more. I know what happened to you back then—everyone around here does."

"You are a good guesser."

"That's part of my extensive intelligence-agent training." Donahue grinned. "Anyway, what I'm saying is if you want to go somewhere, you got it. I'll worry abut the kickback when I get home to Udorn."

"Thank you," Vang said. "I appreciate that." He worked

the buckle of his seatbelt. "But this one is deep infiltration. The only way it will work is if I go in alone."

Donahue shrugged. "Hope you're right," he said neutrally.

It was the truth. Vang had accepted Dennison's assignment: shut down the Golden Triangle connection for good. The Paris firestorm had been the preliminary event; the job was half-complete until the root of the operation was dug up and destroyed, and Vang did not leave jobs half-complete.

Guerrilla tactics were the only way to get to Scanlon; it was a one-man job, and no warrior was better qualified than Vang to go in alone. Still, as Donahue must have sensed, there was more to it than that. . . .

Scanlon was owed a debt of vengeance. He had killed two dozen of Vang's people for money, and now he must pay. The matter concerned Scanlon and the Hmong people, in the person of Vang, and his avenging passion. . . .

"All right," Donahue said. "I don't mean to stick my nose in." Donahue unlatched his door. "I'll give you a hand with your gear."

Vang wore black fatigues and light rigging for quick travel. From Nguyen's description of Scanlon's setup, Vang doubted that any frontal assault could succeed. He had to go in on Scanlon's blind side.

The details would have to be worked out in the field.

On his right hip Vang wore an Ingram M-11 machine pistol in specially designed leather; a fitted pocket hanging just behind it on his web utility belt held the suppressor. A string of kidney pouches contained extra clips, black cosmetic goop, grenades, and a couple of foil-wrapped packets, each about the size of a pack of smokes: C-4 plastic explosive. A sheathed Fairbairn commando knife rode his left hip.

Donahue, lips pursed, watched Vang rig up. "The thing is," Donahue said, "I was wondering when you were coming back out. Maybe you could use a pickup." He grinned. "It's the off season in the spook business around here—has been since seventy-five, they tell me."

He stuck his head inside the cockpit and came out with a

pocket-sized transceiver. "The Udorn boys monitor this frequency twenty-four hours a day, just like old times. We've got relay stations all over the place. What's your sign?"

"V," Vang said, "as in victory."

"Beethoven's Fifth, huh? Okay, I'll tell the signal guys to pass me any messages from V. After you call me in, shoot out a carrier transmission every fifteen minutes or so and I'll use the onboard computer for a rough fix, until we can make voice contact. So," Donahue said, "how long will it take you to wrap up your business?"

"Dawn tomorrow." One way or the other, it would be over by then. "I want your word, though."

"On what?"

"If Udorn monitors no signal by 0700, forget you ever met me."

Donahue looked up at the stars. "Getting late. I don't want to miss breakfast." He offered his hand. "Good luck."

Vang waited until the chopper disappeared below the trees to the south. He turned in the other direction, toward Laos, and marched up toward the ridge.

A rutted cart track ran along the Thailand side of the Mekong, and a ten-minute jog upstream brought Vang to a crossing as the first faint light of dawn began to break. The mouth of the Tha was a hundred meters farther upriver. The bridge was a suspension span with peeled-log supports and a bamboo deck about two meters wide, dotted with water-buffalo manure. Likely it was well used; any customs official who had survived in the Golden Triangle for long had the good sense to take his bribes and keep out of sight.

Near the end of the dry season the Mekong ran low, cutting shifting, meandering channels through exposed mud bars. The broad-leaf jungle came down to each steep cutbank, broken on the other side by a river road running in either direction.

Vang spent five minutes waiting for signs of life; seeing none, he decided to chance exposure on the bridge. He edged silently through the thick growth to the approach, waited another minute, and dogtrotted across. Nothing happened, except that he was in Laos once more.

It was no time for nostalgia. Vang reached the Tha and turned up the narrow track winding along the left-bank bench above the smaller river. He had been through this area once or twice before, though he did not know it well. Groves of bamboo lined the track here and there, enlaced with sinuous vines. Creeks sprang from holes in the limestone valley wall, spontaneous waterwalls glazing the rock. At one point, a colony of termites swarmed hungrily over a deadfall log at the road's edge. The clean fragrant air was invigorating, and for the moment Vang felt good and strong and ready.

Within a couple of klics he came upon the first opium field, the ripe gravid pods waving in the cool morning breeze. Two older women were meticulously gathering the harvest, their cups swinging from neck thongs.

According to the dying Nguyen Van Cao, Thomas Scanlon and a well-trained army controlled the district with an iron hand. What Nguyen could not or would not tell him was the exact location of Scanlon's base. He had never been there, he claimed. He could have been telling the truth. . . .

Vang knew better than most how effectively one could disappear into the hills and valleys and caves of the high country; he could spend weeks searching for Scanlon and never find him. The problem was that he did not have weeks, or even days.

He had to assume that Scanlon knew about Paris by now and would be on alert. From this moment, Vang ran the risk that someone—a Scanlon soldier, contact, stoolie—would spot him and alert the son of a bitch. When that happened, the mission was dead. His own prospects were similarly problematic. . . .

He passed three more poppy fields, carefully keeping out of sight. He guessed there were fields up nearly every draw and creek rill; the Hmong were expert in cultivating land that others could hardly reach, let alone work. The fields controlled by Scanlon must have covered thousands of acres, a hundred at a time, to supply the Paris end of the operation.

The village hugged a slope rising up from the bench at the end of a little spur of track. Vang could see most of it from his position in the cover of a thorny bush: three dozen houses arranged around a community square of hard-packed barren brown dirt. To one side, a milling stone on an axle fashioned from a sturdy branch was mounted above a trough hollowed from half of a four-foot-thick log.

Vang heard movement through the brush to his left, and sensed eyes circling around behind him. Keeping his hands well away from his weapons, he rose carefully to full height.

The movement stopped. Vang stood waiting. Brush rustled again and a gun barrel stabbed into his kidneys. Vang held his hands at shoulder height.

"Good day," he said in Hmong, looking straight ahead. The gun barrel stayed where it was. "Who are you?"

"A kinsman," Vang said evenly. He turned slowly, keeping his hands up. The gun muzzle traced a line along his rib cage.

The woman was in her twenties. She had luxuriant jet-black hair, which she wore in a long braid, and high sculpted cheekbones and fiery dark eyes. She was quite lovely, despite the angry glare with which she looked over Vang and his guns.

Her weapon was a flintlock rifle with a four-foot barrel and a pistol grip instead of a stock, the sort of homemade weapon the Hmong had fashioned for a century and a half, until the Americans had upgraded their armories. . . . The woman looked ready to use it.

"What is your name?" she said.

Vang told her.

She stared back at him. "I know that name." She seemed to come to a decision. "If you are lying I will kill you."

"All right," Vang said. Using one finger, he eased the rifle away from his belly.

"Why have you come back?" she asked.

Vang smiled slightly. "That's three questions. I haven't asked even one."

The woman took two steps back. She did not bring up the rifle again, but held it ready. "Answer me," she said. "What do you want?"

Vang returned her hard gaze. "I want to kill Thomas Scanlon," he said. "Will you help me?"

"You understand," Pao said. "This is my village. I am responsible for these people."

Vang raised his eyebrows. "Of course." As headman, Pao's word ruled; at the same time, by law and tradition, he was charged with the welfare of everyone in Phu Nam Kok.

Pao shared his sister's dark eyes and high clean features, though his hair was cropped short. There was a bandage on his cheek and a bruise under one eye.

"I know who you are," Tsia said. "Or who you were." She stared at Vang.

Vang returned an expressionless gaze. He needed their help, but there was little he could do to convince them that he was an ally. They had to accept him on their own.

"I served in the *bataillons guerriers*," Tsia said. "Near the end, even for a few months into 1976, after the Pathet Lao took over the government. The women were the only ones left— the men were all dead."

Vang glanced at Pao.

"My brother was eleven," Tsia said bitterly. "Nearly old enough, but not quite."

"Our family had saved some silver," Pao said. "I went away to school in Paris two years before the Americans pulled out."

"And you pulled out as well," Tsia said, staring at Vang. "Why?"

"It was the best thing." He had saved the lives of thousands of Hmong, but he would not discuss that—not yet . . . not unless he had to.

"Vientiane would be greatly pleased to get their hands on you." Pao was thinking aloud.

"I'm a war criminal," Vang said. "The penalty for my crimes is death."

"Crimes of humanity," Tsia said. She studied him. "You are risking your life coming back to this country."

"That's right," Vang said.

Everything in the home that Pao and Tsia shared was sparse and neat, and not uncomfortable. The low benches on which they sat were padded with thin mattresses stuffed with dry grass, and in a shallow floor pit charcoal burned against the last of the morning chill. A brightly enameled earthenware pot sat on the floor between the three of them, long curved bamboo straws sprouting from holes in its cover. Vang sipped from his, out of politeness rather than need; the rice wine known as "Iao Iao" was far too potent for him to be guzzling at this hour.

"You saw the villagers," Tsia said. "Except for a few grandparents, I am the oldest person here—and I am twenty-four years old. By the time the war finished, everyone over fifteen, man or woman, had fought. Most of them died."

"The survivors were imprisoned in 'reeducation' camps," Pao said. "The more active you had been in the *Armee Clandestine,* the more difficult they made your stay. For my sister . . ."

"Yes," Vang said to Tsia. "I understand."

"Do you?" But she no longer sounded antagonistic.

"Why did you return from Paris?" Vang asked Pao.

He shrugged. "To do something about . . . what was happening." Pao barked a short, humorless laugh. "People were kept together according to region, and I was placed in the same camp as Tsia. We were only there for a few months, and then we were sent back here."

"To your homes," Vang said slowly.

Tsia shook her head. "This is no longer our home," she said. "It was stolen while we were in the South, and now it will never be a place for Hmong. The good *phi* have fled, and we would do the same, except . . ."

"How many people were sent back here?"

"Thousands, from dozens of villages," Pao said. "Nearly everyone from the province of Houakhong was repatriated."

"And put to work growing opium," Vang guessed.

"Can you guess why?" Tsia said, giving Vang a penetrating look.

"When the Pathet Lao took Vientiane," Vang remembered, "one of their first declarations lifted restrictions against poppy cultivation. Sometime after that, we believe, Scanlon made a bargain with the rebels," Vang reasoned. "In exchange for money—hard currency—he obtained control of the growing and marketing of the opium of the westernmost province."

"Correct," Pao said. "He got the Hmong homeland, and the Hmong as well, to work as his *kha*."

"Have you tasted the soil here?" Tsia asked Vang. "It is sweet on the tongue."

Vang knew that a discriminating farmer could taste the lime in good soil; the sweetness meant excellent crops of rice, or corn—or opium poppies.

"As sweet as any in the high country," Pao said. "Scanlon gets the maximum yield from his acres."

"Pardon me," Vang said, genuinely sorry to have to ask the next question. "Why haven't the Hmong fought Scanlon?"

"The fighters are dead," Pao said. "All but Tsia."

"I am no fighter," Tsia said angrily. "You know that, brother."

"Be quiet," Pao snapped.

But Tsia met Vang's interrogatory gaze. "Every so often," she said levelly, "Scanlon calls for me to come to him." She lowered her eyes. "And I go, and I let him do whatever he wishes."

Pao was red with anger and shame.

"The first time," Tsia said, "when his men came to get me, I struggled, so they knocked me unconscious. I woke up in Scanlon's quarters . . . in his bed."

Pao stood abruptly and began to pace.

"He was repulsive to my senses," she said. "When he tried to touch me, I kicked him. You know where. I clawed at him and tore his skin. His men came running in with guns and jumped on me, tied me up. But then he told them to return me here. I thought it was over.

"The next day," Tsia said, "Scanlon came here with a half-dozen of his men, all Vietnamese. He ordered everyone to the square. He had a pistol."

Pao spun around. "Scanlon pulled an old woman from the

ine, dragged her out to where everyone could see, and shot
her in the head."

"He towed her like a grain sack to where I stood and
threw the body to the ground." Tsia's eyes were moist, her
voice shaky. "He said to me, 'Next time you will do as I tell
you.' And he was right."

"He must be stopped," Pao said.

"That is why I am here."

Pao came and stood before Vang. "There is one more
thing."

Vang looked up at him.

"We know what you did for the Hmong as the war was
lost," Pao said carefully. "There was talk in the camps."

"Yes?"

"You have power. I know what you are able to accomplish."

"I don't think I understand," Vang said.

"I will show you."

Pao went to the door of the hut and pushed it open. Vang
went to stand beside him.

The entire population of the village stood gathered in the
square facing Pao's house, as if waiting for Vang's appearance.
Many of the women had dressed up in their best: high black-
silk hats, paneled skirts, brightly colored sashes. Children
stood silently, wide-eyed and respectful. Nearly all the adults
were in their twenties, with the exception of three or four
elderly women and one skinny old toothless man.

"You understand what I am asking now," Pao said.

"How many?"

"One hundred and sixty-two."

Vang looked at the villagers. Every eye returned his gaze.

"It may not be possible," Vang said.

"I am the headman. I must ask this."

"I'll do my best."

Pao smiled. "Your best, I am told, is very good."

Vang shook his head. It was a logistical question he did not
have time to answer, and yet he had no choice. But for now, he

had to think of Scanlon. "And you must understand," Vang said. "First I have to see to Thomas Scanlon." He turned away and went back to the bench.

"You will need some help." Tsia sat down opposite him.

Vang started to protest.

"I am the only one who has been inside Scanlon's headquarters," she pointed out. "The only one who knows exactly where it is."

"Tell me," Vang said.

Tsia sipped from her straw. "Of course. But there is something else."

Pao sat down on the bench, watching his sister warily.

"I will be there tonight," Tsia said.

"Then I will wait until tomorrow," Vang said.

"No." Tsia pushed aside the straw. "Listen to me, Vang. can help, from inside." She leaned forward, touched his knee.

"I cannot . . ." Vang began.

"You cannot?" Tsia echoed. "What do you imagine it is for me, what that man forces me to do? Can you stand it?— because I cannot, even once more. Not if I do not have to."

Vang shook his head, but he had no good answer. If he were in her position, he would speak as she had.

"My presence within," Tsia said. "It may be the only way to make your plan work."

Vang did not speak for some time. "I do not have a plan," he said finally, smiling slightly.

Tsia returned the smile. "Then we had best get started devising one. We only have a few hours, and there is much I must tell you."

Chapter Ten

Dennison sipped from the tall highball glass of Martel Five Star Brandy and soda, wet a finger on his tongue, and turned a page. He looked up and smiled absently when Miss Paradise came into the room, then went back to his reading. The book was Collier's *Short History of the Second World War*.

Miss Paradise picked up a half-full stemmed glass of Chablis from the glass-topped coffee table and lowered herself into one of the low-slung chairs. She regarded Dennison for a moment: he wore a V-neck sweater over a button-down Brooks Brothers shirt, corduroy slacks, and tassled loafers. His full head of hair was flecked here and there with gray, but his hard stocky body looked as trim and fit as it had when she'd first met him. It seemed to her a lifetime ago, and in a way it was.

They did not see eye to eye with the Agency on methods or results, and they were willing to do something about it; at the beginning, that was what brought them together. They looked down the road, she and Dennison, and saw as clear as a signpost that you could travel this way all your days, and you'd still come up against a dead end. There was no satisfaction—never could be any satisfaction—in Agency ways.

After a time, when they were sure they could stand each other, they quit. They partnered up to do it their own ways. They rerouted their lives along roads that twisted and changed like a philosopher's logic, but always moved forward, not toward a dead end but toward breakthrough.

There was nothing complex or convoluted or theoretical about the new life they had mapped out after their Agency stint; the paths of right and wrong were marked clearly enough for anyone to follow, according to his choice.

There was only this: those who chose the wrong path

could not expect to piss and moan when Dennison's People dropped out of the trees and hit the bastards like ten tons of bad news.

Miss Paradise sipped her wine and made a sour face. *And the hell with them*, she thought. Maybe they'd never be able to fumigate the vermin in every corner of the world, but that didn't mean they couldn't exterminate a nest of them here and there. You took your satisfaction day to day, and wherever it could be found. . . .

"'The most vital quality a soldier can possess is self-confidence, utter, complete and bumptious,'" Dennison quoted, following the passage with his finger. He looked up at Miss Paradise. "Patton." He smiled. "I like that."

"'Bumptious'?"

"That's what it says," Dennison confirmed.

"What's it mean?"

"Obtrusive."

"Thanks. That clears it up for me."

Dennison closed the book, marking his spot with a forefinger, and contemplated her. "We're not doing that badly so far," he said, "all things considered."

She looked startled. "Have I been talking in my sleep?"

Dennison laughed. "Didn't you know I have a mysterious power to cloud women's minds?"

"My mind must have been clouded when I decided to hook up with you, boss dear."

Her platinum hair cascaded down over the shoulders of a plain flannel robe, and on her feet were fat down-filled booties. "What's up?" Dennison asked.

"Peter called. He heard from Vang."

Dennison removed his finger from the book and laid it on the table beside his recliner chair. "When and how?" he asked in a flat voice.

"Vang got to a radio somewhere and called Udorn. They relayed to Peter, and he called us. Vang's original transmission was logged within the last hour."

"Trouble?"

Miss Paradise frowned. "I'm not sure."

"All right, my dear," Dennison said with a tone of put-upon patience. "What did Vang want?"

"He requested that four CH-Forty-sevens meet him at the pickup at 0700 local time."

"Chinooks?" Dennison thought for a moment. "In cargo configuration?"

"Uh-uh." Miss Paradise shook her head. "With troop seats." Her brows formed a V. "You figure he's bringing out an army?"

A smile had begun to dawn on Dennison's face. "No, my dear. I think Vang has added a mission of mercy to the job."

"Peter wants to know what Vang is trying to pull, and he thinks you can tell him. He said he can't send in military birds in any case. If one of our Asian neighbors gets trigger-happy, he's going to have a hell of a time explaining how an American chopper got axed ten years after the war was supposed to be over."

"Is the pickup in Laos?"

"Thailand."

"Then Peter has nothing to worry about." Dennison thought for a moment. "Has he got four Chinooks on hand?"

"Civilian or military?"

Dennison smiled. "Have I ever mentioned that you are cute when you're disingenuous, my dear?"

"The Agency runs a contract company called World Air Transport out of Guam. They can supply the birds."

"Tell Peter to send them in. We'll foot the bill."

"Aw, boss," Miss Paradise said. "You know how I hate it when you start tossing around money as if it were cabbage."

"What's money for?"

"And if Peter argues?"

"Talk him into it, my dear."

Miss Paradise stood and stretched languorously. "Is that the only reason you pay me—for my charm?"

"Sure," Dennison said. "Didn't you know that?"

"You'll pay for that, boss." She went to the door connecting to the office area, but then she turned. "You'll pay, and you'll like it."

"I'm sure I will," Dennison said.

Chapter Eleven

Thomas Scanlon stabbed at the transmit button on the radio transceiver. "Take a second to think it over, son," he said into the mike.

Static sizzled from the speaker. "I have," the other voice said. "I told you: no increase in inventory, no new salesmen. Everything is status quo."

The man on the other end was a Quartermaster Corps sergeant at Udorn. There had been no additional troops brought on base, he was saying, nor any new faces among the spook corps. "You better be damned sure," Scanlon told him.

"Yeah, I know," the sergeant said laconically. "That's what you pay me for. And speaking of which . . ."

"Santa'll put something in your stocking, son," Scanlon drawled. "Out." He flicked the transceiver to "standby" and frowned. The video monitor racked above the radio showed the normal compound activity. The rim sentries were in their usual positions. In the near bowl, a couple of off-duty soldiers were playing one-on-one soccer. Two men came out of the entryway leading to the billets and went in different directions to take their guard shifts. It was four o'clock, and Tsia would be there within the hour. That would help take the edge off. . . .

He had been on the radio for most of the afternoon, trying to track down some answers. When you lived in the middle of nowhere, it paid to have a network—and Scanlon paid well. The various conversations had been reasonably fruitful.

Paris was quiet—too quiet, as the cavalrymen used to say in old Westerns. The police had made not a single arrest, but that figured: they weren't about to bust their asses to nail whoever had done them the favor of wiping out Nguyen. But at the same time, none of Scanlon's people reported any hint of a power shift in the Paris underworld.

Maybe the boys who had so neatly creamed Nguyen were lying low for a time. Or maybe it had been outsiders after all, and the locals were waiting to see how clean the new broom swept.

Scanlon pushed the swivel chair back from the console panel and stood. He still could not completely shake the hunch that the Paris attack had a direct link to him.

Scanlon uncapped the good scotch and splashed two fingers into one of the crystal glasses. Okay, figure the worst-case scenario, he thought: Someone was out to nail him. But first they had to find out where he was, and then they had to get to him. Scanlon grinned and raised his glass. *Good luck, son, whoever you are*, he thought. *Come and try it*. He sipped the whiskey.

No outsider had ever seen his compound, not even Nguyen. The closest anyone had come was U Aung and his shit-sorry merc army, and their bones were fertilizing the jungle now.

The few foreigners whom Vientiane admitted into Laos were never permitted to venture beyond the city limits. If a stranger did somehow make it to this isolated corner of the country, he would stand out like a hooker at a debutante ball, and word would reach Scanlon well before the stranger ever did. For the army it would take to touch him, keeping out of sight would be ten times as difficult. They would be in the same sorry bind as U Aung had been: as conspicuous as Sherman marching through Georgia.

A panel light on the radio blinked. Scanlon flicked it on, picked up the mike, and said, "Talk to me, son."

"I am airborne." It was Vongsaly, lifting off with Tsia from Phu Nam Kok. Scanlon grinned; he had a fresh idea for them. A new videotape had come in, shot in Macao, and he figured it would open her eyes to some possibilities. Hell, there were a couple of positions on that tape even he'd never thought of. . . .

"Flying down, you spot anybody on the ground?" Scanlon said.

"What do you mean?" Vongsaly said.

"What the hell you think I mean?" Scanlon snapped. He was starting to wonder about old Vong, the way he'd acted in the village the day before. Maybe he was too delicate for this kind of work. "I mean," Scanlon said, "did anything catch your eye—anything out of the everyday—from the air or in the village? That simple enough for you, Vong?"

"No."

"No *what?*"

"Everything is normal," Vongsaly said stiffly.

"All right, get your ass in here." Scanlon grinned. "Hey, darlin', we're going to have ourselves a time tonight," he added, knowing Tsia could hear him. Anyway, that kind of crack embarrassed the hell out of Vong. . . .

Scanlon killed the radio and took a long, thoughtful drink. In this place, he was flat-out invulnerable. No force, conventional or guerrilla, could scale the cliff walls of the crater without being picked off like beer bottles on a rail fence. Artillery or mortar would be out in five minutes; that's what the TOW missiles were for. And if anyone had the guts and resources for an airstrike, Scanlon was ready to take one of the choppers up himself for a little air-to-air. Scanlon laughed aloud. One idea that *might* work was a direct hit from a B-52—except that everyone knew a B-52 couldn't hit a toilet with a turd.

The radio blinked again. Scanlon flicked to the local channel. One of the perimeter guards had spotted the chopper coming in; did Scanlon want the woman brought to him?

"I'll be out, son," Scanlon said. "I want to make her feel welcome."

He tossed back the rest of his drink, then unlocked the weaponry cabinet. He selected a Colt Python .357 Magnum and strapped it on, thinking: *A man ought to look his best when his girl comes calling.*

Working the lock of the second steel door outside his quarters, he had to laugh again. He was getting skittery in his old age, seeing monsters under the goddamned bed. The door slid open silently. Scanlon checked the action of the Python, stuck it back in its holster, and headed out for his fun.

From the top of the monadnock dome, Vang watched Scanlon emerge.

Vang studied the man's broad shoulders, his flowing salt-and-pepper mane, the fat handgun on his right hip. He had seen him only once, for a few minutes from a distance, ten years earlier. Scanlon looked around like a southern gentleman surveying his plantation, and Vang got a glimpse of his profile: hard sharp features cut by a bushy mustache, flat stomach, big horseman's hands.

Later there would be a closer look. He wished to study the man before he killed him.

The crown of the big limestone dome above Scanlon's quarters was essentially flat for an area perhaps ten feet in diameter, but from there it dropped off on every side until it was as steep as the compound walls. But there were easier ways to the top. . . .

Pao had guided Vang out of the village at midday, up through the poppy field to the ridge and then down to a tiny dry creekbed at the foot of the next drainage. "My sister . . ." Pao said, staring at the ground.

"I'll bring her back, Pao," Vang said. "Get the others ready."

"Yes," Pao said absently. "Of course." They shook hands.

The creekbed was the trail at first. Farther on it widened to parallel wheel tracks, then narrowed again. At some points it was merely a faint tracing through the ferns and cedars and *tranh* grass, roofed over with leafy branches, tight as a tunnel. When possible, Vang jogged; when necessary, he bushwacked. Occasionally he consulted the map that Pao had drawn for him. One of the grandmothers had hovered over their shoulders, making corrections, noting landmarks; she had lived here all her life, except for a few years in the camps, and seemed to know every square mile of the province.

It was a few minutes before three o'clock when the base of

the mound suddenly loomed up abruptly in front of him, a nearly vertical wall of cracked limestone girded with trees and undergrowth. It curved out of sight a hundred meters over his head. Vang pushed his way on through the brush along its side, scanning the rock at eye level. The mark was a quarter of the way around the base: two overlapping circles, knife etched into the friable stone.

Scanlon had made them his slaves, Tsia had told Vang, but they were not utter sheep. She knew the guerrilla art of moving undetected through the hills and forest, and she and her brother had gone exploring, searching for weakness, learning whatever might aid salvation someday. Then, one time when Scanlon left her alone in his private bedroom, she had discovered the other end of the tunnel, its door hidden behind a framed mural, like a giant wall safe.

According to the grandmother, the passageway dated back over thirty-five years, to the First Indochina War against the French imperialists. Originally a natural drainage channel dissolved into the limestone over the centuries, it had been improved to allow access to the high cave, at the time a major air-raid shelter for the Hmong of the area. Now the tunnel was Scanlon's escape hatch.

Another quarter-arc farther along the base of the road began, abruptly and in the middle of nowhere. It had been graded since the last rainy season, and the forest cut back so that it was wide enough for a single vehicle. The slash was piled off to one side at the road's head. Vang found the Land Rover behind it, covered with a cammie-cloth tarp, parked facing out and ready to roll.

Vang threw back the front end of the tarp and propped open the Rover's hood. He used his knife to pry off the distributor cap, set it on a flat rock, and crushed the plastic under his boot. He flung the rotor into the trees, then lowered the hood and replaced the tarp.

The adit was ten feet directly above the mark, hidden behind an outcropping. Vang set fingers and boot toes into the narrow cracks chasing the wall, then managed to scramble around the overhang and up to the opening, a dark hole barely two feet in diameter. He took a pocket flash from one of the kidney pouches.

For the first five meters he had to belly-crawl, but then the tunnel began to open out. In another ten meters he was able to walk, head down and knees bent. The slope steepened at that point to an angle of close to thirty degrees. The flash's beam illuminated gray-white pocked walls and a trickle of water along the rough-carved floor.

The landing was about fifty meters deep into the mountain, a little platform with two passages branching off from it. The one to the right was nearly level, while the other was sharply steeper, nearly a chimney. Narrow stairsteps were cut into the living rock.

Ten meters down the right-hand passage was the hidden door to Scanlon's quarters. The chimney climbed to the dome's top; during the war it had served for ventilation and as access to the natural lookout post above.

The staircase required both hands and good balance. Vang pocketed the flash and climbed in darkness until he reached a rock ceiling that at first appeared to be a dead end. But then a breath of cool air brushed his face; Vang groped in the blackness and found a small niche cut into the rock to his left. He crawled up on the shelf and reached toward the moving air. A wooden trapdoor was set into the rock. Vang's fingers found a bolt latch. The door opened down toward him, and Vang blinked at the rush of sunlight. After a few moments, he emerged onto the dome roof.

The large rotor-mounted dish antenna provided plenty of cover. Positioned around the other sides of the skylight's steel-plate cover were a video camera, a high-frequency communications aerial, and a gimballed high-intensity spotlight. Ridgelines rippled the forest to Vang's back, the tree cover broken now and again with bomb craters and opium fields in green maturity.

Spread out before him were the double bowls of Scanlon's compound. The catwalk built up on the rim extended around from either side of the front end of the dome like the chelae of a scorpion. The guards walking the perimeter looked like they knew what they were doing.

Vang had been lying motionless and spread-eagled beneath the dish antenna for nearly an hour when the chopper rose from behind the southern rim, and Scanlon stepped from the entryway directly below.

Scanlon watched the chopper hover into position across the bowl near the hangar, then settle toward the prop-washed grass. It was a bright, clear, winter late-afternoon, perhaps an hour shy of sundown. Scanlon stared for a moment at the armed guards to his left and right, then shook his head and muttered, "What the hell, son, it don't cost any extra." He glanced again at the chopper as he crossed to an entry cut into the rock wall to the right.

The domed room was furnished with a large-screen TV, a movie projector and screen, a cooler of Singha beer, two pool tables, and a couple of armchairs and a sofa that had once served time in Scanlon's quarters. Five men were playing cards at a round felt-topped table. Scanlon said, "Hey, Batchay." One of the players popped up as if he were on a string and marched over to Scanlon. Behind him, another player said something inaudible, and the others snickered. If Batchay heard, he gave no indication.

"Yes, sir," he said crisply. The Hmong was in his early twenties. "What can I do for you?"

The kid wore a Hawaiian shirt and counterfeit Levis. He was a real suck-butt, but a couple of weeks earlier Scanlon had promoted him anyway, to second-in-command below Vongsaly. Batchay was a greedy little bastard who'd probably sell him out as soon as someone offered the right price, but before that happened he'd be long gone, or dead, depending on how pissed off he made Scanlon. Meanwhile, he could be used.

"Who's off base right now?" Scanlon asked.

"Two of the Vietnamese—Fa Ngoum and his brother Tung."

"Hanoi?"

"Ho Chi Minh City."

Scanlon laughed. "Seeing how the other half live, huh?"

Batchay stiffened. "They have family in the South—city people, with some education. Their kin have not fared well under the Communist regime."

"I wonder did the Fa boys take a little of the new harvest down with them?"

Batchay returned a bland look. "I wouldn't know, sir. Of course, were I to learn they were stealing from you . . ."

"Cool it, son. I can spare it." Scanlon grinned unpleasantly. "They're probably giving all the money to their poor families anyway, right?"

Batchay nodded.

"The hell they are," Scanlon snapped.

The four men at the card table were taking this all in. Scanlon shot them a look and they turned back to their game. Beyond them, a double-wide gap in the limestone opened on a barracks with neat cots lined up into the dimness. Another tunnel led to a mess hall. "Twenty-one men, including Vongsaly. Right?"

"Yes, sir." Batchay frowned, trying to figure this out.

"Tell everyone to stay sober. I may want to post an extra guard tonight."

"The woman from the village . . . ?" Batchay smiled slightly, to indicate that they were both men of the world.

"Yeah, right. Almost forgot." Scanlon left the unctuous little son gaping at his back.

The next tunnel along the rim opened to the cookhouse, linked inside to the mess hall. Smoke rose through a low venting chimney capped with a tin cone, like a coolie's hat, and outside Scanlon smelled beef roasting. One of the villages raised pigs for the compound, along with a few cows grain-fed according to Scanlon's instructions, for special occasions.

He headed across toward the landing area as the chopper's rotor began to slow. The two mechanics stood by near the hangar door, along with two extra guards who were always there when Tsia came in. Scanlon knew she'd fought with the SGUs, and he didn't put a double-cross past her, like a sneak gun in her knickers. Scanlon figured to get something else into her knickers tonight. . . .

Vongsaly came around to hold the door open for Tsia. She stared straight ahead and waited regally for the rotor to come to a complete stop. When she stepped out, her every move and gesture was stately and dignified. She said something to Vongsaly. He shook his head and turned away, looking annoyed and embarrassed.

Tsia moved her head enough to show Scanlon a fine superior sneer on her handsome chiseled features, as if she were doing him a big favor by condescending to a visit. She wouldn't be so snotty later on, he was willing to bet. She wore traditional Hmong finery: a black silk blouse cut high on the neck; black skirt embellished with bold overlaid stripes of royal blue, its hem embroidered with gold and silver thread; and sandals of shaped bamboo and pigskin leather. Her long hair was piled atop her head and hidden beneath a black silk turban, topped with bright red bunting and highlighted with a band of thin beaten-silver disks.

The girdle at her waist was fashioned of linked patches of smooth silk dyed carmine, jade green, carnelian, vermilion, topaz, azure, ginger—perfect hues in an imperfect world, handworked in the most delicate and subtle fashion: intricate geometric patterns of stairsteps, starbursts, perfect jagged lightning bolts. Ropes of beads hung from it like fobs, each ending in a handworked medallion of silver or gold.

The clothing and jewelry were all gifts from him, and the bitch wore them that way, like she had been forced to dress up for a party she did not want to attend. She stood there as if she were a queen and this was her realm. Scanlon got a kick out of that; it kind of turned him on. . . .

Vongsaly glanced back at her as he came up, as if afraid she might shoot him in the back.

"Any trouble?" Scanlon asked.

Vongsaly looked at him oddly. "Why would there be any trouble?"

"Don't get mouthy, son." Scanlon stared past him to Tsia. "Did everything look normal in Phu Nam Kok?"

"The people are working the fields. They look at me with as much hate as ever. The bad *phi* still inhabit the area."

"Don't give me that Casper the Ghost shit, Vong." Scanlon looked at him. "All right, tell Batchay to post a double guard at dusk. Three-hour shifts, but keep it covered all night."

"The men won't be pleased—"

"Hey, son," Scanlon interrupted. "I think you got me confused with someone who gives a shit."

Vongsaly gave him a narrow look. "What exactly are you expecting?"

"I'm expecting you and everyone else to do what I say, son."

Vongsaly started to say something else, and Scanlon gave him a look that challenged him to go ahead. Vongsaly shut his mouth and stalked away. One of the mechanics drove the Jeep out of the hangar and swung it around, and the other bent to its hitch.

Tsia stared darkly at Scanlon as he came up. "How you doing, sis?" Scanlon said pleasantly. He kissed her, not gently.

Tsia did not resist or react. Scanlon pulled back. Arrant despite burned in her face. "I abhor you," she said.

"Yeah, I know," Scanlon said almost wearily. "But you're the best-looking ginch in these parts, and I'm the hombre who runs things, so it looks like we're stuck with each other."

"I will see you dead."

"No shit," Scanlon said. "When's that going to be?"

"Sooner than you think," Tsia said.

Scanlon gave her a narrow look. "You got something on your mind, sis, or are you just blowing smoke?"

Tsia smiled. "Are you frightened, Scanlon?"

Scanlon slapped her face, not very hard. Her cheek blushed red under her smooth olive skin. Yeah, he was frightened—for about a second and a half. "You must be getting desperate," he sneered. "You're starting to see things."

Tsia's smile had not dissolved with the blow. "That's right," she said. "I wanted to frighten you and I did. A frightened man

is less bother to a woman." She stared up and down his body.
"He has trouble . . . concentrating. He stays soft as a child."

"We'll give it a good shot anyway." Scanlon locked her
forearm in a hard grip and turned her toward the high dome.

"Yes, we will," Tsia said quietly.

Scanlon didn't bother to answer. Inscrutable oriental
bullshit, he decided. Fuck her, and fuck Nguyen and Paris too.
You took the bad breaks with the good in this business. Maybe
he'd been overextended anyway; maybe it was time to think
about easing on out of this racket and on to new ones. Guns
maybe, or coke—hell, he had the money, the experience, and
the balls to do whatever he damned well wanted.

What he wanted right now was a drink or two, some of
that good beef, and then it was show time. . . .

Chapter Twelve

The Vietnamese on the catwalk wasn't that bad a soldier,
considering that he had probably never seen combat. He could
have dogged it, hands in pockets and the AK assault rifle slung
over his shoulder. But he was holding it where he could use it
if he had to, and his head was up, listening for trouble and
scanning the forest dimly reflecting the starlight far below.

Not that it did him any good.

Vang spoke a soft warning in the deepening dusk. The
guard spun around, and Vang caught a brief glimpse of a
youthful open face above the AK swinging around to home in
on him. . . . Vang stroked the trigger of the Ingram, and
there was a little pinpoint flash at the end of the suppressor
and a soft *pffut* sound.

The guard slapped a hand over his heart, as if pledging
allegiance. Before the pain hit, he had time to stare with
disbelief at the dark stain across his palm. Then his features

spasmed in contortion, as if he'd been struck by lightning, and he sunk to one knee. Vang caught him under the arms as he toppled forward, turned the suddenly limp corpse, and lowered it face-down to the dirt-covered bamboo of the platform.

Crouched low, Vang looked around. He heard no sound of alarm, no footsteps racing his way. Stealth and luck could hold for a while, but now the clock was counting down. Before it hit zero, he had to take out as many of Scanlon's force as possible.

He remembered what Jonathan Kay had told him in Paris: "The sole purpose of terrorism is to terrorize."

Now it was time for Thomas Scanlon's terror to begin.

Vang stepped through shadow as he moved out along the canopy, his face blackened to the same color as his fatigues by application of the cosmetic goop; starlight was his ally, illuminating the enemy. The Fairbairn commando knife slid noiselessly from oiled leather and he came up behind the next guard.

The motions were fluid, practiced, executed exactly as every other time: the palm cupped under the chin, the head jerked up and back to guard against noise and expose the neck. Then the steel, between the ribs first for pain and surprise, hard into the reluctant tough kidney and immediately the quick sharp pull to withdraw, and after that the move to the throat, the draw of the wet blade across the taut skin. The guard grunted and gasped, his teeth scraping like a kitten's claws against Vang's hand for a moment. Blood bubbled from the gash and cascaded over the front of the man's tan tunic. Vang eased him down to the bamboo, wiping the blade across the back of his uniform.

Vang stalked on through the night.

An extra guard had come on at nightfall, posted at the mouth of the tunnel running through to the platform overlooking the river road. His head was bent to the flame of a match when Vang dropped from the catwalk above. Vang landed astraddle, and heard a sharp crack as they both went down, his weight driving the guard to earth. Vang rolled away and brought up the Ingram. The guard lay on his stomach, his head turned around too far, so his eyes stared sightlessly over his shoulder. A little bit of blood drooled from the corner of his open mouth.

Vang dragged the broken-necked body inside the cover of the tunnel, flattening himself against the rock wall. He forced himself to wait a full minute this time. No shout went up; no gunfire tracked in his direction.

Vang eased out into shadow. He made the catwalk once more by clambering along one of its shoring brackets far enough to get his hands over the lip and swing up. Each man neutralized eased the odds, but the countdown stopped for nothing. Sooner or later, all hell would break loose, and when it did he had to be in position to keep Tsia out of the crossfire. If he didn't make it—

A Laotian guard turned to face him, not five meters distant, his gun already tracking on Vang's gut. The guard hesitated a second, and peered at Vang through the darkness, expecting a buddy.

Vang took two steps forward and kicked out on the third. The Laotian seemed to rise on tiptoes; his mouth opened but nothing came out except a mousy little squeak. Vang grabbed the Laotian's AK by the barrel, jerked it loose from his numb hands, and drove the butt into the Laotian's face. The Laotian stumbled back, knockkneed, cradling his crotch in both hands, and one foot slipped off the rim of the catwalk.

Vang held his breath. The guard seemed to take a long time to go over, but then he was gliding face-first down the scree slope like a loose ski.

Across the bowl, someone called, "Dao?"

Vang had already moved on, circling back toward the big monadnock dome. The fourth guard position was back on the rim of the far bowl, where the cookhouse vent pipe poked up through a hole bored in the rock. The man there was staring across at whoever had called out. Vang swore to himself for allowing his concentration to split between the fight to be made and concern for Tsia. In these moments there was neither room nor time to entertain twin notions. The guards, and then the woman; everything was the straight line of the mission plan.

Right then the mission plan took a straight line to hell.

Vang had the Ingram up and the last guard framed in its open sights when a man started hollering in Vietnamese, too quickly for Vang to understand the words. But he got the idea.

Someone had tripped over a corpse.

The guard by the vent pipe brought his rifle to his shoulder and looked for a target. Vang shot him in the side. The guard pirouetted and pitched headfirst off the catwalk.

A ratchet of gunfire crackled up toward Vang. He dropped prone, propped an elbow, and put a single silenced shot through a gunman near the middle of the bowl. Vang was on his feet and moving before the triangulating return fire tracked in on the muzzle flash.

It was time to trade subtlety and stealth for as much fire and flash as possible. Vang dug an HE grenade from his pack, jerked the pin on the run, and popped it down the cookhouse vent as he went past. He was climbing on hands and knees back up the mound when the grenade blew.

The thick limestone walls muffled the report to a dull ground-shaking boom. For a long moment its echo decayed toward silence, broken by a strange ponderous creaking. Someone screamed.

Then that part of the rim of the crater collapsed, sending tons of rock cascading down on the cookhouse and mess hall. Chalky dust rose into the night. Men cried out in panic and pain.

Vang was five meters from it when the spotlight atop the mound blazed to life. Vang saw the silhouette of a man behind it. The light swung toward him.

The leading edge of the light beam caught Vang as he fired. The big lens exploded, but the glare had instantly cut Vang's night vision. He jigged to one side instinctively as return fire buzzed past. Vang flipped the Ingram's selector forward to auto and stitched a short burst in the direction of the gimballed stand.

The man behind it dropped his weapon and clutched at

his shoulder. He stared at Vang for a moment, then dropped to one knee and groped for the gun. Vang put a second three-shot cluster across his chest.

The gunman flopped over onto his back, arms and legs flung outward. He started to slide headfirst down the slope, slowly at first but then picking up momentum as the incline steepened, until he shot out of sight like a toboggan down an icy hill.

Vang raced to retake the high ground.

"What do you have for me this time?" Tsia asked.

Scanlon pushed his plate away and leaned back on the low-slung sofa. He smiled ruefully and shook his head. "You know," he said. "You really are a whore at heart."

"We established that years ago," Tsia said. "Now we're discussing price." He enjoyed believing that her scruples matched his, and she let him, because over time he had given her more jewelry than she could wear. As much of it as she could risk "losing" went to Pao for the people of the village. "Come, Scanlon," she said. "Where is my present?"

Scanlon laughed. He took his empty glass to the wall cabinet and set it down on the bar.

Tsia's fingers probed inside the ornate girdle and traced the outline of the knife hidden there, a Ka-Bar fighting blade that had found its way from some U.S. Marine to the Morning Market on Lane Xang Avenue in Vientiane. "Number-one," the Thai kid who sold it to her kept saying. "G.I. Joe number-one cutter." It was that: seven inches long and as sharp as tempered glass.

She had not told Vang she would carry it on this night. She had her claim to vengeance, too. . . .

Scanlon stood with his back to her. She could kill him now—four steps, a quick twisting thrust. But there was the plan, and the timing. Timing was the key. . . .

This was part of a ritual. She had to ask before Scanlon would produce. He crouched and reached for the dial of the safe—

There was a deep thick shuddering explosion. The walls trembled and the floor seemed to shimmy.

Scanlon leaped to his feet and spun around.

The bottle of scotch on the bar teetered and then toppled. It shattered when it hit the floor, and the rich smell of whiskey rose in the air.

Rock grated against rock. A small crevasse chased up one wall, and fine limestone dust puffed from it.

Tsia dropped her drink and sprang up. "Earthquake," she said. She had no trouble sounding frightened. She did not know exactly what was happening, but she knew perfectly well how fragile limestone could be.

Automatic weapons barked, somewhere out in the compound.

"The hell it is," Scanlon snapped. He jerked open the armory door and grabbed an M-203 grenade launcher/M16 rifle tandem rig. He jammed a clip into the receiver, shoved a handful of grenade canisters into his pocket, and headed for the door. "You wait here, goddammit." The door slammed, and Tsia heard the bolt swing to.

She darted to the safe, already knowing that this part of the plan had missed by fifteen seconds. She tried the latch anyway, but it might as well have been frozen solid.

Scanlon came out of the entryway and began to swear in a low steady monotone.

A billowing cloud of dust was mushrooming out of a huge ragged hole in the crater's rim where the cookhouse and mess hall had been. One of his men emerged from it like an apparition. He was so bloodied that Scanlon did not realize for a moment that where the man's left arm should have been was a gory empty socket. Rocks settled, and another huge puff of dust and pebbles gusted from the opening.

Stone groaned behind him, and for a moment Scanlon thought about Tsia, still inside. The hell with the bitch—he had more dire fish to fry.

"Vong! Goddammit, where are you?"

Vongsaly appeared out of the darkness, carrying a rifle.

He looked drawn and frightened. "All the perimeter guards are dead. One was knifed. Four or five more missing, and at least a half-dozen were at mess."

Scanlon looked wildly around. "How many of them?"

"I . . . I don't know."

"Jesus!" Scanlon looked around again. "How did they pull out?"

"No one . . . " Vongsaly gulped. "No one saw them—no one who still lives."

Scanlon brought up the M-203 searching for a target, any target—and suddenly realized that *he* was the target. He could be framed in some bastard's sights right this minute. Scanlon stepped back into the shadows, dragging Vongsaly with him.

"Find them," Scanlon hissed. "Find them, whoever they are."

"What about the woman?"

"Fuck the woman!" Scanlon screamed. But then he stopped himself. "Wait a minute—go get her, Vong. On second thought, I want her right here by my side."

Tsia was crouched by the safe when Vang came out of the bedroom. He said her name softly, but she spun around, a hand to her mouth.

"Are you all right?" Vang said.

"Yes, but it happened too quickly. He didn't open it."

Vang removed one of the little packets of C-4 from his utility belt and began stripping off the foil. He nodded toward the steel door without looking up from his work. "Is that entryway locked?"

"From the other side," Tsia said.

Vang pulled off the lanyard over his head and handed her the Ingram. "Kill anyone who comes in." Vang knelt in front of the half-height safe.

"I hope someone comes." Tsia leveled the pistol on the door. "I hope it is Scanlon."

"There's no time now for vengeance," he said, studying the combination mechanism. "Only survival."

"And results."

Vang broke the claylike bar of plastique in half. "Results," he murmured, molding the explosive around the safe's lock. "Of course."

From out in the compound there was a second muffled cave-in noise; another section of the rim caving in, Vang figured. Rock grated close by, and he glanced up.

Another cleft opened in the wall, a meter above and to one side of the safe.

"Have you ever done this before?" Tsia asked, trying to sound light.

Vang inserted a fuse. "Not exactly," he said, and lit it.

He hustled her across the room, pressed her against the far wall with his body shielding hers. A beat later, the C-4 blew.

The entire cavern trembled and the walls seemed to sway. Dust and pebbles and chips of rock rained down everywhere. The explosion was too loud in the enclosed space. When the echo died, Vang and Tsia were huddled in place, as if the slightest movement might bring down the roof.

Vang said, "Stay here." He stumbled blindly through the dust to the safe. There was a scorched crack around the lock, but beyond that it appeared undamaged. Vang grabbed the latch in frustration and jerked at it. The cylinder came out in his hand, like the core of an apple.

Vang shoved his hand into the opening and ran his fingertips over the locking mechanism, working levers. When he pulled back his hand, the door swung open with it. "In that drawer," Tsia said behind him. "He showed me once, when he was drinking."

Vang took the silenced Ingram from her, set the selector back to single-shot, and put a slug into the drawer lock. A little pocked crater appeared. The second shot tore a hole in the metal, and when Vang pulled, the drawer gave. He stuffed the two bankbooks down inside his fatigues.

Footsteps came toward the door. Vang waved Tsia back toward the bedroom. She stayed where she was.

The big steel door swung open. The young kid—the Hmong called Batchay—came in, flanked by two soldiers. He spotted Tsia standing in the center of the big open living space. Batchay grinned.

"Come," he said in a harsh bullying tone. "He wants you." He smiled; he liked holding a gun on her. "You know, we are alike, you and me. We both do it for money."

"Alike as the chicken and the snake," Tsia spit.

Batchay frowned and took a step toward her, flanked by the two soldiers, and Vang stepped out and let them see him for a moment.

The three men split away and grappled with weapons, and Vang put a dozen shots across the three chests, lining neat red dimples in the tan of their fatigues.

Tsia snatched up Batchay's AK-47. She dropped out the clip, checked to see that it was full, and reseated it. She handled the assault rifle as if she knew it well.

"Let's go," Vang said, and led the way into the bedroom. It was hung with garish silks, and the bed was canopied: this was the place of a man with jaded and perverse tastes. The mural lay face-down on the floor where Vang had dumped it coming in.

Vang's flash picked out the little landing where the main tunnel descended to the exit. "Wait for me at the base," he said. "Give me ten minutes, then go back to the village."

"No," Tsia said. She gestured with the rifle. "I know how to use this, and I can help. I was a soldier too."

The count was running down. If Scanlon had not yet figured out how they were getting out, he would soon. There could already be men on the way to bottle up the tunnel. He didn't have time to argue, yet he feared that her loathing for Scanlon could dilute her warrior skills.

Voices came from the other end of the tunnel. "Let's go," Tsia said urgently, and started climbing up the steep chimney stairway.

The sky above was peppered with stars as they emerged into the night. "Cover the tunnel," Vang ordered. He belly-crawled forward to command a view of the compound below.

In the dawning starlight he saw a corpse draped half-off the canopy to the right, the cookhouse site to the left. Now it was a shallow bowl filled with huge chunks of broken stone. The lower half of a man's torso stuck out from under a boulder rimmed with blood.

Vang put the rough body count at eighteen men minimum, at least three-quarters of Scanlon's private army. But body count was not the object of this engagement. Only one body counted: the head and heart of Thomas Scanlon.

An electric motor hummed somewhere across the compound. Near the gap between the two bowls, the big hangar door began to swing open.

The mechanics were nowhere to be seen; if they had any sense, they'd fled through the tunnel and down to the road at the first explosion. One guard flanked the hangar, looking nervous and outnumbered. The deeper noise of a vehicle motor drifted to Vang, and the Jeep emerged, headlights out, towing one of the armed Hughes choppers out into the compound.

Vang swore. He could not let Scanlon get clear that way. This had to be finished, here, tonight.

Behind him, Tsia screamed.

Vang twisted around, brought up the Ingram, and barely stopped himself from firing. Two men and Tsia were bunched in a knot for that moment. Then one of the men jerked her down into the tunnel; the other was aiming at Vang.

Vang dived and rolled, fired, and caught the gunner in the gut. The man flopped over, the upper half of his body facedown on rock. Vang flung out an arm. He was still moving, beginning to slip down the backside of the slope. He crabbed both hands, fingertips scraping rock until somehow they found a crack and dug in. He hung like that for a moment, his cheek against the rough surface, his breath coming quickly. He pulled, found purchase with his feet, and crawled carefully back to the plateau.

The chopper motor sputtered to life. Vang pushed the guard's corpse back into the chimney and heard it rattle down the chimney and hit below with a hard thunk. Vang dropped in and climbed down after it.

* * *

Scanlon peered into the darkness and said, "Move, goddammit." He stood just inside the cover of the hangar, the M-203 fire-ready with a full clip in the automatic rifle and an HE grenade seated in the breech of the launcher ganged to it. The Hughes sat idling in front of the open hangar door. *Home free*, he thought, but then he remembered the blown safe, the punctured drawer, the missing bankbooks. . . . Those were numbered accounts; anyone walked in with those books, talked the right trash, there was a chance they'd actually hand over the money—*his* money, dammit.

Across the far bowl, Vongsaly came out of the tunnel entryway from his quarters. Scanlon grinned in the darkness. It was horsetrading time, son. Vongsaly dragged the woman toward him.

She was muttering a monotonal stream of curses, twisting and jerking against Vongsaly's grip as he pulled her along. Scanlon stepped from his cover. Tsia looked up and gasped, and Scanlon slapped her across the face very hard. Her head snapped around and she cried out.

Vongsaly pulled back just inside the proscenium arch of the hangar door and covered the compound with his AK. One guard's body was slumped in front of the exit tunnel; another head lolled off the edge of the catwalk a little farther on. Scanlon grabbed Tsia's arm and shook her, and she went silent.

"Who are they?" Scanlon said. His voice was a bit unsteady and cut by a note of desperation.

Tsia clawed at his eyes.

Scanlon tried to punch her in the face, but Tsia ducked away and the blow glanced off one ear. Vongsaly shot a look at her and licked his lips. Scanlon drew back his fist, and Vongsaly opened his mouth to stop him.

A single, sharp, flat crack split the quiet, and a hole appeared in Vongsaly's throat, below his gaping mouth and above his Adam's apple. A pencil-thin line of blood jetted three feet into the air, drops flecking Scanlon's fist. Vongsaly half-turned and went down on his back. More blood pulsed from the wound.

Scanlon pulled Tsia up tight against him, his left arm

locked around her neck. He glanced at the chopper, maybe six steps distant, then pulled back into the hangar's cover. He had to have time, dammit. . . .

"Just tell me," he said, almost reasonably. "Who the hell are those guys?"

Tsia laughed. "One man, Scanlon. One man did all of this."

"Who?" He shook her roughly.

"Before too many minutes more," Tsia said, "he will kill you."

"If he does," Scanlon said, "you won't be around to cheer." One part of his mind was racing: *One man . . . Nguyen and the Paris shitstorm—it was part of a line to me after all. . . . Who, goddammit? Who the hell owes me like this and has the brass balls to pull it off?*

"All right, you bastard," Scanlon hollered. "Time to make medicine."

A bubble of blood formed in the hole in Vongsaly's neck, trembled, and burst. There was no sound or movement from the compound.

Scanlon jerked Tsia hard against him and jammed the barrel of the autorifle up under her chin, forcing her head up and back. Her teeth grated together and she grunted with pain. "Here we go, honey," Scanlon said in her ear. "Mexican-standoff time."

Scanlon walked her out of the hangar's shadow, her body covering his.

"Five seconds, pal," Scanlon screamed. "Five seconds to show yourself, or I'll blow the bitch's head off."

Nothing moved.

Scanlon jerked the rifle away and a short burst of autofire shattered the night. He stuck the warm barrel back up under Tsia's chin. "The next one comes out the top of her head, asshole," Scanlon shouted.

Tsia screamed, "No!"

Scanlon jerked his head around in the direction in which she was staring. Someone had come out of the tunnel; in the starlight Scanlon made out a slight, compact man carrying a small automatic weapon.

"First the chattergun," Scanlon called. For a long beat the other man did not move. Then he unclipped the weapon from his neck lanyard and bent to lay it on the ground. Scanlon felt better already.

"That's good, son," he called. "Now come over where we can have a look at you."

Scanlon watched the figure move across the open bowl, squinting to make out the son of a bitch's features. The guy's head was down and his shoulders slumped, like he knew he was whipped. "That's close enough," Scanlon said. The guy was twenty meters distant, off to the side away from the purring chopper. Tsia moaned softly. Scanlon kept the rifle barrel where it was.

The guy raised his head, and Scanlon said, "Jesus fucking Christ."

"Every one of your men is dead," Vang said evenly.

Scanlon pushed Tsia forward. *Play it careful with this son,* he told himself; he kept Tsia in front of him. He jerked her to a stop beside the idling chopper. "Vang," he said, with something like awe. "I never forget a face."

"Do you remember the faces of the people you murdered?"

For a moment Scanlon did not get it, did not connect the man with the time. Then he saw him: standing beside an APC, on the Laotion bank of the Mekong, watching a couple of dozen of his people climb aboard that old monitor boat. . . .

"That was ten years ago, son." Scanlon drew back his lips in a lupine smile. "You hold a long grudge." His mouth felt dry, his tongue a little thick. "It was you who took out Nguyen, right?"

"You killed twenty-three of my tribespeople, Scanlon."

This wasn't getting anyone anywhere; the thing to do was take care of business, get the hell out, and regroup. There was something mesmeric in the bastard's steady gaze, his soft, almost toneless voice.

Tsia tried to loosen his grip around her neck. Scanlon

jerked her arm up hard and she grunted. He shook his head impatiently. "That's old news, Vang," he said.

"You are a murderer," Vang said.

"You're next, son," Scanlon snapped. Sweat burned his eyes, and he blinked. "First off, where are my goddamn bankbooks?"

Vang stood immobile. He saw Tsia's left hand creep toward her ornate wide waistband sash.

Scanlon swung the rifle down on Vang. "Your gooks aren't going to come back to life, son—and neither are you. Produce, or I'll take them off your corpse."

Vang's hand inched up and inside his black fatigues. He kept his eyes locked with Scanlon's, and saw only peripherally Tsia's hand start to move—

Tsia came out with the Ka-Bar knife and slashed wildly at Scanlon's face.

Scanlon screamed madly. Tsia jerked free, and Scanlon swung blindly, and the rifle barrel caught her between the shoulder blades. She stumbled a few steps and went down, crying out in pain.

A wide gash split Scanlon's cheek from beneath his mane of hair behind his ear to the corner of his mouth, the two clean-cut edges of skin drawn back like the peel of an overripe tomato. There was blood all over one side of his face and in one eye. Through it he saw Vang moving. He tracked his weapon on the blur of motion and clamped down on the trigger. Vang was down, but then he rolled and came up again. The woman grabbed at his ankle. Scanlon stumbled off balance and the rest of the clip went up into the night sky. Scanlon kicked at the woman, missed. She scuttled away. He wiped at his face with the back of his sleeve, and instantly the cloth was soaked with blood. But he could see the bastard now.

Scanlon dropped to one knee, butted the stock against his thigh, and stroked the launcher's trigger. The HE grenade whistled and flamed, slammed into the crater wall near the tunnel entrance, and blew dust and rock into the air.

Scanlon could not see Vang anywhere, but at least there was no return fire. He felt dizzy and sick to his stomach, and knew he had to get out of there, right that moment. He stumbled to the chopper, jerked the seatbelt hard around his waist, and engaged the rotor. Dust swirled and covered the woman as the chopper lifted off.

Tsia sat up as Vang knelt beside her. There was a livid purple bruise all over one side of her face, and tears of pain in her eyes. "Are you all right?" Vang said.

"Dammit," Tsia swore fervently. "I am so sorry. I could have killed him." She sounded near to weeping.

She was not seriously hurt; Vang felt a quick wash of relief, and set the emotion aside. "Come on," he ordered.

Tsia looked up. "What . . . ?"

"This isn't over yet."

Tsia scrambled to her feet. Vang was already climbing into the second Hughes, parked back inside the hangar, flipping controls, checking gauges. Tsia clambered in the other side. "Strap in," Vang said, watching the fuel indicator come up.

"Can you fly this?" Tsia said.

"Flying it isn't the problem," Vang said. "Getting it out of here might be." The engine fired, and the rotor began to turn. Immediately, rock dust rose all around; in seconds they were engulfed in a cloud of it.

"Hold your breath," Vang said grimly.

The chopper's skids eased off the hangar floor, the machine rising almost imperceptibly. Three meters of clearance at best, Vang thought. He moved the stick, and the chopper eased blindly forward through the dust. It settled a few inches, and the skids scraped the rock. Vang moved the stick a hair. The chopper crept forward again. Vang listened for the awful tearing noise of the rotor cutting into solid limestone wall or ceiling. The chopper eased another meter.

The dust cleared slightly, and the TOW nose sight poked through the cloud. Vang pushed forward a bit more, and the chopper slipped out of the hangar and into the open night.

The other Hughes disappeared to the south.

Vang full-powered. The chopper shot up, slewed around, headed after Scanlon.

Thailand was no more than a few minutes away; they had to stop Scanlon before he crossed the frontier. A firefight in Laotian airspace was one thing, but Thailand was in the U.S. camp. There was too much chance of turning a personal vendetta into an international incident. . . .

Scanlon's bird was skimming the ridgelines a half-mile ahead.

Vang swung out to one side, hit the arming switch, and turned on the TOW's tracker. Dark forest reeled by beneath the skids. Vang flipped up the cap and hit the "launch" button.

Smoke back-blasted from under the stab wing, and the missile shot out past the chopper's nose, spitting fire and trailing its guide wire. Vang watched the tracker, adjusted the cross-hairs on the aircraft ahead, saw the range close. . . .

Scanlon jinked hard left and nosed up steeply. The TOW shot beneath his skids, slammed into a hillside, and blew with a blinding flash. Scanlon was circling back now as he climbed.

He pulled up just shy of a stall, hung for a moment, and dived, coming down over Vang's shoulder. One of Scanlon's TOWs spewed from its tube. But he was too close; before Scanlon could control the wire-guidance system, the missile was already past on Vang's left side as he slewed away and brought his nose around. The TOW exploded somewhere below, the concussion rocking the chopper slightly.

Scanlon's chopper was side-on to Vang now, and as he started to evade, Vang loosed a burst from the 30mm Chain Gun. The big slugs raked across Scanlon's tail. His chopper yawed and started to drop away. Vang was close enough to see Scanlon's face illuminated by the dial lights, one side glistening red with fresh blood, his long hair matted with it. . . . Vang's Hughes shot past over Scanlon's whirling rotor, skidded sideways in the air, and came back around.

Scanlon got the chopper pulled up, but one of the control lines must have been hit. Scanlon tried to maneuver the craft around, and it lugged and labored. He launched another TOW almost blindly. It shot off to the side and hit somewhere over the horizon.

Vang sprayed another burst from the Chain Gun. Holes

dimpled the chopper's body metal in a diagonal line behind the compartment. Vang shot past above Scanlon's hamstrung craft.

Scanlon turned away beneath him and cut a straight line south. Smoke began to dribble from his engine mount. His chopper was limping badly now.

Vang flanked it and held speed for a moment, peering across at Scanlon. Smoke filled the compartment. A small gun cracked and the side window of Scanlon's chopper starred, then shattered outward. Vang saw the Colt in Scanlon's hand, chopping at the glass. Smoke poured out the broken window. The chopper stumbled and leveled again.

Vang pulled ahead, then swung abruptly around and hit the Chain Gun's trigger.

The bubble front of Scanlon's chopper exploded and disappeared. More smoke billowed out into the night. Scanlon's chopper slowed, fell over nearly on its side, then somehow righted again.

Vang turned and dropped down. His chopper faced Scanlon's across a hundred meters of open airspace.

"Oh my God," Tsia murmured.

Blood soaked Scanlon's hair and covered his face like a mask, where flying glass had chewed into it. He clawed madly at his eyes. One was glazed with blood. The other was an empty, dripping socket.

Vang reached for the TOW firing button.

Scanlon blinked his good eye and peered across the void at Vang. His bloody raw face was twisted with impotent rage, and his broken mouth opened in a silent scream.

Vang fired, then glanced at the tracker. But no adjustment was necessary.

The TOW slammed into the front of Scanlon's chopper and through its length. Scanlon simply disappeared. The chopper shot backward and flipped over, as if it had been swatted by an immense hand. Then the tanks went, and there was nothing left but a greasy ball of flame that became a comet plummeting into the forest below.

"Okay," Vang said. His voice sounded strange in his ears, thick and strained. Scanlon's chopper slammed into the ground, and flames plumed for the sky. Up ahead, no more than a half-mile, was the dark smooth line of the Mekong.

Tsia began to weep softly in shock and relief.

Vang turned the chopper north, back toward the village. "Let's go home," he said.

Dennison's Compound
April 15

"How are they doing?" Dennison asked.

Vang shrugged. "It's always difficult for newcomers—the culture, language, climate." Vang smiled. "Imagine being taken halfway around the world and told this is your new home. Of course," he added, "it is better than being Scanlon's slave."

"All of them got in without any trouble?" Miss Paradise asked. "The five hundred in the camp, as well as the people from Phu Nam Kok?"

"Yes." Vang stood at the rail, looking off across the compound's big front lawn. "Thank you."

"You're the one who's due thanks," Dennison said.

"You're too modest, boss dear," Miss Paradise said lightly.

"Many people—many more than are aware of it—owe thanks to you, Dennison," Vang insisted.

Dennison felt himself redden slightly, and turned toward the front door. "Let's have a drink on it."

"You'll have to fetch, boss," Miss Paradise said languidly. "I'm too comfortable."

She was stretched out in one of the front-porch lounge chairs, wearing a pair of satin jogging shorts over a Danskin leotard, and teardrop sunglasses. March had gone out like a lamb this year, and something a lot like summer had come on its heels. Across the valley, snow still frosted the mountain ridge, but around the compound it had all melted weeks before. This day was cloudless, bright, and brisk, the sun slanting its warmth under the porch's eave.

Dennison came back out carrying a tray: Martel Five Star Brandy highballs for him and Vang, a stemmed glass of chilled Chablis for Miss Paradise. Dennison lowered himself into a rattan deck chair.

"We came up roses," he said, sipping his drink. "Everything dovetailed pretty neatly at the end."

"Through Peter, we saw that the DEA was briefed," Miss Paradise said almost dreamily. "They had an inkling about the Scanlon connection, but we filled them in on chapter and verse, and made sure they knew that Dennison's People were responsible for busting it up so it will stay busted."

"It's good public relations," Dennison said. "They were damned grateful, and gracious enough to tacitly admit that they couldn't have achieved our kind of results. So we asked them to return the favor by going across the street to ask the INS boys to expedite the clearances on your Hmong."

"The money helped," Miss Paradise said. "Thanks to Scanlon, your people weren't exactly indigent."

Vang turned and leaned back against the porch rail. "Any difficulties with the numbered accounts?"

"Jonathan Kay handled it. Zurich was routine, but apparently Algiers was a little dicey. Kay worked it out—something to do with a rented chopper, a bank vice-president, and the threat of a three-hundred-mile walk home across the northern Sahara." Dennison smiled his pleasant smile. "The total take was right around seven million."

"Not that much, once it was divvied," Miss Paradise said. "Besides airfares and processing costs for nearly seven hundred of your people, we had to reimburse Peter for the charter costs on that 'civilian' force that met you and the villagers on the Thailand side of the Mekong. It was only fair. And Kay got a commission on the collection job."

"I've deposited your share of the remainder—including

your usual fee—to your account," Dennison said. "With all those new folks on your hands, it should come in handy."

"And your share . . ."

"I'm going to buy a new frock," Miss Paradise chirped. "You know how we girls are."

"It goes into the war chest, my dear," Dennison said. "Against the next time the slime starts oozing under the door."

"Tomorrow or the day after," Miss Paradise said, "the way the world is headed lately."

Vang straightened. "I should get home."

"Take the chopper," Dennison offered. "I'll have it ferried back from Libby."

"Thanks." They shook hands. Miss Paradise pushed her sunglasses up over her forehead and sat up. "You sure you have to run?"

Vang nodded. "There is one more problem I must see to."

"The Hmong?"

Vang shook his head. "Fishman, Berger, and Rabinowitz," he said. "During my absence, they seem to have developed a close personal relationship with my liquor cabinet."

Relive the American Experience in Viet Nam

BANTAM VIET NAM WAR BOOKS